The black mask turned toward him. "Stark."

He spurred the beast again. "I claim my sword-right, bastard!"

The remembered voice spoke from behind the barred slot. "Claim it, then!" The black axe swept a circle, warning friend and foe alike that this was a single combat. And all at once they two were alone in a little space at the heart of the battle.

Their mounts shocked together. The axe came down in a whistling curve, and the red swordblade flashed to meet it. There was a ringing clash of metal, and the blade was shattered and the axe fallen to the ground.

There was a strange sound from the tribesmen. Stark ignored it. He spurred his mount ruthlessly, pressing in.

Ciaran reached for his sword, but his hand was numbed by the force of the blow and lacked its usual split-second cunning. The hilt of Stark's weapon, still clutched in his own numb grip and swung viciously by the full weight of his arm, fetched Ciaran a stunning blow on the helm so that the metal rang like a flawed bell. He reeled back in the saddle, only for a moment, but for long enough. Stark grasped the war-mask and ripped it off, and got his hands around the naked throat.

He did not break that neck, as he had planned to do. And the clansmen all around the circle stopped and stared and did not move.

Stark knew now why the Lord Ciaran had never shown his face.

Praise for Leigh Brackett

"There's only one Leigh Brackett and there's only one
Eric John Stark—both stand alone in their field!"
—*Ray Bradbury*

"Brackett is absolutely at the top of her genre."
—*Publisher's Weekly*

"Leigh Brackett was one of the most influential women writers for the
pulps (along with C. L. Moore), her work being an inspiration to Marion
Zimmer Bradley, Lin Carter, Jo Clayton, Moorcock and many others."
—*The Encyclopedia of Fantasy*

"Leigh Brackett combines the best of A. Merritt and Edgar
Rice Burroughs with much that is uniquely her own!"
—*Lester del Rey*

"Fluid and lovely."
—*Lin Carter*

"Brackett not only continued the great romantic tradition of Edgar
Rice Burroughs (though with infinitely more sophistication), but she
managed to sneak into the Puritan pulps... a sensuousness which
the male writers of the period couldn't seem to achieve, both in
descriptive ability and hints that the hero and heroine wanted more
than for the former to save the latter from a bug-eyed monster....
Brackett's works are adventurous world-creating at its best."
—*A Reader's Guide to Science Fiction*

"She approached all she wrote with economy and vigor: everything
about her early stories—their color, their narrative speed, the
brooding forthrightness of their protagonists—made them an ideal
and fertile blend of traditional space opera and sword and sorcery."
—*The Encyclopedia of Science Fiction*

THE PLANET STORIES LIBRARY

STRANGE ADVENTURES ON OTHER WORLDS

AVAILABLE MONTHLY EXCLUSIVELY FROM PLANET STORIES!

FOR AUTHOR BIOS AND SYNOPSES,
VISIT PAIZO.COM/PLANETSTORIES

The Secret of Sinharat

and

People of the Talisman

by Leigh Brackett

Introduction by Michael Moorcock

Cover by Andrew Hou

PLANET STORIES
Seattle
Erik Mona, Publisher

Planet Stories is a division of Paizo Publishing, LLC
2700 Richards Road, Suite 201
Bellevue, WA 98005

PLANET STORIES is a trademark of Paizo Publishing, LLC

Visit us online at paizo.com/planetstories

Printed in China

Planet Stories #5, *The Secret of Sinharat*, by Leigh Brackett
First Printing December, 2007

10 9 8 7 6 5 4 3 2 1   2007

TABLE OF CONTENTS

Stark Rides Again

BY MICHAEL MOORCOCK

THEY ALL CAME out of Edgar Rice Burroughs, of course—Brackett, Bradbury, even Ballard—and Burroughs came out of the Western desert lands as obviously as Hammett and Chandler came out of the Western cities—San Francisco and Los Angeles. Those ochre vistas of Nevada, New Mexico, Arizona and California, broken by old, eroded mountains and inhabited by a mysterious people, who left cities and monuments behind them before vanishing forever, were Burroughs's inspiration just as they inspired native Californians Leigh Brackett and her protégé Ray Bradbury. In both cases the original inspiration of Burroughs was modified by later Californians. In Leigh Brackett's case it was Sam Spade and Philip Marlowe who clearly gave something to Eric John Stark and her other lone adventurers. In Bradbury's it was Steinbeck's characters, especially those who lived on Tortilla Flats or Cannery Row. There's a strong argument for claiming that the majority of the best and most influential fiction of the twentieth century (at least the first half) came out of California, from Jack London to Philip K. Dick.

Leigh Brackett is probably best known now for her involvement in movies, from *The Big Sleep* to *The Empire Strikes Back*, but it was as a writer of "sword and planet" fiction that I first knew her. As a boy I would scour the second-hand bookshops of South London for copies of *Planet Stories*, *Startling Stories* or *Thrilling Wonder Stories*, eager for more tales of Eric John Stark, whose adventures I had first come across in the rather thin UK versions of those magazines. I'm not sure if the titles were Leigh's or the choice of the editors but they had a great resonance for me—*Queen of the Martian Catacombs, Black Amazon of Mars, The Enchantress of Venus,* and others. For me, Stark was even more of a hero than John Carter and, of course, he was much more in tune with my own times when the screen was filled with movies like *The Maltese Falcon, The Killers,* and *Pickup on South Street,* what Leigh's husband Edmond Hamilton called "urban adventure tales" and what we these days call simply "noir"—movies full of grim-eyed men and taunting, beautiful, exotic women united against the system and frequently put, through no fault of their own, on the wrong side of the Law. Even the westerns of those days, like *Shane,* took on that same romantic quality. Later, in the movies of Clint Eastwood, for instance, those qualities would emerge again and again, for these were men a bored woman could love and an adventurous man emulate.

For half my youth I yearned to be riding some strange, complaining reptilian steed across the dead sea bottoms of Mars while for the other half I longed to be wearing a trench coat and a snap-brim fedora, walking the rain-sodden streets of the big city. Even when I could afford the trench coat and the fedora (I was already in the rain-sodden big city) I was still wondering if it would ever be possible to find a Mars whose vast red deserts were interrupted by low, broken bluffs and the ruins of cities that were ancient before Man first emerged on Earth. If my very earliest teenage stories were influenced by Burroughs, there was no doubt that my first published adult fantasy stories were influenced by Brackett. And I wasn't the only one. Half the British SF writers I knew could quote Brackett verbatim and had written their own versions of Stark, the best known of which today is Edward C. Tubb's *Dumarest of Terra,* perhaps the longest running single-character series in UK SF.

Edmond Hamilton, whose reputation in science fiction preceded Leigh's, was one of her first mentors, as was the great Henry Kuttner. Kuttner's own fantasy hero Elak of Atlantis was never as convincing as any Leigh gave us. Like Hamilton, he was at heart a true science fiction man. But both recognised the originality of Leigh's imagination and encouraged her to write the stories which are best described as science fantasy, incorporating elements of both science fiction and fantasy, as well as the old-fashioned scientific romance. Of course, she could write straight science fiction and often did. She could also write hard-boiled detective thrillers in the manner of Carroll John Daly, Lester Dent, and the more sophisticated *Black Mask* writers who followed them. She published several including her first, *No Place for a Corpse*, and one ghosted for the actor George Sanders, as *Stranger at Home*, which showed that she could have pursued a perfectly lucrative career as a full-time crime novelist had she wished. But interplanetary adventure fiction remained her first love and by the time she was encouraging the young Ray Bradbury (who co-wrote *Lorelei of the Red Mist* with her) she had become a star of *Planet Stories* and the other pulps.

I considered those pulps far superior to the more respectable SF magazines like *Astounding* (later *Analog*) and *The Magazine of Fantasy and Science Fiction*. I think my preference was mostly to do with the unchecked vividness of the writing. *Astounding* was too wooden, too evidently written by enthusiastic engineers. *F&SF* struck me as too pretentious.

I have often argued that the language and music of *Black Mask* came out of California, along with the imagery. James M. Cain, originally from Maryland, used to say that "Californian" was what made him write as he did. The author of *Double Indemnity* and *Mildred Pierce* claimed that his noir stories were inspired by hearing the language of the California streets. He would become irritable when people suggested he copied Chandler. His stories, he said, sounded like Chandler's because both writers (along with Hammett) were subject to the same daily, casual influences. They heard "Californian" all around them and the language of the West Coast cities was as vivid and as vital as anything you could hear in twentieth-century New York. Brackett's experiences, of course, were the same. She grew up with that language. She didn't live too far from where Burroughs settled (on land he christened "Tarzana"). And she grew up admiring, along with Douglas Fairbanks, characters who weren't a million miles from Sam Spade. Burroughs could never, for instance, have made John Carter smoke a cigarette and grind it out in the sand of a dead sea bottom as Stark does in the opening pages of

The Secret of Sinharat, for all the world like some character out of *Casablanca.*

It was a few years before I realised that Leigh was a woman, just as I didn't know that C. L. Moore, creator of Northwest Smith (also something of an ancestor of Stark's) was of the opposite sex to my own. They became known as the "Queens of the SF Pulps" and both certainly knew how to write a great embittered romantic man as well as any Brontë. Stark was a role model for me long before I had read *Wuthering Heights* and discovered Heathcliff or Mr. Rochester. Stark was Humphrey Bogart playing Douglas Fairbanks parts. Leigh had a photograph of herself as a little girl with Fairbanks. She grew up loving those dashing sword-wielding adventurers, as I did. Later, she would get to know Bogart, too. While decades and thousands of miles apart, we developed the same enthusiasms and when together could be like a couple of kids recollecting our favourite scenes from *The Thief of Baghdad* or *The Warlord of Mars.* We loved Westerns, too, and you'll find resonances of Max Brand in her stories, while some of my first fiction was about Kit Carson and other heroes of the borderlands.

The story of how Howard Hawks sent for "this guy Brackett," wanting to work with him on *The Big Sleep,* is today very well known. To his credit (and somewhat typically—for in Hawks's world women divided into strong ones he could work with and weak ones he could romance) he went on to get her to do the lion's share of that script and she would later write some of his finest films with John Wayne, beginning with the magnificent *Rio Bravo.* She was in some ways a typical Hawks heroine. She had a big, steady voice and a way of looking at you directly which made you decide to cut out the bullshit, should you be thinking of offering her any. You could easily imagine her staring down an Apache war-chief while she forked a cartridge into her Winchester. She and I became very close friends, in spite of our considerable political differences (she tended to share Wayne's views) and we frequently met, often visiting one another's houses when I was in the US or she and Ed were in England, which they loved. We would swap favorite food—I'd send her English tea (then hard to get) and she'd send me maple syrup from their own farm. During the years of the Vietnam War we had quite distinctly opposing views, but somehow they never got in the way of a deepening friendship which was fueled by all the many things we did have in common, including a powerful respect for the individual. This respect colored all Leigh's fiction, whether it was about lone sword-wielding outlaws like Stark or black frontiersmen like the hero of her historical novel *Follow the Free Wind*.

Whatever her powers of synthesis, Leigh emerged as a great original almost from the moment she started publishing. Her name on the cover of *Planet* would put sales up in a moment. And if it was an Eric John Stark story, people would go to enormous trouble to seek a copy out. I remember some SF writers at a convention quoting whole passages aloud and competing together to produce a pastiche on a typewriter borrowed from somewhere. Stark was one of the most influential characters to come out of the SF pulps, and Brackett's style influenced more than one generation: you can, of course, hear echoes of it in Ray Bradbury, who in turn influenced the likes of Harlan Ellison and J. G. Ballard.

As already noted, Leigh was a screenwriter of the first rank and her script for *The Long Goodbye* with Elliot Gould was more than a faithful adaptation of Chandler. She took Chandler's original into areas he might have taken it himself if he had been working in Brackett's age. It is a movie whose reputation has continued to grow, at once an homage and an interpretation of Philip Marlowe very different to the one she did for Bogart. When Leigh was asked to write the script of *The Empire Strikes Back* for George Lucas, she saw a version of Stark in Han Solo and might have done something very interesting with the character had she not died prematurely only a year after her husband, Ed. As it is, there was always an element of Stark in Solo, just as there is in every other planet-hopping outlaw who rides the space-lanes and is as handy with a sword (or lightsaber) as he is with a ray-gun.

Stark's planetary system was one in which most worlds were just about inhabitable, but the majority of his adventures took place on Mars (the desert world) or Venus (by common consent of the times a world of seas and swamps). This is a system which was largely sketched out by Burroughs and Otis Adelbert Kline and their followers and developed through the 1930s and 40s in the romantic SF pulps. For me, it remains the actuality no rational astronomer will ever challenge. And Brackett gave us memorable heroines and villainesses worthy of her great heroes, the greatest of whom is Eric John Stark. Not until the cyberpunks of the 1980s did anyone combine the definitive style of 40s noir with the wilder reaches of SF romanticism and in this, as in so many ways, Leigh was an innovator and an inspiration.

Her work lives precisely because of her ability to combine full-strength technicolor imagery with all-out power prose that was written at top speed, rarely revised, and had a clarity and punch few of her pulp peers ever mastered, let alone bettered. What she did in these stories, expanded from their original *Planet Stories* appearance and all the better for that, was to offer a generation of writers and readers a gold standard for the production of uninhibited imaginative adventure fiction which has yet to be improved upon. If you're reading her for the first time, I envy you.

Michael Moorcock
Lost Pines, TX
July, 2007

MICHAEL MOORCOCK, *creator of the character Elric of Melniboné, is considered one of the most important living speculative fiction authors. His honors include the Nebula Award, the World Fantasy Award, the British Fantasy Award, the Bram Stoker Lifetime Achievement Award, and a 2002 induction into the Science Fiction and Fantasy Hall of Fame.*

The Secret
of Sinharat

CHAPTER ONE

FOR HOURS THE hard-pressed beast had fled across the Martian desert with its dark rider. Now it was spent. It faltered and broke stride, and when the rider cursed and dug his heels into the scaly sides, the brute only turned its head and hissed at him. It stumbled on a few more paces into the lee of a sandhill, and there it stopped, crouching down in the dust.

The man dismounted. The creature's eyes burned like green lamps in the light of the little moons, and he knew that it was no use trying to urge it on. He looked back the way he had come.

In the distance there were four black shadows grouped together in the barren emptiness. They were running fast. In a few minutes they would be upon him.

He stood still, thinking what he should do next. Ahead, far ahead, was a low ridge, and beyond the ridge lay Valkis and safety, but he could never make it now. Off to his right, a lonely tor stood up out of the blowing sand. There were tumbled rocks at its foot.

"They tried to run me down in the open," he thought. "But here, by the Nine Hells, they'll have to work for it!"

He moved then, running toward the tor with a lightness and speed incredible in anything but an animal or a savage. He was of Earth stock, built tall, and more massive than he looked by reason of his leanness. The desert wind was bitter cold, but he did not seem to notice it, though he wore only a ragged shirt of Venusian spider silk, open to the waist. His skin was almost as dark as his black hair, burned indelibly by years of exposure to some terrible sun. His eyes were startlingly light in color, reflecting back the pale glow of the moons.

With the practiced ease of a lizard he slid in among the loose and treacherous rocks. Finding a vantage point, where his back was protected by the tor itself, he crouched down.

After that he did not move, except to draw his gun. There was something eerie about his utter stillness, a quality of patience as unhuman as the patience of the rock that sheltered him.

The four black shadows came closer, and resolved themselves into mounted men.

They found the beast, where it lay panting, and stopped. The line of the man's footprints, already blurred by the wind but still plain enough, showed where he had gone.

The leader motioned. The others dismounted. Working with the swift precision of soldiers, they removed equipment from their saddle-packs and began to assemble it.

The man crouching under the tor saw the thing that took shape. It was a Banning shocker, and he knew that he was not going to fight his way out of this trap. His pursuers were out of range of his own weapon. They would remain so. The Banning, with its powerful electric beam, would take him—dead or senseless, as they wished.

He thrust the useless gun back into his belt. He knew who these men were, and what they wanted with him. They were officers of the Earth Police Control, bringing him a gift—twenty years in the Luna cell-blocks.

Twenty years in the gray catacombs, buried in the silence and the eternal dark.

He recognized the inevitable. He was used to inevitables—hunger, pain, loneliness, the emptiness of dreams. He had accepted a lot of them in his time. Yet he made no move to surrender. He looked out at the desert and the night sky, and his eyes blazed, the desperate, strangely beautiful eyes of a creature very close to the roots of life, something less and more than man. His hands found a shard of rock and broke it.

The leader of the four men rode slowly toward the tor, his right arm raised.

His voice carried clearly on the wind. "Eric John Stark!" he called, and the dark man tensed in the shadows.

The rider stopped. He spoke again, but this time in a different tongue. It was no dialect of Earth, Mars or Venus, but a strange

speech, as harsh and vital as the blazing Mercurian valleys that
bred it.

"*Oh N'Chaka, oh Man-without-a-tribe, I call you!*"

There was a long silence. The rider and his mount were motionless under the low moons, waiting.

Eric John Stark stepped slowly out from the pool of blackness
under the tor.

"Who calls me N'Chaka?"

The rider relaxed somewhat. He answered in English, "You
know perfectly well who I am, Eric. May we meet in peace?"

Stark shrugged. "Of course."

He walked on to meet the rider, who had dismounted, leaving
his beast behind. He was a slight, wiry man, this EPC officer, but
there was about him the rawhide look of the planetary frontiers.
Those planets, Earth's sister worlds, were not quite as forbidding
as they had once seemed when peered at from millions of miles
away, and they had their peoples, descendants of some parent
human stock that long ago had seeded the whole System. But
they were still cruel worlds and even as they had left their mark
on Stark, they had left it on this man, on his grizzled hair and
sun-blackened skin, in his hard good-humored face and keen
dark eyes.

"It's been a long time, Eric," he said.

Stark nodded. "Sixteen years." The two men studied each
other for a moment, and then Stark said, "I thought you were
still on Mercury, Ashton."

"They've called all us experienced hands in to Mars." He held
out cigarettes. "Smoke?"

Stark took one. They bent over Ashton's lighter, and then stood
there smoking while the wind blew red dust over their feet and
the three men of the patrol waited quietly beside the Banning.
Ashton was taking no chances. The electro-beam could stun
without injury.

Presently Ashton said, "I'm going to be crude, Eric. I'm going
to remind you of some things."

"Save it," Stark retorted. "You've got me. There's no need to talk about it."

"Yes," said Ashton, "I've got you, and a damned hard time I've had doing it. That's why I'm going to talk about it."

His dark eyes met Stark's cold stare and held it.

"Remember who I am—Simon Ashton. Remember who came along when the miners in that valley on Mercury had a wild boy in a cage, and were going to finish him off like they had the tribe that raised him. Remember all the years after that, when I brought that boy up to be a civilized human being."

Stark laughed, not without a certain humor. "You should have left me in the cage. I was caught a little old for civilizing."

"Maybe. I don't think so. Anyway, I'm reminding you," Ashton said.

Stark said, with no particular bitterness, "You don't have to get sentimental. I know it's your job to take me in."

Ashton said deliberately, "I won't take you in, Eric, unless you make me." He went on then, rapidly, before Stark could answer. "You've got a twenty-year sentence hanging over you, for running guns to the Middle-Swamp tribes when they revolted against Terro-Venusian Metals, and a couple of similar jobs. All right. So I know why you did it, and I won't say I don't agree with you. But you put yourself outside the law, and that's that. Now you're on your way to Valkis. You're headed into a mess that'll put you on Luna for life, the next time you're caught."

"And this time you don't agree with me."

"No. Why do you think I broke my neck to catch you before you got there?" Ashton bent closer, his face very intent. "Have you made any deal with Delgaun of Valkis? Did he send for you?"

"He sent for me, but there's no deal yet. I'm on the beach. Broke. I got a message from this Delgaun, whoever he is, that there was going to be a private war back in the Drylands, and he'd pay me to help fight it. After all, that's my business."

Ashton shook his head.

"This isn't a private war, Eric. It's something a lot bigger and nastier than that. The Martian Council of City-States and the

Earth Commission are both in a cold sweat, and nobody can find out exactly what's going on. You know what the Low-Canal towns are—Valkis, Jekkara, Barrakesh. No law-abiding Martian, let alone an Earthman, can last five minutes in them. And the back-blocks are absolutely *verboten*. So all we get is rumors.

"Fantastic rumors about a barbarian chief named Kynon, who seems to be promising heaven and earth to the tribes of Kesh and Shun—some wild stuff about the ancient cult of the Ramas that everybody thought was dead a thousand years ago. We know that Kynon is tied up somehow with Delgaun, who is a most efficient bandit, and we know that some of the top criminals of the whole System are filtering in to join them. Knighton and Walsh of Terra, Themis of Mercury, Arrod of Callisto Colony—and, I believe, your old comrade in arms, Luhar the Venusian."

Stark gave a slight start, and Ashton smiled briefly.

"Oh, yes," he said. "I heard about that." Then he sobered. "You can figure that set-up for yourself, Eric. The barbarians are going to go out and fight some kind of a holy war, to suit the entirely unholy purposes of men like Delgaun and the others. Half a world is going to be raped, blood is going to run deep in the Drylands—and it will all be barbarian blood spilled for a lying promise, and the carrion crows of Valkis will get fat on it. Unless, somehow, we can stop it."

He paused, then said flatly, "I want you to go on to Valkis, Eric—but as my agent. I won't put it on the grounds that you'd be doing civilization a service. You don't owe anything to civilization, Lord knows. But you might save a lot of your own kind of people from getting slaughtered, to say nothing of the border-state Martians who'll be the first to get Kynon's axe.

"Also, you could wipe that twenty-year hitch on Luna off the slate, maybe even work up a desire to make a man of yourself, instead of a sort of tiger wandering from one kill to the next." He added, "If you live."

Stark said slowly, "You're clever, Ashton. You know I've got a feeling for all planetary primitives like those who raised me, and you appeal to that."

"Yes," said Ashton, "I'm clever. But I'm not a liar. What I've told you is true."

Stark carefully ground out the cigarette beneath his heel. Then he looked up. "Suppose I agree to become your agent in this, and go off to Valkis. What's to prevent me from forgetting all about you, then?"

Ashton said softly, "Your word, Eric. You get to know a man pretty well when you know him from boyhood on up. Your word is enough."

There was a silence, and then Stark held out his hand. "All right, Simon—but only for this one deal. After that, no promises."

"Fair enough." They shook hands.

"I can't give you any suggestions," Ashton said. "You're on your own, completely. You can get in touch with me through the Earth Commission office in Tarak. You know where that is?"

Stark nodded. "On the Dryland Border."

"Good luck to you, Eric."

He turned, and they walked back together to where the three men waited. Ashton nodded, and they began to dismantle the Banning. Neither they nor Ashton looked back, as they rode away.

Stark watched them go. He filled his lungs with the cold air, and stretched. Then he roused the beast out of the sand. It had rested, and was willing to carry him again as long as he did not press it. He set off again, across the desert.

The ridge grew as he approached it, looming into a low mountain chain much worn by the ages. A pass opened before him, twisting between the hills of barren rock.

He traversed it, coming out at the farther end above the basin of a dead sea. The lifeless land stretched away into the darkness, a vast waste of desolation more lonely than even the desert. And between the sea-bottom and the foothills, Stark saw the lights of Valkis.

CHAPTER TWO

THERE WERE MANY lights, far below. Tiny pinpricks of flame where torches burned in the streets beside the Low-Canal—the thread of black water that was all that remained of a forgotten ocean.

Stark had never been here before. Now he looked at the city that sprawled down the slope under the low moons, and shivered, the primitive twitching of the nerves that an animal feels in the presence of death.

For the streets where the torches flared were only a tiny part of Valkis. The life of the city had flowed downward from the cliff-tops, following the dropping level of the sea. Five cities, the oldest scarcely recognizable as a place of human habitation. Five harbors, the docks and quays still standing, half buried in the dust.

Five ages of Martian history, crowned on the topmost level with the ruined palace of the old pirate kings of Valkis. The towers still stood, broken but indomitable, and in the moonlight they had a sleeping look, as though they dreamed of blue water and the sound of waves, and of tall ships coming in heavy with treasure.

Stark picked his way slowly down the steep descent. There was something fascinating to him in the stone houses, roofless and silent in the night. The paving blocks still showed the rutting of wheels where carters had driven to the marketplace, and princes had gone by in gilded chariots. The quays were scarred where ships had lain against them, rising and falling with the tides.

Stark's senses had developed in a strange school, and the thin veneer of civilization he affected had not dulled them. Now it seemed to him that the wind had the echoes of voices in it, and the smell of spices and fresh-spilled blood.

He was not surprised when, in the last level above the living town, armed men came out of the shadows and stopped him.

They were lean, dark men, very wiry and light of foot, and their faces were the faces of wolves—not primitive wolves at all but beasts of prey that had been civilized for so many thousands of years that they could afford to forget it.

They were most courteous, and Stark would not have cared to disobey their requests.

He gave his name. "Delgaun sent for me."

The leader of the Valkisians nodded his narrow head. "You're expected." His sharp eyes had taken in every feature of the Earthman, and Stark knew that his description had been memorized down to the last detail. Valkis guarded its doors with care.

"Ask in the city," said the sentry. "Anyone can direct you to the palace."

Stark nodded and went on, down through the long-dead streets in the moonlight and the silence.

With shocking suddenness, he was plunged into the streets of the living.

It was very late now, but Valkis was awake and stirring. Seething, rather. The narrow twisting ways were crowded. The laughter of women came down from the flat roofs. Torchlight flared, gold and scarlet, lighting the wine-shops, making blacker the shadows of the alley-mouths.

Stark left his beast at a *serai* on the edge of the canal. The paddocks were already jammed. Stark recognized the long-legged brutes of the Dryland breed, and as he left a caravan passed him, coming in, with a jangling of bronze bangles and a great hissing and stamping in the dust.

The riders were tall barbarians—Keshi, Stark thought, from the way they braided their tawny hair. They wore plain leather, and their blue-eyed women rode like queens.

Valkis was full of them. For days, it seemed, they must have poured in across the dead sea bottom, from the distant oases and the barren deserts of the back-blocks. Brawny warriors of Kesh and Shun, making holiday beside the Low-Canal, where there was more water than any of them had seen in their lives.

They were in Valkis, these barbarians, but they were not part of it. Shouldering his way through the streets, Stark got the peculiar flavor of the town, that he guessed could never be touched or changed by anything.

In the square, a girl danced to the music of harp and drum. The air was heavy with the smell of wine and burning pitch and incense. A little, swart Valkisian in his bright kilt and jeweled girdle leaped out and danced with the girl, his teeth flashing as he whirled and postured. In the end he bore her off, laughing, her black hair hanging down his back.

Women looked at Stark. Women graceful as cats, bare to the waist, their skirts slit at the sides above the thigh, wearing no ornaments but the tiny golden bells that are the particular property of the Low-Canal towns, so that the air is always filled with their delicate, wanton chiming.

Valkis had a laughing, wicked soul. Stark had been in many places in his life, but never one before that beat with such a pulse of evil, incredibly ancient, but strong and gay.

He found the palace at last—a great rambling structure of quarried stone, with doors and shutters of beaten bronze closed against the dust and the incessant wind. He gave his name to the guard and was taken inside, through halls hung with antique tapestries, the flagged floors worn hollow by countless generations of sandaled feet.

Again, Stark's half-wild senses told him that life within these walls had not been placid. The very stones whispered of age-old violence, the shadows were heavy with the lingering ghosts of passion.

He was brought before Delgaun, the lord of Valkis, in the big central room that served as his headquarters.

Delgaun was lean and catlike, after the fashion of his race. His black hair showed a stippling of silver, and the hard beauty of his face was strongly marked, the lines drawn deep and all the softness of youth long gone away. He wore a magnificent harness, and his eyes, under fine dark brows, were like drops of hot gold.

He looked up as the Earthman came in, one swift penetrating glance. Then he said, "You're Stark."

There was something odd about those yellow eyes, bright and keen as a killer hawk's yet somehow secret, as though the true thoughts behind them would never show through. Instinctively, Stark disliked the man.

But he nodded and came up to the council table, turning his attention to the others in the room. A handful of Martians—Low Canallers, chiefs and fighting men from their ornaments and their proud looks—and several outlanders, their conventional garments incongruous in this place.

Stark knew them all, Knighton and Walsh of Terra, Themis of Mercury, Arrod of Callisto Colony—and Luhar of Venus. Pirates, thieves, renegades, and each one an expert in his line.

Ashton was right. There was something big, something very big and very ugly, shaping between Valkis and the Drylands.

But that was only a quick passing thought in Stark's mind. It was on Luhar that his attention centered. Bitter memory and hatred had come to savage life within him as soon as he saw the Venusian.

The man was handsome. A cashiered officer of the crack Venusian Guards, very slim, very elegant, his pale hair cropped short and curling, his dark tunic fitting him like a second skin.

He said, "The aborigine! I thought we had enough barbarians here without sending for more."

Stark said nothing. He began to walk toward Luhar.

Luhar said sharply, "There's no use in getting nasty, Stark. Past scores are past. We're on the same side now."

The Earthman spoke, then, with a peculiar gentleness.

"We were on the same side once before. Against Terro-Venus Metals. Remember?"

"I remember very well!" Luhar was speaking now not to Stark alone, but to everyone in the room. "I remember that your innocent barbarian friends had me tied to the block there in the swamps, and that you were watching the whole thing with honest pleasure. If the Company men hadn't come along, I'd be screaming there yet."

"You sold us out," Stark said. "You had it coming."

He continued to walk toward Luhar.

Delgaun spoke. He did not raise his voice, yet Stark felt the impact of his command.

"There will be no fighting here," Delgaun said. "You are both hired mercenaries, and while you take my pay you will forget your private quarrels. Do you understand?"

Luhar nodded and sat down, smiling out of the corner of his mouth at Stark, who stood looking with narrowed eyes at Delgaun. He was still half blind with his anger against Luhar. His hands ached for the kill. But even so, he recognized the power in Delgaun.

A sound shockingly akin to the growl of a beast echoed in his throat. Then, gradually, he relaxed. The man Delgaun he would have challenged. But to do so would wreck the mission that he had promised to carry out here for Ashton.

He shrugged and joined the others at the table.

Walsh of Terra rose abruptly and began to prowl back and forth. "How much longer do we have to wait?" he demanded.

Delgaun poured wine into a bronze goblet. "Don't expect me to know," he snapped. He shoved the flagon along the table toward Stark.

Stark helped himself. The wine was warm and sweet on his tongue. He drank slowly, sitting relaxed and patient, while the others smoked nervously or rose to pace up and down.

Stark wondered what, or who, they were waiting for. But he did not ask.

Time went by.

Stark raised his head, listening. "What's that?"

Their duller ears had heard nothing, but Delgaun rose and flung open the shutters of the window near him.

The Martian dawn, brilliant and clear, flooded the dead sea bottom with harsh light. Beyond the black line of the canal a caravan was coming toward Valkis through the blowing dust.

It was no ordinary caravan. Warriors rode before and behind, their spearheads blazing in the sunrise. Jewelled trappings on the beasts, a litter with curtains of crimson silk, barbaric splendor. Clear and thin on the air came the wild music of pipes and the deep-throated throbbing of drums.

Stark guessed without being told who it was that rode out of the desert like a king.

Delgaun made a harsh sound in his throat. "It's Kynon, at last!" he said, and swung around from the window. His eyes sparkled with some private amusement. "Let us go and welcome the Giver of Life!"

Stark went with them, out into the crowded streets. A silence had fallen on the town. Valkisian and barbarian alike were caught now in a breathless excitement, pressing through the narrow ways, flowing toward the canal.

Stark found himself beside Delgaun in the great square of the slave market, standing on the auction block, above the heads of the throng. The stillness, the expectancy of the crowd were uncanny....

To the measured thunder of drums and the wild skirling of desert pipes, Kynon of Shun came into Valkis.

CHAPTER THREE

STRAIGHT INTO THE square of the slave market the caravan came, and the people pressed back against the walls to make way for them. Stamping of padded hoofs on the stones, ring and clash of harness, brave glitter of spears and the great two-handed broadswords of the Drylands, with drumbeats to shake the heart and the savage cry of the pipes to set the blood leaping. Stark could not restrain an appreciative thrill in himself.

The advance guard reached the slave block. Then, with deafening abruptness, the drummers crossed their sticks and the pipers ceased, and there was utter silence in the square.

It lasted for almost a minute, and then from every barbarian throat the name of Kynon roared out until the stones of the city echoed with it.

A man leaped from the back of his mount to the block standing at its outer edge where all could see, his hands flung up.

"I greet you, my brothers!"

And the cheering went on.

Stark studied Kynon, surprised that he was so young. He had expected a gray-bearded prophet, and instead, here was a brawny-shouldered man of war standing as tall as himself.

Kynon's eyes were a bright, compelling blue, and his face was the face of a young eagle. His voice had deep music in it—the kind of voice that can sway crowds to madness. Stark looked from him to the rapt faces of the people—even the Valkisians had caught the mood—and thought that Kynon was the most dangerous man he had ever seen. This tawny-haired barbarian in his kilt of bronze-bossed leather was already half a god.

Kynon shouted to the captain of his warriors, "Bring the captive and the old man!" Then he turned again to the crowd, urging them to silence. When at last the square was still, his voice rang challengingly across it.

"There are still those who doubt me. Therefore I have come to Valkis, and this day—now! I will show proof that I have not lied!"

A roar and a mutter from the crowd. Kynon's men were lifting to the block a tottering ancient so bowed with years that he could barely stand, and a youth of Terran stock. The boy was in chains. The old man's eyes burned, and he looked at the boy beside him with a terrible joy.

Stark settled down to watch. The litter with the crimson curtains was now beside the block. A girl, a Valkisian, stood beside it, looking up. It seemed to Stark that her green eyes rested on Kynon with a smouldering anger. He glanced away from the serving girl, and saw that the curtains were partly open. A woman lay on the cushions within. He could not see much of her, except that her hair was like dark flame and she was smiling, looking at the old man and the naked boy. Then her glance, very dark in the shadows of the litter, shifted away and Stark followed it and saw Delgaun. Every muscle of Delgaun's body was drawn taut, and he seemed unable to look away from the woman in the litter.

Stark smiled, very slightly. The outlanders were cynically absorbed in what was going on. The crowd had settled again to that silent, breathless tension. The sun blazed down out of the empty sky. The dust blew, and the wind was sharp with the smell of living flesh.

The old man reached out and touched the boy's smooth shoulder, and his gums showed bluish as he laughed.

Kynon was speaking again.

"There are still those who doubt me, I say! Those who scoffed when I said that I possessed the ancient secret of the Ramas of long ago—the secret by which one man's mind may be transferred into another's body. But none of you after today will doubt that I hold that secret!"

"I, myself, am not a Rama." He glanced down along his powerful frame, half-consciously flexing his muscles, and laughed. "Why should I be a Rama? I have no need, as yet, for the Sending On of Minds!"

Answering laughter, half ribald, from the crowd.

"No," said Kynon. "I am not a Rama. I am a man like you. Like you, I have no wish to grow old, and in the end, to die."

He swung abruptly to the old man.

"You, Grandfather! Would you not wish to be young again—to ride out to battle, to take the woman of your choice?"

The old man wailed, "Yes! Yes!" and his gaze dwelt hungrily upon the boy.

"And you shall be!" The strength of a god rang in Kynon's voice. He turned again to the crowd and cried out, "For years I suffered in the desert alone, searching for the lost secret of the Ramas. And I found it, my brothers! I alone—in these two hands I hold it, and with it I shall begin a new era for our Dryland races!"

"There will be fighting, yes. There will be bloodshed. But when that is over and the men of Kesh and Shun are free from their ancient bondage of thirst and the men of the Low Canals have regained their own—then I shall give new life, unending life, to all who have followed me. The aged and lamed and wounded can choose new bodies from among the captive. There will be no more age, no more sickness, no more death!"

A rippling, shivering sigh from the crowd. Eyeballs gleaming in the bitter light, mouths open on the hunger that is nearest to the human soul.

"Lest anyone still doubt my promise," said Kynon, "watch. Watch—and I will show you!"

They watched. Not stirring, hardly breathing, they watched.

The drums struck up a slow and solemn beat. The captain of the warriors, with an escort of six men, marched to the litter and took from the woman's hands a bundle wrapped in silks. Bearing it as though it were precious beyond belief, he came to the block and lifted it up, and Kynon took it from him.

The silken wrappings fluttered loose, fell away. And in Kynon's hands gleamed two crystal crowns and a shining rod. He held them high, the sunlight glancing in cold fire from the crystal.

"Behold!" he said. "The Crowns of the Ramas!"

The crowd drew breath then, one long rasping *Ah!*

The solemn drumbeat never faltered. It was as though the pulse of the whole world throbbed within it. Kynon turned. The old man began to tremble. Kynon placed one crown on his wrinkled scalp, and the tottering creature winced as though in pain, but his face was ecstatic. Relentlessly, Kynon crowned with the second circlet the head of the frightened boy.

"Kneel," he said.

They knelt. Standing tall above them, Kynon held the rod in his two hands, between the crystal crowns.

Light was born in the rod. It was no reflection of the sun. Blue and brilliant, it flashed along the rod and leaped from it to wake an answering brilliance in the crowns, so that the old man and the youth were haloed with a chill, supernal fire.

The drumbeat ceased. The old man cried out. His hands plucked feebly at his head, then went to his breast and clenched there. Quite suddenly he fell forward over his knees. A convulsive tremor shook him. Then he lay still.

The boy swayed and then fell forward also, with a clashing of chains.

The light died out of the crowns. Kynon stood a moment longer, rigid as a statue, holding the rod which still flickered with blue lightening. Then that also died.

Kynon lowered the rod. In a ringing voice he cried, "Arise, grandfather!"

The boy stirred. Slowly, very slowly, he rose to his feet. Holding out his hands, he stared at them, and then touched his thighs, and his flat belly, and the deep curve of his chest. Up the firm young throat the wondering fingers went, to the smooth cheeks, to the thick fair hair above the crown. A cry broke from him.

With the perfect accent of the Drylands, the Earth boy cried in Martian, "I am in the youth's body! I am young again!'

A scream, a wail of ecstasy, burst from the crowd. It swayed like a great beast, white faces turned upward. The boy fell down and embraced Kynon's knees.

Eric John Stark found that he himself was trembling slightly. He glanced at Delgaun and the outlanders. The Valkisian wore a look of intense satisfaction under his mask of awe. The others were almost as rapt and open-mouthed as the crowd.

Stark turned his head slightly and looked down at the litter. One white hand was already drawing the curtains, so that the scarlet silk appeared to shake with silent laughter. The serving girl beside it had not moved. She looked up at Kynon, and there was nothing in her eyes but hate.

After that there was bedlam, the rush and trample of the crowd, the beating of drums, the screaming of pipes, deafening uproar. The crowns and the crystal rod were wrapped again and taken away. Kynon raised up the boy and struck off the chains of captivity. He mounted, with the boy beside him. Delgaun walked before him through the streets, and so did the outlanders.

The body of the old man was disregarded, except by some of Kynon's barbarians who wrapped it in a white cloth and took it away.

Kynon of Shun came in triumph to Delgaun's palace. Standing beside the litter, he gave his hand to the woman, who stepped out and walked beside him through the bronze door.

The women of Shun are tall and strong, bred to stand beside their men in war as well as love, and this red-haired daughter of the Drylands was enough to stop a man's heart with her proud step and her white shoulders, and her eyes that were the color of smoke. Stark's gaze followed her from a distance.

Presently in the council room were gathered Delgaun and the outlanders, Kynon and his bright-haired queen—and no other Martians but those three.

Kynon sprawled out in the high seat at the head of the table. His face was beaming. He wiped the sweat off it, and then filled a goblet with wine, looking around the room with his bright blue eyes.

"Fill up, gentlemen. I'll give you a toast." He lifted the goblet. "Here's to the secret of the Ramas, and the gift of life!"

Stark put down his goblet, still empty. He stared directly at Kynon.

"You have no secret," said Stark deliberately.

Kynon sat perfectly still, except that, very slowly, he put his own goblet down. Nobody else moved.

Stark's voice sounded loud in the stillness.

"Furthermore," he said, "that demonstration in the square was a lie from beginning to end."

CHAPTER FOUR

STARK'S WORDS HAD the effect of an electric shock on the listeners. Delgaun's black brows went up, and the woman came forward a little to stare at the Earthman with profound interest.

Kynon asked a question, of nobody in particular. "Who," he demanded, "is this great black ape?"

Delgaun told him.

"Ah, yes," said Kynon. "Eric John Stark, the wild man from Mercury." He scowled threateningly. "Very well—explain how I lied in the square!"

"Certainly. First of all, the Earth boy was a prisoner. He was told what he had to do to save his neck, and then was carefully coached in his part. Second, the crystal rod and the crowns are a fake. You used a simple Purcell unit in the rod to produce an electronic brush discharge. That made the blue light. Third, you gave the old man poison, probably by means of a sharp point on the crown. I saw him wince when you put it on him."

Stark paused. "The old man died. The boy went through his sham. And that was that."

Again there was a flat silence. Luhar crouched over the table, his face avid with hope. The woman's eyes dwelt on Stark and did not turn away.

Then, suddenly, Kynon laughed. He roared with it until the tears ran.

"It was a good show, though," he said at last. "Damned good. You'll have to admit that. The crowd swallowed it, horn, hoofs and hide."

He got up and came round to Stark, clapping him on the shoulder, a blow that would have laid a lesser man flat.

"I like you, wild man. Nobody else here had the guts to speak out, but I'll give you odds they were all thinking the same thing."

Stark said, "Just where were you, Kynon, during those years you were supposed to be suffering alone in the desert?"

"Curious, aren't you? Well, I'll let you in on a secret." Kynon lapsed abruptly into perfectly good colloquial English. "I was on Terra, learning about things like the Purcell electronic discharge." Reaching over, he poured wine for Stark and held it out to him. "Now you know. Now we all know. So let's wash the dust out of our throats and get down to business."

Stark said, "No."

Kynon looked at him. "What now?"

"You're lying to your people," Stark said flatly. "You're making false promises, to lead them into war."

Kynon was genuinely puzzled by Stark's anger. "But of course!" he said. "Is there anything new or strange in that?"

Luhar spoke up, his voice acid with hate. "Watch out for him, Kynon. He'll sell you out, he'll cut your throat, if he thinks it best for the barbarians."

Delgaun said, "Stark's reputation is known all over the system. There's no need to tell us that again."

"No." Kynon shook his head, looking very candidly at Stark. "We sent for you, didn't we, knowing that? All right."

He stepped back a little, so that the others were included in what he was going to say.

"My people have a just cause for war. They go hungry and thirsty, while the City-States along the Dryland border hog all the water sources and grow fat. Do you know what it means to watch your children die crying for water on a long march, to come at last to the oasis and find the well sanded in by a storm, to go on again, trying to save your people and your herd? Well, I do! I was born and bred in the Drylands, and many a time I've cursed the border states with a tongue like a dry stick.

"Stark, you should know the workings of the barbarian mind as well as I do. The men of Kesh and Shun are traditional enemies. Raiding and thieving, open warfare over water and grass. I had to give them a rallying point—a faith strong enough to unite them. Resurrecting the old Rama legend was the only hope I had. And it has worked. The tribes are one people now. They can go on and take what belongs to them—the right to live. I'm not really so far out in my promises, at that. Now do you understand?"

Stark studied him, with his cold cat-eyes. "Where do the men of Valkis come in—the men of Jekkara and Barrakesh? Where do *we* come in, the hired bravoes?"

Kynon smiled. It was a perfectly sincere smile, and it had no humor in it, only a great pride and a cheerful cruelty.

"We're going to create an empire," he said softly. "The City-States are disorganized, too starved or too fat to fight. And Earth is taking us over. Before long, Mars would be hardly more than another Luna. We're going to fight that. Drylander and Low-Canaller together, we're going to build a power out of dust and blood—and there will be loot in plenty to go round."

"That's where my men come in," said Delgaun, and laughed. "We Low-Canallers live by rapine."

"And you," said Kynon, "the 'hired bravoes,' are in it to help. I need you and the Venusian, Stark, to train my men, to plan campaigns, to give me all you know of guerilla fighting. Knighton has a fast cruiser. He'll bring us supplies from outside. Walsh is a genius, they tell me, at fashioning weapons. Themis is a mechanic, and also the cleverest thief this side of hell—saving your presence, Delgaun! Arrod organized and bossed the Brotherhood of the Little Worlds, which had the Patrol going mad for years. He can do the same for us. So there you have it. Now, Stark, what do you say?"

The Earthman answered slowly, "I'll go along with you—as long as no harm comes to the tribes."

Kynon laughed. "No need to worry about that."

"Just one more question," Stark said. "What's going to happen when the people find out that this Rama stuff of yours is just a fake?"

"They won't," said Kynon. "The crowns will be destroyed in battle, and it will be very tragic, but very final. No one knows how to make more of them. Oh, I can handle the people! They'll be happy enough, with good land and water."

He looked around and then said plaintively, "And now can we sit down and drink like civilized men?"

They sat. The wine went round, and the vultures of Valkis drank to each other's luck and loot, and Stark learned that the woman's name was Berild. Kynon was happy. He had made his point with the people, and he was celebrating. But Stark noticed that though his tongue grew thick, it did not loosen.

Luhar grew steadily more morose and silent, glancing covertly across the table at Stark. Delgaun toyed with his goblet, and his yellow gaze which gave nothing away moved restlessly between Berild and Stark.

Berild drank not at all. She sat a little apart, with her face in shadow, and her red mouth smiled. Her thoughts, too, were her own secret. But Stark knew that she was still watching him, and he knew that Delgaun was aware of it.

Presently Kynon said, "Delgaun and I have some talking to do, so I'll bid you gentlemen farewell for the present. You, Stark, and Luhar—I'm going back into the desert at midnight, and you're going with me, so you'd better get some sleep."

Stark nodded. He rose and went out, with the others. An attendant showed him to his quarters, in the north wing. Stark had not rested for twenty-four hours, and he was glad of the chances to sleep.

He lay down. The wine spun in his head, and Berild's smile mocked him. Then his thoughts turned to Ashton, and his promise. Presently he slept, and dreamed.

He was a boy on Mercury again, running down a path that led from a cave mouth to the floor of a valley, one of the deep, interconnecting valleys of air. Above him the mountains rose into the sky and were lost beyond the shallow atmosphere. The rocks danced in the terrible heat, but the soles of his feet were like iron, and trod them lightly. He was quite naked.

The blaze of the sun between the valley walls was like the shining heart of Hell. It did not seem to the boy N'Chaka that it could ever be cold again, yet he knew that when darkness came there would be ice on the shallows of the little stream. The gods were constantly at war.

He passed a place, ruined by earthquake. It was a mine, and N'Chaka remembered that when he had been very small he had lived there, with several white-skinned creatures shaped like himself. He went on without a second glance.

He was searching for Tika. When he was old enough, he would mate with her. He wanted to hunt with her now, for she was fleet and as keen as he at scenting out the great lizards. He heard her voice calling his name. There was terror in it, and N'Chaka began to run. He saw her, crouched between two huge boulders, her light fur stained with blood.

A vast black-winged shadow swooped down upon him. It glared at him with its yellow eyes, and its long beak tore at him. He thrust his spear at it, but talons hooked into his shoulder, and the golden eyes were close to him, bright and full of death.

He knew those eyes. Tika screamed, but the sound faded, everything faded but those eyes. He sprang up, grappling with the thing....

A man's voice yelling, a man's hands thrusting him away. The dream receded. Stark came back to reality, dropping the scared attendant who had come to waken him.

The man cringed away from him. "Delgaun sent me—he wants you, in the council room." Then he turned and fled.

Stark shook himself. The dream had been terribly real. He went down to the council room. It was dusk now, and the torches were lighted.

Delgaun was waiting, and Berild sat beside him at the table. They were alone there. Delgaun looked up, with his golden eyes.

"I have a job for you Stark," he said. "You remember the captain of Kynon's men, in the square today?"

"I do."

"His name is Freka, and he's a good man, but he's addicted to a certain vice. He'll be up to his ears in it by now, and somebody has to get him back by the time Kynon leaves. Will you see to it?"

Stark glanced at Berild. It seemed to him that she was amused, whether at him or at Delgaun he could not tell. He asked.

"Where will I find him?"

"There's only one place where he can get his particular poison—Kala's, out on the edge of Valkis. It's in the old city, beyond the lower quays." Delgaun smiled. "You may have to be ready with your fists, Stark. Freka may not want to come."

Stark hesitated. Then, "I'll do my best," he said, and went out into the dusky streets of Valkis.

He crossed a square, heading away from the palace. A twisting lane swallowed him up. And quite suddenly, someone took his arm and said rapidly, "Smile at me, and then turn aside into the alley."

The hand on his arm was small and brown, the voice very pretty with its accompaniment of little chiming bells. He smiled, as she had bade him, and turned aside into the alley, which was barely more than a crack between two rows of houses.

Swiftly, he put his hands against the wall, so that the girl was prisoned between them. A green-eyed girl, with golden bells braided in her black hair, and impudent breasts bare above a jeweled girdle. A handsome girl, with a proud look to her.

The serving girl who had stood beside the litter in the square, and had watched Kynon with such bleak hatred.

"Well," said Stark. "And what do you want with me, little one?"

She answered, "My name is Fianna. And I do not intend to kill you, neither will I run away."

Stark let his hands drop. "Did you follow me, Fianna?"

"I did. Delgaun's palace is full on hidden ways, and I know them all. I was listening behind the panel in the council room. I heard you speak out against Kynon, and I heard Delgaun's order, just now."

"So?"

"So, if you meant what you said about tribes, you had better get away now, while you have the chance. Kynon lied to you. He will use you, and then kill you, as he will use and then destroy his own people." Her voice was hot with bitter fury.

Stark gave her a slow smile that might have meant anything, or nothing.

"You're a Valkisian, Fianna. What do you care what happens to the barbarians?"

Her slightly tilted green eyes looked scornfully into his.

"I'm not trying to trap you, Earthman. I hate Kynon. And my mother was a woman of the desert."

She paused, then went on somberly, "Also I serve the lady Berild and I have learned many things. There is trouble coming, greater trouble than Kynon knows." She asked, suddenly, "What do you know of the Ramas?"

"Nothing," he answered, "except that they don't exist now, if they ever did."

Fianna gave him an odd look. "Perhaps they don't. Will you listen to me, Earthman from Mercury? Will you get away, now that you know you're marked for death?"

Stark said, "No."

"Even if I tell you that Delgaun has set a trap for you at Kala's?"

"No. But I will thank you for your warning, Fianna."

He bent and kissed her, because she was very young and honest. Then he turned and went on his way.

CHAPTER FIVE

NIGHT CAME SWIFTLY. Stark left behind him the torches and the laughter and the sounding harps, coming into the streets of the old city where there was nothing but silence and the light of the low moons.

He saw the lower quays, great looming shapes of marble rounded and worn by time, and went toward them. Presently he found that he was following a faint but definite path, threaded between the ancient houses. It was very still, so that the dry whisper of the drifting dust was audible.

He passed under the shadow of the quays, and turned into a broad way that had once led up from the harbor. A little way ahead, on the other side, he saw a tall building half fallen in ruin. Its windows were shuttered, barred with light, and from it came the sound of voices and a thin thread of music, very reedy and evil.

Stark approached it, slipping through the ragged shadows as though he had no more weight to him than a drift of smoke. Once a door banged and a man came out of Kala's and passed by, going down to Valkis. Stark saw his face in the moonlight. It was the face of a beast, rather than a man. He muttered to himself as he went, and once he laughed, and Stark felt a loathing in him.

He waited until the sound of footsteps had died away. The ruined houses gave no sign of danger. A lizard rustled between the stones, and that was all. The moonlight lay bright and still on Kala's door.

Stark found a little shard of rock and tossed it, so that it made a sharp snicking sound against the shadowed wall beyond him. Then he held his breath, listening.

No one, nothing, stirred. Only the dry wind stirred in the empty houses.

Stark went out, across the open space, and nothing happened. He flung open the door of Kala's dive.

Yellow light spilled out, and a choking wave of hot and stuffy air. Inside, there were tall lamps with quartz lenses, each of which poured down a beam of throbbing, gold-orange light. And in the little pools of radiance, on filthy furs and cushions on the floor, lay men and women whose faces were slack and bestial.

Stark realized now what secret vice Kala sold here. Shanga— the going-back—the radiation that caused temporary artificial atavism and let men wallow for a time in beasthood. It was suppose to have been stamped out, years ago. But it still persisted, in places like this outside the law.

He looked for Freka and recognized the tall barbarian. He was sprawled under one of the Shanga lamps, eyes closed, face brutish, growling and twitching in sleep like the beast he had temporarily become.

A voice spoke from behind Stark's shoulder. "I am Kala. What do you wish, Outlander?"

He turned. Kala might have been beautiful once, a thousand years ago as you reckon sin. She wore still the sweet chiming bells in her hair, and Stark thought of Fianna. The woman's ravaged face turned him sick. It was like the reedy, piping music, woven out of the very heart of evil. Yet her eyes were shrewd, and he knew that she had not missed his searching look around the room, nor his interest in Freka. There was a note of warning in her voice.

He did not want trouble, yet. Not until he found some hint of the trap Fianna had told him of.

He said, "Bring me wine."

"Will you try the lamp of Going-back, Outlander? It brings much joy."

"Perhaps later. Now, I wish wine."

She went away, clapping her hands for a slatternly wench who came between the sprawled figures with an earthen mug. Stark sat down beside a table, where his back was to the wall and he could see both the door and the whole room. Kala had returned to her own heap of furs by the door, but her basilisk eyes were alert.

Stark made a pretense of drinking, but his mind was very busy, very cold.

Perhaps this, in itself, was the trap. Freka was temporarily a beast. He would fight, and Kala would shriek, and the other dull-eyed brutes would rise and fight also.

But he would have needed no warning about that—and Delgaun himself had said there would be trouble.

No. There was something more.

He let his gaze wander over the room. It was large, and there were other rooms off of it, the openings hung with ragged curtains. Through the rents, Stark could see others of Kala's customers sprawled under Shanga-lamps, and some of these had gone so far back from humanity that they were hideous to behold. But still there was no sign of danger to himself.

There was only one odd thing. The room nearest to where Freka sat was empty, and its curtains were only partly drawn.

Stark began to brood on the emptiness of that room. He beckoned Kala to him. "I will try the lamp," he said. "But I wish privacy. Have it brought to that room, there."

Kala said, "That room is taken."

"But I see no one!"

"It is taken, it is paid for, and no one may enter. I will have the lamp brought here."

"No," said Stark. "The hell with it. I'm going."

He flung down a coin and went out. Moving swiftly outside, he placed his eye to a crack in the nearest shutter, and waited.

Luhar of Venus came out of the empty room. His face was worried, and Stark smiled. He went back and stood flat against the wall beside the door.

In a moment, it opened and the Venusian came out, drawing his gun as he did so.

Stark jumped him.

Luhar let out one angry cry. His gun went off, a vicious streak of flame across the moonlight, and then Stark's great hand crushed the bones of his wrist together so that he dropped it clashing on the stones. He whirled around, raking Stark's face with his nails as he clawed for the Earthman's eyes, and Stark hit him. Luhar fell, rolling over, and before he could scramble up again Stark had picked up the gun and thrown it away into the ruins across the street.

Luhar came up from the pavement in one catlike spring. Stark fell with him, back and through Kala's door, and they rolled together among the foul fur and cushions. Luhar was built of spring steel, with no softness in him anywhere, and his long fingers were locked around Stark's throat.

Kala screamed with fury. She caught a whip from among her cushions—a traditional weapon along the Low Canals—and began to lash the two men impartially, her hair flying in tangled locks across her face. The bestial figures under the lamps shambled to their feet, and growled.

The long lash ripped Stark's shirt and the flesh of his back beneath it. He snarled and staggered to his feet, with Luhar still clinging to the death grip on his throat. He pushed Luhar's face away from him with both hands and threw himself forward, over a table, so that Luhar was crushed beneath him.

The Venusian's breath left him with a whistling grunt. His fingers relaxed. Stark struck his hands away. He rose and bent over Luhar and picked him up, gripping him cruelly so that he turned white with pain, and raised him high and flung him bodily into the growling, beast-faced men who were shambling toward him.

Kala leaped at Stark, cursing, striking him with the coiling lash. He turned. The thin veneer of civilization was gone from Stark now, erased in a second by the first hint of battle. His eyes blazed with a cold light. He took the whip out of Kala's hand and laid his palm across her evil face, and she fell and lay still.

He faced the ring of bestial, Shanga-sodden men who walled him off from what he had been sent to do. There was a reddish tinge to his vision, partly blood, partly sheer rage. He could see Freka standing erect in the corner, his head weaving from side to side brutishly.

Stark raised the whip and strode into the ring of men who were no longer quite men.

Hands struck and clawed him. Bodies reeled and fell away. Blank eyes glittered, and red mouths squealed, and there was a mingling of snarls and bestial laughter in his ears. The blood-lust had spread to these creatures now. They swarmed upon Stark and bore him down with the weight of their writhing bodies.

They bit him and savaged him in a blind way, and he fought his way up again, shaking them off with his great shoulders, trampling them under his boots. The lash hissed and sang, and the smell of blood rose on the choking air.

Freka's dazed, brutish face swam before Stark. The Martian growled and flung himself forward. Stark swung the loaded butt of the whip. It cracked solidly on the Shunni's temple, and he sagged into Stark's arms.

Out of the corner of his eyes, Stark saw Luhar. He was behind Stark now, and there was a knife in his hand.

Hampered by Freka's weight, Stark could not leap aside. As Luhar rushed in, he crouched and went backward, his head and shoulders taking the Venusian low in the belly. He felt the hot kiss of the blade in his flesh, but the wound was glancing, and before Luhar could strike again, Stark twisted like a great cat and struck down. Luhar's skull rang on the flagging. The Earthman's fist rose and fell twice. After that, Luhar did not move.

Stark got to his feet. He stood with his knees bent and his shoulders flexed, looking from side to side, and the sound that came out of his throat was one of pure savagery.

He moved forward a step or two, half naked, bleeding, towering like a dark colossus over the lean Martians, and the brutish throng gave back from him. They had taken more mauling than they liked, and there was something about the Outlander's simple desire to rend them apart that penetrated even their Shanga-clouded minds.

Kala sat up on the floor, and snarled, "Get out."

Stark stood a moment or two longer, looking at them. Then he lifted Freka to his feet and laid him over his shoulder like a sack of meal and went out, moving neither fast nor slow, but in a straight line, and way was made for him.

He carried the Shunni down through the silent streets, and into the twisting, crowded ways of Valkis. There, too, the people stared at him and drew back, out of his path. He came to Delgaun's palace. The guards closed in behind him, but they did not ask that he stop.

Delgaun was in the council room, and Berild was still with him. It seemed that they had been waiting, over their wine and their private talk. Delgaun rose to his feet as Stark came in, so sharply that his goblet fell and spilled a red pool of wine at his feet.

Stark let the Shunni drop to the floor.

"I have brought Freka," he said. "Luhar is still at Kala's."

He looked into Delgaun's eyes, golden and cruel, the eyes of his dream. It was hard not to kill.

Suddenly the woman laughed, very clear and ringing, and her laughter was all for Delgaun.

"Well done, wild man," she said to Stark. "Kynon is lucky to have such a captain. One word for the future, though—watch out for Freka. He won't forgive you this."

Stark said thickly, looking at Delgaun, "This hasn't been a night for forgiveness." Then he added, "I can handle Freka."

Berild said, "I like you, wild man." Her eyes dwelt on Stark's face, curious, compelling. "Ride beside me when we go. I would know more about you."

And she smiled.

A dark flush crept over Delgaun's face. In a voice tight with fury, he said, "Perhaps you've forgotten something, Berild. There is nothing for you in this barbarian, this creature of an hour!"

He would have said more in his anger, but Berild said sharply, "We will not speak of time. Go now, Stark. Be ready at midnight."

Stark went. And as he went, his brow was furrowed deep by a strange doubt.

CHAPTER SIX

AT MIDNIGHT, IN the great square of the slave market, Kynon's caravan formed again and went out of Valkis with thundering drums and skirling pipes. Delgaun was there to see them go, and the cheering of the people rang after them on the desert wind.

Stark rode alone. He was in a brooding mood and wanted no company, least of all that of the Lady Berild. She was beautiful, she was dangerous, and she belonged to Kynon, or to Delgaun, or perhaps to both of them. In Stark's experience, women like that were sudden death, and he wanted no part of her. At any rate, not yet.

Luhar rode ahead with Kynon. He had come dragging into the square at the mounting, his face battered and swollen, an ugly look in his eyes. Kynon gave one quick look from him to Stark, who had his own scars, and said harshly,

"Delgaun tells me there's a blood feud between you two. I want no more of it, understand? After you're paid off you can kill each other and welcome, but not until then. Is that clear?"

Stark nodded, keeping his mouth shut. Luhar muttered assent, and they had not looked at each other since.

Freka rode in his customary place by Kynon, which put him near to Luhar. It seemed to Stark that their beasts swung close together more often than was necessary from the roughness of the track.

The big barbarian captain sat rigidly erect in his saddle, but Stark had seen his face in the torchlight, sick and sweating, with the brute look still clouding his eyes. There was a purple mark on his temple, but Stark was quite sure that Berild had spoken the truth—Freka would not forgive him either the indignity or the hangover of his unfinished wallow under the lamps of Shanga.

The dead sea bottom widened away under the black sky. As they left the lights of Valkis behind, winding their way over the sand and the ribs of coral, dropping lower with every mile into the vast basin, it was hard to believe that there could be life any-where on a world that could produce such cosmic desolation.

The little moons fled away, trailing their eerie shadows over rock formations tortured into impossible shapes by wind and water, peering into clefts that seemed to have no bottom, turn-ing the sand white as bone. The iron stars blazed, so close that the wind seemed edged with their frosty light. And in all that endless space nothing moved, and the silence was so deep that the coughing howl of a sand-cat far away to the east made Stark jump with its loudness.

Yet Stark was not oppressed by the wilderness. Born and bred to the wild and barren places, this desert was more kin to him than the cities of men.

After a while there was a jangling of bangles behind him and Fianna came up. He smiled at her, and she said rather sullenly, "The Lady Berild sent me, to remind you of her wish."

Stark glanced to where the scarlet-curtained litter rocked along, and his eyes glinted.

"She's not one to let go of a thing, is she?"

"No." Fianna saw that no one was within earshot, and then said quietly, "Was it as I said, at Kala's?"

Stark nodded. "I think, little one, that I owe you my life. Luhar would have killed me as soon as I tackled Freka."

He reached over and touched her hand where it lay on the bri-dle. She smiled, a young girl's smile that seemed very sweet in the moonlight, honest and comradely.

It was odd to be talking of death with a pretty girl in the moonlight.

Stark said, "Why does Delgaun want to kill me?"

"He gave no reason, when he spoke to the man from Venus. But perhaps I can guess. He knows that you're as strong as he is, and so he fears you. Also, the Lady Berild looked at you in a certain way."

"I thought Berild was Kynon's woman."

"Perhaps she is—for the time," answered Fianna enigmati-cally. Then she shook her head, glancing around with what was almost fear. "I have risked much already. Please don't let it be known that I've spoken to you, beyond what I was sent to say."

Her eyes pleaded with him, and Stark realized with a shock that Fianna, too, stood on the edge of a quicksand.

"Don't be afraid," he said, and meant it. "We'd better go."

She swung her beast around, and as she did so she whispered, "Be careful, Eric John Stark!"

Stark nodded. He rode behind her, thinking that he liked the sound of his name on her lips.

The Lady Berild lay among her furs and cushions, and even then there was no indolence about her. She was relaxed as a cat is, perfectly at ease and yet vibrant with life. In the shadows of the litter her skin showed silver-white and her loosened hair was a sweet darkness.

"Are you stubborn, wild man?" she asked. "Or do you find me distasteful?"

He had not realized before how rich and soft her voice was. He looked down at the magnificent supple length of her, and said, "I find you most damnably attractive—and that's why I'm stubborn."

"Afraid?"

"I'm taking Kynon's pay. Should I take his woman also?"

She laughed, half scornfully. "Kynon's ambitions leave no room for me. We have an agreement, because a king must have a queen—and he finds my counsel useful. You see, I am ambitious too! Apart from that, there is nothing."

Stark looked at her, trying to read her smoke-gray eyes in the gloom. "And Delgaun?"

"He wants me, but..." She hesitated, and then went on, in a tone quite different from before, her voice low and throbbing with a secret pleasure as vast and elemental as the star-shot sky.

"I belong to no one," she said. "I am my own."

Stark knew that for the moment she had forgotten him. He rode for a time in silence and then he said slowly, repeating Delgaun's words, "Perhaps you have forgotten something, Berild. There is nothing for you in me, the creature of an hour."

He saw her start, and for a moment her eyes blazed and her breath was sharply drawn. Then she laughed, and said,

"The wild man is also a parrot. And an hour can be a long time—as long as eternity, if one wills it so."

"Yes," said Stark, "I have often thought so, waiting for death to come at me out of a crevice in the rocks. The great lizard stings, and his bite is fatal."

He leaned over in the saddle, his shoulders looming above hers, naked in the biting wind.

"My hours with women are short ones," he said. "They come after the battle, when there is time for such things. Perhaps then I'll come and see you."

He spurred away and left her without a backward look, and the skin of his back tingled with the expectancy of a flying knife. But the only thing that followed him was an echo of disturbing laughter down the wind.

Dawn came. Kynon beckoned Stark to his side, and pointed out at the cruel waste of sand, with here and there a reef of basalt black against the burning white.

"This is the country you will lead your men over. Learn it." He was speaking to Luhar as well. "Learn every water hole, every vantage point, every trail that leads toward the Border. There are no better fighters than the Dryland men when they're well led, and you must prove to them that you can lead. You'll work with their own chieftains—Freka, and the others you'll meet after we reach Sinharat."

Luhar said, "Sinharat?"

"My headquarters. It's about seven days' march—an island city, old as the moons. The Rama cult was strong there, legend has it, and it's a sort of holy, taboo place to the tribesmen. That's why I picked it."

He took a deep breath and smiled, looking out over the dead sea bottom toward the Border, and his eyes held the same pitiless light as the sun that baked the desert.

"Very soon, now," he said, more to himself than the others. "Only a handful of days before we drown the Border States in their own blood. And after that..."

He laughed, very softly, and said no more. Stark could believe that what Berild said of him was true. There was a flame of ambition in Kynon that would let nothing stand in its way. He measured the size and the strength of the tall barbarian, the eagle look of his face and the iron that lay beneath his joviality. Then Stark, too, stared off toward the Border and wondered if he would ever see Tarak or hear Simon Ashton's voice again.

For three days they marched without incident. At noon they made a dry camp and slept away the blazing hours, and then went on again under a darkening sky, a long line of tall men and rangy beasts, with the scarlet litter blooming like a strange flower in the midst of it. Jingling bridles and dust, and padded hoofs trampling the bones of the sea, toward the island city of Sinharat.

Stark did not speak again to Berild, nor did she send for him. Fianna would pass him in the camp, and smile sidelong, and go on. For her sake, he did not stop her.

Neither Luhar nor Freka came near him. They avoided him pointedly, except when Kynon called them all together to discuss some point of strategy. But the two seemed to have become friends, and drank together from the same bottle of wine.

Stark slept always beside his mount, his back guarded and his gun loose. The hard lessons learned in his childhood had stayed with him, and if there was a footfall near him in the dust he woke often before the beast did.

Toward morning of the fourth night the wind, that never seemed to falter from its steady blowing, began to drop. At dawn it was dead still, and the rising sun had a tinge of blood. The dust arose under the feet of the beasts and fell again where it had risen.

Stark began to sniff the air. More and more often he looked toward the north, where there was a long slope as flat as a his palm that stretched away farther than he could see.

A restless unease grew within him. Presently he spurred ahead to join Kynon.

"There is a storm coming," he said, and turned his head northward again.

Kynon looked at him curiously.

"You even have the right direction," he said. "One might think you were a native." He, too, gazed with brooding anger at the long sweep of emptiness.

"I wish we were close to the city. But one place is as bad as another when the storm wind blows, and the only thing to do is to keep moving. You're a dead dog if you stop—dead and buried."

He swore, with a curious admixture of Anglo-Saxon in his Martian profanity, as though the storm were a personal enemy.

"Pass the word along to force it—dump whatever they have to to lighten the loads. And get Berild out of that damned litter. Stick by her, will you, Stark? I've got to stay here, at the head of the line. And don't get separated. Above all, *don't get separated!*"

Stark nodded and dropped back. He got Berild mounted, and they left the litter there, a bright patch of crimson on the sand, its curtains limp in the utter stillness.

Nobody talked much. The beasts were urged on to the top of their speed. They were nervous and fidgety, inclined to break out of line and run for it. The sun rose higher.

One hour.

The windless air shimmered. The silence lay upon the caravan with a crushing hand. Stark went up and down the line, lending a hand to the sweating drovers with the pack animals that now carried only water skins and a bare supply of food. Fianna rode close beside Berild.

Two hours.

For the first time that day there was a sound in the desert.

It came from far off, a moaning wail like the cry of a giantess in travail. It rushed closer, rising as it did so to a dry and bitter shriek that filled the whole sky, shook it, and tore it open, letting in all the winds of hell.

It struck swiftly. One moment the air was clear and motionless. The next, it was blind with dust and screaming as it fled, tearing with demoniac fury at everything in it path.

Stark spurred toward the women, who were only a few feet away but already hidden by the veil of mingled dust and sand.

Someone blundered into him in the murk. Long hair whipped across his face and he reached out, crying "Fianna! Fianna!" A woman's hand caught his, and a voice answered, but he could not hear the words.

Then, suddenly, his beast was crowded by other scaly bodies. The woman's grip had broken. Hard masculine hands clawed at him. He could make out, dimly, the features of two men, close to him.

Luhar, and Freka.

His beast gave a great lurch, and sprang forward. Stark was dragged from the saddle, to fall backward into the raging sand.

CHAPTER SEVEN

HE LAY HALF-STUNNED for a moment, his breath knocked out of him. There was a terrible reptilian screaming sounding thin through the roar of the wind. Vague shapes bolted past him, and twice he was nearly crushed by their trampling hoofs.

Luhar and Freka must have waited their chance. It was so beautifully easy. Leave Stark alone and afoot, and the storm and the desert between them would do the work, with no blame attaching to any man.

Stark got to his feet, and a human body struck him at the knees so that he went down again. He grappled with it, snarling, before he realized that the flesh between his hands was soft and draped in silken cloth. Then he saw that he was holding Berild.

"It was I," she gasped, "And not Fianna."

Her words reached him very faintly, though he knew she was yelling at the top of her lungs. She must have been knocked from her own mount when Luhar thrust between them.

Gripping her tightly, so that she should not be blown away, Stark struggled up again. With all his strength, it was almost impossible to stand.

Blinded, deafened, half strangled, he fought his way forward a few paces, and suddenly one of the pack-beasts loomed shadow-like beside him, going by with a rush and a squeal.

By the grace of Providence and his own swift reflexes, he caught its pack lashings, clinging with the tenacity of a man determined not to die. It floundered about, dragging them, until Berild managed to grasp its trailing halter rope. Between them, they fought the creature down.

Stark clung to its head while the woman clambered to its back, twisting her arm through the straps of the pad. A silken scarf whipped toward him. He took it and tied it over the head of the beast so it could breathe, and after that it was quieter.

There was no direction, no sight of anything, in that howling inferno. The caravan seemed to have been scattered like a drift of autumn leaves. Already, in the few brief moments he had stood still, Stark's legs were buried to the knees in a substratum of sand that rolled like water. He pulled himself free and started on, going nowhere, remembering Kynon's words.

Berild ripped her thin robe apart and gave him another strip of silk for himself. He bound it over his nose and eyes, and some of the choking and the blindness abated.

Stumbling, staggering, beaten by the wind as a child is beaten by a strong man, Stark went on, hoping desperately to find the main body of the caravan, and knowing somehow that the hope was futile.

The hours that followed were nightmare. He shut his mind to them, in a way that a civilized man would have found impossible. In his childhood there had been days, and nights, and the problems had been simple ones—how to survive one span of light that one might then survive the span of darkness that came after. One thing, one danger, at a time.

Now there was a single necessity. Keep moving. Forget tomorrow, or what happened to the caravan, or where the little Fianna with her bright eyes may be. Forget thirst, and the pain of breathing, and the fiery lash of sand on naked skin. Only don't stand still.

It was growing dark when the beast fell against a half-buried boulder and snapped its foreleg. Stark gave it a quick and merciful death. They took the straps from the pad and linked themselves together. Each took as much food as he could carry, and Stark shouldered the single skin of water that fortune had vouchsafed them.

They staggered on, and Berild did not whimper.

Night came, and still the storm wind blew. Stark wondered at the woman's strength, for he had to help her only when she fell. He had lost all feeling himself. His body was merely a thing that continued to move only because it had been ordered not to stop.

The haze in his own mind had grown as thick as the black obscurity of the night. Berild had ridden all day, but he had walked, and there was an end even to his strength. He was approaching it now, and was too weary even to be afraid.

He became aware at some indeterminate time that Berild had fallen and was dragging her weight against the straps. He turned blindly to help her up. She was saying something, crying his name, striking at him so that he should hear her words and understand.

At last he did. He pulled the wrappings from his face and breathed clean air. The wind had fallen. The sky was growing clear.

He dropped in his tracks and slept, with the exhausted woman half dead beside him.

Thirst brought them both awake in the early dawn. They drank from the skin, and then sat for a time looking at the desert, and at each other, thinking of what lay ahead.

"Do you know where we are?" Stark asked.

"Not exactly." Berild's face was shadowed with weariness. It had changed, and somehow, to Stark, it had grown more beautiful, because there was no weakness in it.

She thought a minute, looking at the sun. "The wind blew from the north," she said. "Therefore we have come south from the track. Sinharat lies that way, across the waste they call the Belly of Stones." She pointed to the north and east.

"How far?"

"Seven, eight days, afoot."

Stark measured their supply of water and shook his head. "It'll be dry walking."

He rose and took up the skin, and Berild came beside him without a word. Her red hair hung loose over her shoulders. The rags of her silken robe had been torn away by the wind, leaving her only the loose skirt of the desert women, and her belt and collar of jewels.

She walked erect with a steady, swinging strike, and it was almost impossible for Stark to remember her as she had been, riding like a lazy queen in her scarlet litter.

There was no way to shelter themselves from the midday sun. The sun of Mars at its worst, however, was only a pale candle beside the sun of Mercury, and it did not bother Stark. He made Berild lie in the shadow of his own body, and he watched her face, relaxed and unfamiliar in sleep.

For the first time, then, he was conscious of a strangeness in her. He had seen so little of her before, in Valkis, and almost nothing on the trail. Now, there was little of her mind or heart that she could conceal from him.

Or was there? There were moments, while she slept, when the shadows of strange dreams crossed her face. Sometimes, in the unguarded moment of waking, he would see in her eyes a look he could not read, and his primitive senses quivered with a vague ripple of warning.

Yet all through those blazing days and frosty nights, tortured with thirst and weary to exhaustion, Berild was magnificent. Her white skin was darkened by the sun and her hair became a wild red mane, but she smiled and set her feet resolutely by his, and Stark thought she was the most beautiful creature he had ever seen.

On the fourth day they climbed a scarp of limestone worn in ages past by the sea, and looked out over the place called the Belly of Stones.

The sea-bottom curved downward below them into a sort of gigantic basin, the farther rim of which was lost in shimmering distance. Stark thought that never, even on Mercury, had he seen a place more cruel and utterly forsaken of gods or men.

It seemed as though some primal glacier must have met its death here in the dim dawn of Mars, hollowing out its own grave. The body of the glacier had melted away, but its bones were left. Bones of basalt, of granite and marble and porphyry, of every conceivable shape and color and size, picked up by the ice as it marched southward from the pole and dropped here as a cairn to mark its passing.

The Belly of Stones. Stark thought that its other name was Death.

For the first time, Berild faltered. She sat down and bent her head over her hands.

"I am tired," she said. "Also, I am afraid."

Stark asked, "Has it ever been crossed?"

"Once, that I know of. But they were a war party, mounted and well supplied."

Stark looked out across the stones. "We will cross it, " he said.

Berild raised her head. "Somehow I believe you." She rose slowly and put her hands on his breast, over the strong beating of his heart.

"Give me your strength, wild man," she whispered. "I shall need it."

He drew her to him and kissed her, and it was a strange and painful kiss, for their lips were cracked and bleeding from their terrible thirst. Then they went down together into the place called the Belly of Stones.

CHAPTER EIGHT

THE DESERT HAD been a pleasant and kindly place. Stark looked back upon it with longing. And yet this inferno of glaring rock was so like the valleys of his boyhood that it did not occur to him to lie down and die.

They rested for a time in the sheltered crevice under a great leaning slab of blood-red stone, moistening their swollen tongues with a few drops of stinking water from the skin. At nightfall they drank the last of it, but Berild would not let him throw the skin away.

Darkness, and a lunar silence. The chill air sucked the day's heat out of the rocks and the iron frost came down, so that Stark and the red-haired woman must keep moving or freeze.

Stark's mind grew clouded. He spoke from time to time, in a croaking whisper, dropping back into the harsh mother-tongue of the Twilight Belt. It seemed to him that he was hunting, as he had so many times before, in the waterless places—for the blood of the great lizard would save him from thirst.

But nothing lived in the Belly of Stones. Nothing, but the two who crept and staggered across it under the low moons.

Berild fell, and could not rise again. Stark crouched beside her. Her face stared up at him, white in the moonlight, her eyes burning and strange.

"I will not die!" she whispered, not to him, but to the gods. *"I will not die!"*

And she clawed the sand and the bitter rocks, dragging herself onward. It was uncanny, the madness that she had for life.

Stark raised her up and carried her. His breath came in deep, sobbing gasps. After a while he, too, fell. He went on like a beast on all fours, dragging the woman.

He knew dimly that he was climbing. There was a glimmering of dawn in the sky. His hands slipped on a lip of sand and he went rolling down a smooth slope. At length he stopped and lay on his back like a dead thing.

The sun was high when consciousness returned to him. He saw Berild lying near him and crawled to her, shaking her until her eyes opened. Her hands moved feebly and her lips formed the same four words. *I will not die.*

Stark strained his eyes to the horizon, praying for a glimpse of Sinharat, but there was nothing, only emptiness and sand and stone. With great difficulty he got the woman to her feet, and for a while he had to support her.

He tried to tell her that they must go on, but he could no longer form the words. He could only gesture and urge her forward, in the direction of the city.

But she refused to go. "Too far... die... without water..."

He knew that she was right, but still he was not ready to give up.

She began to move away from him, toward the south, and he thought that she had gone mad and was wandering. Then he saw that she was peering with awful intensity at the line of the scrap that formed this wall of the Belly of Stones. It rose into a great ridge, serrated like the backbone of a whale, and some three miles away a long dorsal fin of reddish rock curved out into the desert.

Berild made a little sobbing noise in her throat. She began to plod toward the distant promontory.

Stark caught up with her. He tried to stop her but she would not be stopped, turning a feral glare upon him.

She croaked, "Water!" and pointed.

He was sure now that she was mad. He told her so, forcing the painful words out of his throat, reminding her of Sinharat and that she was going away from any possible help.

She said again, "Too far. Two—three days, without water." She pointed. "Very old well—a chance—"

Stark hesitated, standing with his head swaying drunkenly. He could not think very well. But he thought that the chances were a hundred to one that this was all only a hallucination born of Berild's thirst-madness.

Yet they had very little to lose by taking the gamble. He knew now that they were not going to reach Sinharat. He nodded slowly, and went with her toward the curve of rock.

The three miles might have been three hundred. Each time either of them fell, they lay now for a longer time before struggling up again. Each time, Stark thought that it was the end for the woman. But every time, Berild finally got up and staggered forward again, and he went with her, forcing his body painfully forward on this last throw of the dice.

The sun was setting by the time they came up under the ragged cliffs, onto a little crest. The long, streaming light showed everything, pitilessly.

There was no well. There was a carven pillar, half buried on one side, and the mounded shape of an incalculably ancient ruin of which only the foundations and a few broken columns were left. That was all.

Berild pitched forward and lay still. Stark stood and stared, knowing that this was the end of everything, but unable to think, unable even to remember. He sagged down on his knees beside the woman, and the darkness slid over his mind.

He awoke later, and it was night, and cold. He was vaguely surprised to awaken at all, and he lay for some moments before he tried to raise his head. The two little moons cast a shifting brilliance. He looked for Berild, beside him.

She was gone.

Stark stared at the place in the sand where she had lain, and then after a moment he struggled up to his feet. He looked around and saw Berild.

She was down there below the little crest on which he was. He saw her quite clearly in the moonlight, standing beside the half-buried pillar at the edge of the shapeless ruins. She leaned on the pillar, and her head hung downward as though she could not raise it. He wondered what last well-spring of strength had enabled her to awake and make her way down there.

As Stark watched, he saw Berild's head come up. She looked this way and that through the flattened ruins, turning her head very slowly. After a little while, Stark got an uncanny feeling that she was trying to visualize the place as it had been, even though the walls must have been dust a thousand years ago.

Berild moved. She went inward into the ruin, slowly, carefully, and then she put out her hand as though she was touching the long-vanished wall, as though she was feeling along it for doorway that had not been there for ages. She turned right after so many steps, and again moved carefully in a straight line, and then turned again to her left.

It almost seemed to Stark as though she could see the vanished walls, and was following them. He watched her, a white shape moving in the moonlight, stopping now and then to gather a little strength, but carefully, surely, threading through the desolation of the ancient flattened ruin.

Finally she halted, in a broad flat place that might once have been a central courtyard. There she fell on her knees and began to dig weakly.

The vagueness suddenly left Stark's brain, and his body screamed with its need. There was only one thing Berild would dig for with dying strength. He lurched his way down the little slope, and got down beside her.

"Well," she gasped. "Dig..."

They scrabbled like a pair of dogs in the yielding sand. Stark's nails slipped across something hard, and the moonlight struck a metallic glint from something beneath the dust. Within a few minutes they had bared a golden cover six feet across, very massive and wonderfully carved with the symbols of some lost god of the sea.

Stark struggled to lift the thing away. He could not move it. Then Berild pressed a hidden spring and the cover slid back of itself. Beneath it, wet and cold, protected through all these ages, water stirred gently against mossy stones.

An hour later, Stark and Berild lay sleeping, soaked to the skin, their very hair dripping with the blessed dampness.

Next night, when the low moons roved again over the desert, they sat by the well, drowsy with an animal sense of rest and repletion. Stark looked at the woman, and said, "Who are you, Berild?"

"But you know that. I am a Shunni woman, and I am to be Kynon's queen."

"Are you, Berild? I think you are a witch. Only a witch could find a well hidden for ages, here in a place where you have never been."

She became very still. But when she answered, it was with a laugh.

"No witchcraft, wild man. I told you that a war-party once crossed the Belly of Stones. They followed old tradition, and finally found the well. My father was of that party."

It could be, Stark thought. The secret of a well was a treasure beyond price in these Drylands, to be handed down from father to child.

"I did not know we were near the place," she added, "until I saw the landmark, the fin of rock that juts from the great ridge. But I feared we would die before we reached it."

Yes, thought Stark, it could very well be as she said.

But why did she walk through this place as though she knew and saw the walls as they were a thousand years ago? She does not know that I watched her, moving familiarly through this ancient ruin as one who lived here when it was whole would move.

"What are you dreaming of, wild man?" The moon is in your eyes."

"I don't know," said Stark.

Dreams, delusions, the unearthly suspicions that had crossed his mind? It could be that he had heard too much talk of old Martian legends, in this deathly wilderness where the dark memory of the Ramas haunted the minds of men.

"Forget your dreams, wild man. That which is real is better."

He looked down at her in the pale light, and she was young, and beautifully made, and her lips were smiling.

He bent his head. Her arms went around him. Her hair blew soft against his cheek. Then, suddenly, she set her teeth cruelly into his lip. He cried out and thrust her away, and she sat back on her heels, mocking him.

Stark cursed her. There was a taste of blood in his mouth. He reached out and caught her, and again she laughed, a peculiarly sweet, wicked sound.

"That," she said, "is because you called Fianna's name instead of mine, when the storm broke."

The wind blew over them, sighing, and the desert was very still.

For two days they remained among the ruins. At evening of the second day Stark filled the water skin, and Berild replaced the golden cover on the well. They began the last long march toward Sinharat.

CHAPTER NINE

STARK SAW IT rising against the morning sky—a city of marble, high on an island of coral laid bare by the vanishing of the sea. The coral island stood up tall in the hard clear sunlight, its naked cliffs beautifully striated with deep rose and white and delicate pink. And from this lovely pedestal there rose walls and towers so perfectly built from many-shaded marble and so softly sculptured by time that it was difficult to tell where the work of men began and ended. Sinharat, the Ever-living....

Yet it had died. As he came closer to it, plodding slowly through the sand with Berild, he saw that the place was now no more than a beautiful corpse, many of the lovely towers broken, many of the palaces roofless and open to the sky. The only signs of life were outside and below the city, on the dry lagoon that surrounded it. Here were beasts and tents and men, a huddle of them that looked small and unimportant under the loom of the dead city.

"The caravan," said Berild. "Kynon... and the others... are here."

"Why are they camped below the city instead of in it?" asked Stark.

She gave him a mocking sidelong glance. "This was the old city of the Ramas, and its name still has power. The people of the Drylands don't like to enter it. When the hordes gather here, you will see. They will camp outside."

"For fear of the Ramas? But the Ramas are gone, long ago."

"Of course—but old fears die slowly." Berild laughed. "Kynon has no such superstitions. He will be up there in the city."

As they plodded nearer, they were seen. Riders started to race out toward them from the encampment, and figures hurried between the skin tents. Soon they were near enough to hear a distant crying of excited voices.

Stark walked stolidly on, his face set straight ahead. It seemed to him that the shimmering haze around them had darkened, a little. A vein in his temple had begun to throb.

The racing Shunni riders reached them, voices shouted to them. Berild answered, but Stark said nothing. He walked on, and his eyes were on the city.

Berild plucked his arm, and spoke his name urgently, repeating it so that he would listen.

"Stark! I know what is in your mind, but it is not the way. You must wait...."

He plodded on and did not answer, or look at her. Now they were near enough the camp that tribesmen were all around them, calling Berild's name in a rising uproar of excitement, while others of them ran toward the great stairway, carved in the coral, that led up into Sinharat.

The camp of the caravan was below that stairway, and not far from the encampment was a big arched opening in the coral cliff, a natural cavern. Men came from it with heavy water-skins, so that it was evident that there was a well in the cavern. But Stark saw only the great stairway that led upward, and as he walked on toward it, the tribesmen around them stopped the excited shouting. They fell silent, watching Stark's face, and drew away from him as he set foot upon the lowest step of the stair.

"You must *listen!*" Berild, somewhere in the darkening haze beside him, was clinging to his arm, speaking almost in his ear. "Kynon will kill you if you do this thing. I know him, Stark."

But he was not Stark any more, he was N'Chaka. The enemies of N'Chaka had dealt him a cruel death, but it had passed him by, he had not died and now it was his turn. They were up there, on the cliffs where even the great lizards did not go, and they thought they were safe from him but he would climb, and climb, and slay....

He climbed, and the darkness of his vision deepened, and then of a sudden it cleared away and he stood in the hard clear sunlight in a great square of the city Sinharat.

All around the square rose the sculptured fronts of buildings, dazzling in the morning light. On them marched files of carven figures in the dress of ancient Mars, and the sun struck glints from jeweled eyes, and harshened the outlines of the faces so

that it seemed that all the pride and glory and cruelty of the Ramas of old still held sway here.

But Stark had eyes only for the living, for the men who were
coming across the square. Kynon, a gun in his hand, was walking
out from the biggest palace, and ahead of him came Luhar.

Luhar.

"Stark, stop!" Kynon's voice rang.

Stark did not even look at him. He had eyes only for Luhar, who
stood there fresh from sleep, his pale hair tumbled, his eyes still
drowsy but now, sharply, awakening.

"I will shoot you unless you stop, Stark!" warned Kynon.

From beside him, Stark vaguely heard Berild's cry. "But for
him, I'd be dead in the desert, Kynon!"

Kynon made a decisive gesture. "If he saved you, I will thank
him. But he must not touch Luhar! Come here, Berild!"

Voices. And what were voices to N'Chaka when the time for
slaying, for vengeance, had come?

Berild had left him, had hurried forward to run past Luhar in
the direction of Kynon, who stood, grim with the leveled gun.
And still Stark moved on.

He saw the first sharp alarm in Luhar's face now replaced by
a triumphant, taunting smile. The man whom Luhar had killed
had come back to life, but he was going to be killed a second
time, here and now, and all was well. Luhar's smile deepened.

Berild, running past Luhar, seemed to stumble and pitch
against him, and then recovered herself.

Luhar's smile of triumph suddenly blanked out. In his face was
only an incredulous astonishment. He stood, and looked down
at the slash in his tunic from which his heart's blood was spurting, and then he crashed down the flagging.

Stark stopped, then. He did not understand. But Kynon did
and his voice came in a wrathful shout.

"*Berild!*"

Berild calmly threw away the little knife in her hand. Its thin
blade glittered redly in the sun, and it rattled and tinkled on the
stone paving. Her back was to Stark and he could not see her

face, but he could hear the bitter passion that throbbed in her voice as she said to Kynon, "He was nearly my death. Do you understand that? He would have *ended* me!" She spoke the word as though she was uttering the most blackly blasphemous thing in the world. "What now, Kynon? Will you shoot *me*?"

There was a silence. N'Chaka was gone, and Eric John Stark stood looking down at the dead Venusian. He was not thinking of Luhar now. He was thinking that Berild must have had that little knife hidden in the waistband of her skirt all this time, and he was wondering how close he had come to getting it in his back.

And why, in the moment of her passion, had she spoken that odd word, accusing Luhar of nearly "ending" her?

Stark went on, toward Kynon. He saw the rage in Kynon's face and he thought that he was going to shoot, after all. There was nothing of the jovial barbarian and hail-fellow about Kynon now. He looked as friendly as a frustrated tiger.

"Damn you, Berild, I needed that man!" he said.

Berild's eyes blazed. "Why don't you get down beside him and cry and cover your head? In his desire to murder Stark, he did not scruple to leave me to die also. Am I to forgive that?"

Kynon looked as though he was tempted to strike her. But Stark spoke, and asked, "Where is Freka?"

Kynon turned on him, and his face now was dark and dangerous. "Listen, Stark, you'd be dead on the stones right now instead of Luhar, if Berild hadn't such a passion for revenge. You're alive, you're lucky. Don't push it."

Stark merely waited. Kynon went on, in a voice that cut as coldly as a wind from the pole.

"Freka is out with others, raising the Dryland fighting-men who will gather here. Freka will return. When he returns, I'll kill the first of you two who makes a move at the other. Do you hear?"

Stark said, "I hear."

Kynon's piercing gaze hung on him, but apparently he decided not to push it either. He growled, "Hell take such allies! Old hatred, old feuds, always at each other's throats."

"I thought you wanted tough fighters," said Stark. "If you wanted dear hearts and loving friendship, you sent for the wrong men."

"I'm beginning to think I did," said Kynon, scowling. "Well, it's done for now. But it isn't done for good. Delgaun was close with Luhar and he'll want blood for this when he finds out about it. He and his cursed Low-Canallers have been difficult enough to handle, as it is."

He turned angrily and started back toward the building from which they had come. Berild gave Stark an unfathomable look as they followed.

There came a sound that made the hair bristle a little on Stark's neck. It was a murmuring, seeming to come from all the silent, dead white city around them, a sound not human in tone but rising and falling like distant voices. The morning breeze had begun to blow and the vague whispering seemed brought by it. Stark did not like it at all.

They went with Kynon into a room of polished marble, with faded frescoes of the same figures in ancient dress that marched in the carvings outside. The frescoes were much more faded in some places than in others, so that only here and there did a shadowy face leap suddenly into being, prideful and mocking with smiling lips, or a procession pass solemnly toward some obliterated worship.

Kynon had here a folding wooden desk, with papers scattered on it, which looked utterly incongruous in this place.

"I sent riders back," Kynon said abruptly, "to search for you. They didn't find you. You were nowhere near Sinharat. And now you pop up out of nowhere."

Berild said, "Your riders wouldn't have found us. We came across the Belly of Stones."

"With one skin of water? It's impossible!"

Berild nodded. "But we had three skins, that were on the pack-beast that Stark caught. They were our life."

So Berild had her secrets from Kynon, and one of them was the hidden well? Stark was not surprised. She was the kind of woman who would have many secrets.

But I have my secrets too, Berild. And I will not tell even you how I saw you walking in the moonlight with too great a knowledge of dead ages.

"It was not," Berild was saying to Kynon, "exactly a pleasure journey. I want to rest. Was Fianna saved?"

Kynon came out of some inner abstraction to answer, with a nod, "Yes, she and most your things."

Berild left. Kynon's eyes followed her, and when she had gone he looked at Stark.

"Even with water, only a wild man could have done it," he said. "But again I warn you—curb your wildness, Stark. Especially when Delgaun comes."

Stark said, "Drylanders and Low-Canallers and outland mer-cenaries—can you keep them from each other's throats?"

"By all the gods, I'll do it if I have to tear throats out myself!" Kynon swore viciously. "We can grab a world and only one thing could prevent it—the old feuds that have brought so many brave plans to wreck, in the past. They'll not wreck *my* plans!"

They would if he could encompass it, Stark thought. He had known from the time that Ashton had given him his mission of stopping this thing, that the only possible leverage he would have was the ancient quarrels of Mars, that his only chance would be to turn these old enemies against each other. How he would do this, he did not know.

He found that he was swaying, and Kynon saw it and exclaimed, "Go get some rest before you drop here. I'll say this, that you may be a wild man but you are indeed a man, to have come the way you did."

He stepped closer and added flatly, "And I'll tell you also, that I don't quite like men who are as tough or almost as tough as I am. Get out."

Stark went the way he pointed, into a broad and shadowy hallway. The first room he looked into had a sleeping-pad in the corner. He stumbled to it and fell, rather than lay down.

But even as he plunged into sleep, he heard the faint echoing whisper from outside, the uncanny murmurs, rising now into a strange, pulsating singing of sound that seemed to moan through the whole dead city like a dirge.

CHAPTER TEN

STARK AWOKE TO find the room in semi-dusk, a narrow shaft of red sunset light striking in from a high loophole window. He sensed that a presence had awakened him and then he saw Fianna, sitting on a carved stone bench across the room. She was looking at him, her eyes serious and dark.

"You growled, before you awoke," she said. "Like a great beast."

"Perhaps that is what I am," he said.

"Perhaps it is," Fianna said, and nodded. "But if so, I will tell you this, beast: You have come into a trap."

He got to his feet, every nerve waking to alertness. He went and stood looking down at her.

"What do you mean, little one?"

"Don't call me 'little one,'" she flashed. "It is not I who am foolish and young—it is you. If you were not, you would not be in Sinharat."

"But you are here also, Fianna."

She sighed. "I know. It is not a place where I would wish to be. But I serve the lady Berild, and must go where she takes me."

He looked keenly down at her for a moment. "You serve her. Yet you hate her."

She hesitated. "I don't hate her. Sometimes, for all her wickednesses, I envy her—she lives so passionately and fully. But I fear her—I fear what she and Kynon may do to my people."

Eric John Stark feared that too but he did not say so. Instead, he said, "Being a beast, I'm concerned for my hide. You spoke of a trap."

"It is this," said Fianna. "You are valuable to Kynon, to train his hordes, when they gather, in outland fighting-skills. But Delgaun and his support are even more valuable to Kynon. If Delgaun asks your death for Luhar's…"

She did not finish, and Stark finished for her, "Why, then Kynon will very likely regretfully sacrifice one guerilla fighter, to keep the Low-Canallers happy. Thanks for the warning. But this was already in my mind."

Fianna said hopefully, "You could slip away before Delgaun comes. If you stole a mount and took water, you could escape."

No, thought Stark. It is the sensible thing to do, if I want to save my skin, but Simon Ashton will be waiting in Tarak and I can't go to him and say that I've quit the whole thing, it's just too dangerous.

Besides, he thought, there's something here and I can't understand and that I must find out. Something...

Fianna, watching his face, said suddenly, "You're going to stay. But don't give me the lying reasons you're now thinking up. You stay because of Berild."

Stark smiled. "All women think that men do nothing except for a woman."

"And all men deny it when it is true," she said. "Tell me, were you and Berild lovers in the desert?"

"Jealous, Fianna?"

He expected her to sputter resentment at that, but she did not. Instead an enigmatic, almost pitying look came into her eyes, and she said softly, "No, not jealous, Eric John Stark. But saddened."

She rose suddenly to her feet and said, formally, "I am sent to bring you to the Lady Berild."

Stark's eyes narrowed slightly. "With Kynon right here? Will he like that?"

Fianna smiled mirthlessly. "That's a clever, cautious beast, to think of that. But Kynon is down in the camp below the city. And the Lady Berild does not like this place, and lives elsewhere. I will take you."

He went out with her into the great square. There was no one in it at all, and its sculptured walls and towers rose into the flaring red sunset, wrapped in a silence that was oppressive. As they walked, their footfalls sounded loud upon the ancient flagstones, and it seemed to Stark that all the stones of dead Sinharat that loomed around them were listening, and watching.

The evening wind sprang up and touched his face. Suddenly, he stopped. He had heard a sound that began as an inaudible vibration and rose stealthily into his hearing. A whispering, a vast, vague murmuring that came from everywhere and nowhere, so that it seemed that Sinharat was not only listening and watching, but was now speaking also.

Of a sudden, the whispering swelled up into musical voices. Organ-voices, that seemed to come from the very coral on which the city stood. Flute-voices, from the tall towers that caught the last red light. Shrill, distant voices as of the desert pipes, raging from the carven cornices of buildings far across the city.

Stark caught Fianna's arm. "What is it?"

"The voices of the Ramas."

He said roughly, "Make sense."

She shrugged. "So all Drylanders believe. That is why they hate to come here. But others have said that it is only the wind that sings in the hollow coral."

Stark understood. The massive coral pedestal on which the city stood was indeed a vast honeycomb of tiny air-passages, and the wind forcing up through them could create this eery effect.

"No wonder your barbarians don't like it," he muttered. "I'm a barbarian. I don't like it."

They went through streets that ran like topless tunnels between the walls and the towers that reached impossibly thin and tall into the evening sky. Some of them had lost their upper stories, and some had fallen entirely, but in the main they were still beautiful, the colors of the marble still lovely. And as the wind changed, the singing voices of Sinharat changed with it. Sometimes those voices were soft and gentle, murmuring about everlasting youth and its pleasures. And then they became strong and fierce with pride, crying *You die, but I do not!* Sometimes they swelled up, mad, laughing and hateful. But always their song was subtly evil.

In the outside world, even in Valkis, the Ramas had been only a legend, a shadowy tradition that a clever barbarian was using to give glamour to his leadership. But here in Sinharat, the Ramas seemed very real, and he began to understand why all this world in the long ago had feared them, and hated them, and envied them.

Fianna led him toward the western battlement of the high city, a point a little distance away from the great stair. She took him into a building that loomed in the gathering darkness like a white dream-castle, and along a hallway where flaring torches in sockets threw a shaking light over the carven dancing-girls that seemed in that illumination to be moving along the walls. She opened a door and stepped aside for Stark to enter.

The room was low and long, and the soft glow that lighted it came from the lamps with shades of alabaster as thin as paper. Berild came toward him, but not the Berild of the desert. She wore a jeweled girdle, and a wide collar of green jewels above her breasts, and a white cloak hanging from her shoulders.

"I hate that gloomy ruin where Kynon hold his councils," she said. "This is better. Do you think it was the apartment of a queen?"

"It is now," said Stark.

Her eyes softened. He took her by the shoulders, and her mocking smile flashed and she said, "But if I am a queen, I am not for you, wild man."

Then, with a startling abruptness, the smile left her face and she put his hands away. "There is no time for this," she said. "I sent for you to speak of danger. You may not live out this night."

"If you wanted to take my mind off you," said Stark, "that statement is just the thing to do it."

His grim humor awakened no answer in her sober face. She took his hand and led him to an open window.

This westward face of the building rose sheer from the edge of the coral cliff. Out beyond the window stretched the vastness of the deepening Martian night, with no moons yet up but a great vault of stars tenting the desert. A little to the left, down at the base of the cliff, were the torches of the camp, winking and shaking in the wind.

Up from beneath them came the murmurours, whistling, piping voices of the wind in the hollow coral. But also there came the sounds of the camp, of squealing beasts, of a voice bawling an order, of picket-pins being driven deeper.

"Kynon is there," said Berild. "He waits to welcome Delgaun and the others from Valkis, who arrive tonight."

The skin between Stark's shoulders tightened slightly. The crisis had come sooner than he expected.

He shrugged. "Well, then, Delgaun is coming. I wasn't afraid of him in Valkis, and I don't fear him here."

Berild looked at him steadily. "Fear him," she said. "I know Delgaun."

Their faces were only inches apart and there was something in hers that he had glimpsed there once before.

"How can you know him so well?" he asked. "You're a Shunni woman, and he is a Valkis."

"Do you think Kynon hasn't been plotting with Delgaun for months?" She demanded impatiently. "Do you think I can watch a man all those times and not know whether he is dangerous?"

"Your concern for me is moving, Berild," said Stark. "That is—if it's sincere."

He half-expected her to flare out at him for that, but she did not. She looked at him levelly, and said, "You're strong. And it may be that I shall need a strong man at my side."

"To protect you? But you have Kynon!"

Berild said impatiently, "I need no one to *protect* me. As for Kynon, I come always second with him, and his ambitions first. He would put me aside without a thought, if it helped to realize his plans of conquest."

"And you don't intend to be put aside," said Stark.

Her eyes flashed. "I do not."

"So, the wild man may be useful," said Stark. "I'll say this for you, Berild—you have a certain honesty that I admire."

She smiled wickedly. "It's only the least of my attractions."

Stark thought for a moment. "When Delgaun arrives, will the tribesmen down there come up into Sinharat with him and Kynon?"

Berild nodded. "Yes, for this night Kynon is to raise his standard. For that, they'll come—even though they have a superstitious fear of this place."

He looked at her curiously, and said, "You talk to tribesmen's superstitions—yet you yourself are a woman of the Shunni."

"Yes. But I do not believe what they believe. Kynon taught me better—he had education, in outland places, and I learned from him."

"You didn't learn ambition from him," said Stark.

"No," she said. "I'm tired of being just another woman. I too would like to hold a world between my hands."

Looking at her, it came to Stark that Ashton might have more to fear than he knew, that this woman might be as great a threat to the peace of Mars as Kynon and Delgaun.

Of a sudden, the cold night wind brought through the open window a sound of excited voices from the encampment underneath the cliff.

Stark and Berild went to the window. Far out in the darkness of the desert there were little points of ruddy light that moved in a long line toward Sinharat.

Drums suddenly boomed hoarsely down in the camp below, drowning with their clamor the piping of the wind in the coral. Torches sprang to light between the tents, and the drums grew louder.

"Delgaun has come," said Berild.

"And I must go," said Stark.

He turned and went out of the room. In the corridor of the carven dancing-girls, he came face to face with Fianna.

"You were listening," he said.

She did not deny it. "I hate to see foolish beasts run their throats toward the knife," she said. "So I have a word for you, Eric John Stark."

"Yes?"

"Don't trust Berild too far. She is not all she seems."

Fianna paused, and then in a whisper, she added, "Did you ever think that all of the Ramas of old might *not* be dead?"

All the half-formed, vague suspicions that had haunted Stark since the desert surged up in a cold tide within him. He grasped for her, demanding, "What do you mean?"

But Fianna eluded him, and was gone like a shadow. After a moment, he turned and went out into the dark, silent street.

The drums were echoing across dead Sinharat, but as Stark went through the streets it seemed to him that above them he could hear, louder than ever before, the mocking sounds, the pipings and flutings and whisperings, that seemed to echo from the past.

CHAPTER ELEVEN

SHATTERING THE NIGHT, light and sound crashed up the grand stairway of Sinharat. First came massed torch-bearers, holding their flaring brands high. Then the thundering skin drums and shrilling pipes, and then Kynon and his newcome allies, and after them the tribesmen.

As the procession climbed, the dark western face of the cliff-top city leaped into the quivering light. The ancient carven faces that had for centuries looked out on nothing but darkness and silence and desert, now glared triumphantly in the shaking red rays. And despite the proud, loud clamor of drums and pipes, the eyes of climbing tribesmen glinted with doubt as they looked up and beheld the old stone faces of the Ramas.

Stark heard the uproar approaching through the streets, as he waited patiently in the darkness of a deep doorway of the building that was Kynon's headquarters. He saw the torches, drummers, pipers, warriors, march into the great square and across it toward him. He thought that Kynon was putting on a brave show indeed, to impress everyone that the men of Kesh and Shun and the men of the Low Canals were now friends and allies.

Kynon came up onto the steps in front of the old building, only a score of yards from where Stark stood in shadows. He turned and faced the torches and the glinting spears and the fierce faces.

"Bring the banner!" he cried in his bull voice.

A tall barbarian came promptly, with a black silken banner rolled on a long staff. With a gesture totally theatrical, and yet nonetheless impressive, Kynon shook the silk loose so that it flowed out on the cold wind.

"Here I raise the Banner of Death and Life!" he cried. "Death for our enemies, and life—unending life—for us who shall rule this world!"

The silken standard, unfolding on the wind, showed two white crowns, and below them a red sword, on a field of dead black.

The cry of the crowd was like the baying of a great hound.

Stark's eyes had been searching the faces in the torchlight and now he saw the little knot of men in outland dress—Walsh, Themis, Arrod—and in front of them, Delgaun.

"I bring you not only a banner, but strong allies!" roared Kynon. "In the new era that begins, old enmities are forgotten. Delgaun of Valkis stands shoulder to shoulder with us in this conquest, and with him will march the men of the Low Canals!"

Delgaun came up beside Kynon and faced the crowd and raised his hand. There was a response, but not a wildly enthusiastic one.

Shrewdly, Kynon did not give them time to start muttering. He said loudly, "And when Kesh and Shun, and Valkis and Jekkara, march together against the Border States, with us will fight brave men from far away!"

Walsh and the other two heard their cue and started up the steps. But Stark stepped out of the shadows and came up beside Delgaun and Kynon, and looked at them and smiled. He said loudly, so that all could hear, "I will follow your banner—and I greet my brother and comrade-in-arms, Delgaun of Valkis!"

He put his hand on Delgaun's shoulder in the traditional gesture. Delgaun's gold-colored eyes flared hot as an eagle's, and his hand went under his cloak. He said thickly,

"You bastard...."

"Do you want to ruin everything?" said Kynon in a low voice charged with agony and anger. "Return the greeting!"

Slowly, as though he would rather have torn his arm from its socket, Delgaun raised his hand and placed it on Stark's shoulder. There was sweat on his face.

Stark grinned at him sardonically. He thought his timing had been rather good. Delgaun would try to kill him, but would not now dare to do it openly. Comradeship in arms was a sacred thing to the barbarians.

"The riders are out in the Drylands this night!" Kynon shouted to the crowd. "The fighting-men of all the tribes will soon gather here! Go back down and prepare for them. And remember..." He paused dramatically, then continued, "Remember that it is not only the loot of a world we march for, but unending life to enjoy it in, through the Sending On of Minds!"

The crowd raised a storm of cheers. But it seemed to Stark that the carven stone faces of the Ramas high above them looked down at them with secret mirth.

Kynon turned abruptly and led the way into his council hall. They followed. In the torchlit room, he turned on them, looking dangerous as an angry lion.

"We'll have this out once and for all," he said between his teeth, "Stark, you've brought nothing but dissension to us, since you came."

Stark answered flatly. "An old enemy tried to kill me—and when I survived, I tried to kill him. Would you yourself have done differently?"

He looked then at Delgaun. "Luhar was my enemy, but I do not know why Delgaun should hate me. Let's have this thing out, as you say. Delgaun, if you have cause for anger against me, say now what it is. Speak out!"

The golden eyes glared at him out of a face that had become livid. Delgaun's lips twisted, but he did not speak.

Damn you, you can't speak, thought Stark. You hate me because you're jealous over Berild, but you daren't say that out.

Delgaun finally muttered, "I may have been wrong. It could be that Luhar poisoned my mind against Stark."

"Then that is that," said Kynon.

He went over to the table and sat down behind it and let his bleak gaze rove over their faces before he spoke.

"The fighting-men will start arriving tomorrow," he said. "I want them trained in detachments as they come in. Arrod, you'll help Stark do that. Knight's cruiser should be here in two days, with the weapons we need. I want our force on the march from Sinharat two weeks from now, no later."

A glow came into Kynon's eagle eyes, although his voice remained hard and harsh.

"The Border States we'll hit first will be Varl and Kathuun. They're bound to get warning enough to close their gates. My Drylanders will make a pretense of siege. Then we'll retreat, a little, as help comes from the two cities."

A slow smile curved Delgaun's lips. "Yes, help from Valkis and Jekkara. My Low-Canallers will nobly come to the assistance of the Border States. When they joyfully open their gates to us— then we all go in together."

"Clever," said Walsh admiringly, a smile on his coarse face.

Kynon's big hand squeezed shut. "The fall of Varl and Kathuun will breach the whole line of the Border States. We'll roll up that line, and in six months we'll be in Kabora."

Themis, a man with a dark, saturnine face who spoke little, asked, "What about the government of Earth?"

Kynon grinned. "Principle of non-intervention in Martian affairs has been their policy for a long time. They'll deplore, they'll protest—but nothing more, and we'll have our hands on the throat and the loot of a world."

Stark felt cold. He could not fault this plan. It would work, and red destruction would run along the Border like a spreading flame. Men would die in those cities, and most of them would be the warriors of the Drylands, so that the clever thieves of the Low Canals could reap the plunder.

There came to Stark the determination to kill Kynon with his own hand before he let this thing happen.

Kynon rose. "That's it. You've got your jobs, and they won't be easy. Get to them by the first light of morning."

His voice stopped them as they were going. "One more thing. The soul and spirit of this whole war is the hunger for eternal life, the secret of the Ramas. If any of you let on that I don't have that secret, if any of you even as much as smile when the Sending On of Minds is mentioned—"

He did not finish. He did not have to. What was in Kynon's face was a threat more deadly than any he could have spoken.

Stark thought that if what he suspected was true, the joke was on Kynon, and a grim and terrible joke it was. If Berild…

He would not let himself finish that thought. It was impossible. To dream that the old, dark secret of Mars had survived, that some of the Ramas had survived, just because he saw a woman walking in moonlight and heard a serving-girl's sullen insinuation—it was too fantastic. He would forget it.

But Stark could not forget it in the days that followed. He spent each day down in the dust and glare of the desert, teaching the techniques of modern guerilla warfare to the men of Kesh and Shun who rode constantly in from the wastes. He heard the talk of these warriors, and more even than loot they talked of unending life. He saw how their eyes followed the great black banner, with its white crowns above the crimson sword, when it went with Kynon through the camp.

Knighton's little cruiser came in, its weapons were unloaded, and it went away again for more. Men came from Valkis and Jekkara and Barrakesh, and with these Kynon and Delgaun talked long, setting the times and routes for the great stroke against the Border, and then these too went away again.

Freka came, with the last of the fighting men of Shun. Stark saw the tall barbarian chieftain riding with his men through the camp that had now grown great, and he heard the shouts that hailed him. He went a little later to report to Kynon, and Freka was standing with him by the banner.

Stark felt the Shunni's eyes glaring at him through half-drooping lids, yet Freka made no move.

"You've both had your warning," Kynon said curtly. "Remember it. I won't repeat it."

Stark made his report on the readiness of the warriors, and went away, and felt Freka's gaze burning a hole in his back.

He had not seen Berild, in these days of hurry and toil. One evening when he left Kynon and Delgaun in the camp, and climbed the great stairway in the red sunset light, Stark turned aside and went toward the building where she had her quarters. He felt that he had to put the dark, impossible doubt in his mind at rest.

The wind was talking through the hollow coral, the streets of Sinharat vibrated to the murmuring voices that strengthened as the light faded and the wind rose. From the marble walls, the stone faces of the Ramas watched him with fixed and secret smiles.

Stark came into the street he sought and then stopped suddenly. At the far end of the dusky street, he saw the flutter of a white cloak that disappeared as he watched.

He thought that it was Berild, and he followed. But without being conscious of it, he made his footfalls softer and softer, going through the silent, dusky streets after her like a hunting sand-cat.

Where a street turned, he lost her.

Stark stood, undecided which way to search, and the whispering voices in the coral mocked and jeered him.

A narrow way beside him led to a wider street on which rose a great domed white pile. There was a track in the blown dust and sand that way. He followed it, and reached the gaping open doorway of the building, and peered cautiously.

It was not much more shadowy inside than in the dusking street. Light still struck through tall windows set above a gallery that ringed the great dome, high up above the floor. The light was enough to show a round, perfectly empty hall, whose only feature was a crumbling inscription that covered all one wall. Berild stood, her back to him, looking up and reading this inscription.

She was silent, but he knew that she was reading from the way her head turned slightly, inclining forward with each few lines. And for a moment, Stark felt a coldness like that of outer space.

For the inscription was in that ancient language of the Ramas which no one for millennia had been able to read.

"Witch-woman," his instincts clamored. *"Not human, not really human. Run!"*

He forced himself to stand silent, there in the shadows outside the door. He saw Berild, after a few more minutes of concentration, droop her head as though in pain.

Then she turned brusquely away from the inscription, and her sandals tapped the dusty flagstones. She went toward a stair that spiraled up the side of the vast room, to the encircling gallery. Stark saw her go to one of the tall windows there, and stand looking out with her back still toward him.

The wind chuckled and muttered through the gaping doors and windows, and it covered the sound of Stark's soft footfalls as he went across the room and up the stair. He came up and stopped, a dozen feet behind the silent woman.

"It's not as you remembered it, is it, Berild?" he said. "What was it like before, with the blue ocean around it, and the ships?"

CHAPTER TWELVE

BERILD DID NOT turn around. It was as though she had not heard his voice. She stood absolutely still—too still.

Stark went to the window and stood beside her. The dying light from across the desert showed her face, with its mocking smile.

"What are you dreaming about now, wild man?"

To Stark's ears, it seemed as though there was a thin edge of brittleness in her mockery.

"You're a Rama," he said flatly.

"But the Ramas were long ago," she said. "If I were one, I would be very old. How old?"

He disregarded the derision in her tone. He said, "That's what I want to know, Berild. How old? A thousand years ... ten thousand? How many bodies have you inhabited?"

Instantly, the moment that he put the thought into spoken words, it seemed immeasurably more horrible to Stark than it had before. Something of that horror must have shown in his face, for he saw a dangerous flash in her eyes.

"What you say is madness," she said. "Who has put this thought into your head?"

"A woman walking in the moonlight," he muttered. "A woman who threaded her way through walls and doorways that hadn't been there for centuries, and that she could only know because she remembered them."

Berild's tension seemed to relax a little. She said impatiently, "So that's it! In the Belly of Stones—you were awake, when I hunted for and found the well."

Then she laughed. "Why didn't you say so, why did you keep it to yourself? I could have told you that it was the secret my father gave me—to walk this way, so many steps, then that way, and so on, until I was where the well was buried. And you thought ..." Her laughter came again.

"I don't believe you," he said. "You were not measuring your steps—you were groping, remembering." The shadows were deepening. He took a step toward her, peering into her face. "You've been laughing at Kynon all along, haven't you? The real Rama, laughing at the pretend one?"

Berild said, in a slow voice that had now no laughter in it at all, "Forget this thing, Eric John Stark. It is madness, and it could be your death."

"How many of you are there, Berild? How many have come down through the ages, secretly stealing the bodies of others, laughing at the world that thought they were all gone long ago?"

In a whisper that was full of infinite menace, Berild said, "I tell you again, forget this."

"There would have to be at least two of you, so one could use the Sending On of Minds on the other," Stark said, and nodded. "And who but the jealous one, the one who said, 'There is nothing for you in this creature of an hour.' It is he, isn't it? Delgaun?"

In a voice sibilant with passion, Berild said, "I will hear no more of your delusions. Don't come with me—I want no madman for an escort."

And she turned swiftly and left him, almost running down the stair that was in heavy darkness now, and so out of the building.

Stark stood, his mind awhirl. She had been warm and living, her arms around him that night, but inside the Shunni woman's vibrant body—a Rama woman of long ago?

He turned and looked back out the open window. The moons were rising, and their shifting light slanted across the vague desert. Down beneath the cliffs of Shinharat, the far-flung torches of the Drylanders' camp pricked the gloom, and voices came upon the piping wind, and the squeal of beasts, and the sounds of a sane and normal world. He told himself that he was deluded, obsessed. But he knew that it was not so.

Looking down there, another thought came slowly to Stark. If it was true, if Berild and Delgaun were Ramas of old, then this barbarian campaign to loot and conquer half of Mars was steered by intelligence as old and evil as Sinharat. Yet Kynon would be the conqueror, the ruler, and he was no Rama. Was that why Berild had become Kynon's woman, to influence his every move, plotting all the while with Delgaun?

He turned abruptly around, away from the window. The great, ancient hall was now a well of utter darkness, and the wind that moaned and whispered through it seemed cold with the cold of dead ages. A detestation of the place seized Stark, and he went down the stairs and out of the building, feeling all the way as though eyes watched him in the blackness.

As he walked through the silent, moon-splashed streets of Sinharat, Stark tried to think. He had to stop Kynon's plan of conquest—was more bound to do so, if age-old evil was behind it. Should he tell Kynon and the others, about Delgaun and Berild?

They would laugh at him. He had no proof to show them, none in the world.

But there must be some way. He...

Stark suddenly stopped walking, all his nerves alert. He listened, turning his head this way and that.

There was no sound at all, but the wind and its whisperings. Nothing moved in the shadow-blotched, moonlit streets of the dead city.

But Stark was not reassured. His senses had spoken and had told him that someone, something, was stalking him.

He moved on, after a moment, heading toward the distant glow of light that came from Kynon's palace in the great square. But after a dozen steps he suddenly froze again.

This time, he heard it. A scutter and scuffle of feet, back down the narrow street in the shadows.

Stark put his hand on his gun and his voice rang down the street. "Come out!"

A stooping figure came out of the shadow, toward him. For a moment he did not realize that this was the tall barbarian chieftain, Freka, for the man was hunched, bent forward.

Then as Freka came across a bar of moonlight, Stark saw his face, slack-jawed, grinning, inexpressibly repulsive. He knew then. Freka, the addict of an ancient vice, was a long way into

Shanga, and in his animalism he cared not the least about the gun facing him. He cared only about his brute hatred.

"Go back." Stark said softly. "I'll kill you."

But he knew that he could not, that the threat was an empty one. If he killed Freka, he would incur the death penalty himself.

With a flash of insight, Stark realized the neatness of the trap. Delgaun had set it, without a doubt—no one else would have brought Freka the Shanga lamp. Whoever of the two killed the other, must himself die by Kynon's decree. Delgaun could not lose.

Stark suddenly took to his heels and ran. He ran in the direction of the distant torch-glow. If he could get that far, so that Kynon and the others saw Freka pursuing and attacking him...

He did not get that far. Freka, half an animal, could run as fast as he, and faster. With an animal-like sound, he caught up to Stark, and his long arms went around Stark's head, and his teeth sank into the back of Stark's neck.

Stark, feeling himself going down, dived to the pavement to help the movement. The side of his head rang on the time-worn cobbles and he felt half-stunned but he kept on rolling in a somersault that shook off the thing on his back. It shook the gun out of his hand, also. He scrambled to his feet.

Freka, mewing, reached from the street where he had fallen and his long arms grabbed Stark's knees and pulled him down again.

A kind of horror possessed Stark. He had been called a half-beast, in his lifetime, but the thing he fought was all beast.

The teeth were trying for his throat. Stark's hand grabbed the long hair of the barbarian and snapped his head back. Still holding Freka's hair, he banged his head onto the cobbles.

Freka still clawed and mewed, and a shivering conviction that this creature was invulnerable came to Stark. He heard vague voices yelling somewhere. In a kind of hysterical fury he banged Freka's head again and again on the cobblestones.

The voice of Kynon roared close by, and Stark was hauled to his feet and blinked his eyes at the tossing torches.

"He's murdered Freka—give me a spear!" screamed a Shunni warrior.

Stark saw other tribesmen, all with fury on their faces, and saw also the horrified face of Walsh, and then Kynon's head blotted out the others as Kynon came close to him.

"I warned you, Stark!"

"The man was in Shanga, he was an animal set upon me!" gasped Stark. "And I know who set him! Delgaun..."

The flat of Kynon's great hand cracked across his mouth and he reeled backward. Hard hands held him when he would have struck back.

"Blood for Freka's blood!" the Shunni warrior was screeching to Kynon. "Unless all the men of Shun see this man die, we do not march with you!"

"You will see it," Kynon said, "All will see it. And yours, brother, will be the weapon that wipes out Freka's blood."

Stark, raging, roared to Kynon, "You idiot! Pretending to the Rama knowledge, while all the time you're a puppet dangled by..."

A spear-haft hit Stark on the back of his head and he fell into blackness.

He came to in a place of cold, dry stone. There was an iron collar around his neck, and a five-foot chain ran from it to a ring in the wall. The cell was small. A gate of iron bars closed the single entrance. Beyond was a well, with other cell doors around it, and above were thick stone gratings. He guessed that the place was built beneath some inner court of the palace.

A torch lit the room. There were no other prisoners. But there was a guard, a thick-shouldered barbarian who sat on what looked like an execution block in the center of the well, with a sword and a jug of wine. It was the Shunni warrior who had screamed for a spear, and he looked at Stark and smiled.

"You should not have slept so long, outlander," he said. "For you have only three hours till morning. And when morning comes, you will die on the great stair, where all the men of Shun can see."

He drank from the jug, and set it down, and smiled again.

"Death comes easily if the thrust is sure," he said. "But if the thrust wobbles, death is very slow, and very painful. I think yours will be slow."

Stark did not answer. He waited, with the same unhuman patience he had shown when he waited for his captors under the tor.

The man on the block laughed, and raised the jug again.

Stark's eyes narrowed slightly. He saw the movement of a shadow, in the darkness beyond the drinking man

He thought he knew who it was that came to this place so stealthily. Delgaun would make very sure that he never stood upon the great stair, to shout mad accusations to the Drylanders before he died.

He thought that he had not even three hours, now.

CHAPTER THIRTEEN

THEN, AS THOUGH she had suddenly taken shape there, Fianna stood in the shadows behind the Shunni. Her young face was very pale, but her hand did not tremble as she brought up the little gun she held.

The gun coughed, and the Shunni warrior pitched forward and lay without moving, while his sword rattled along the stone floor. The jug, upset, sent out bright crawling loopings of red.

Fianna stepped over the body and unlocked the iron collar with a key she took from her girdle.

Stark took her slender shoulders between his hands. "Listen, Fianna. It could be your death if it becomes known that you have done this."

She gave him a deep, strange look. In the dusky light, her proud young face was unfamiliar, touched with something fey and sad. He wished that he could see her eyes more clearly.

"I think that the death of many things is close," she said. "Tonight is a black and evil time in Sinharat, which has known so much of darkness and evil. And I risked freeing you because I think you are my only hope—perhaps the only hope of Mars."

He drew her to him, and kissed her, and stroked her dark head. "You're too young to concern yourself with the destiny of worlds."

He felt her tremble. "The youth of the body is only illusion, when the mind is old."

"And is yours old, Fianna?"

"Old," she whispered. "As old as Berild's."

The words vibrated away and were lost in silence. But to Stark, it seemed that suddenly a world-deep abyss had been opened between him and this girl who looked up at him from dark, unguessable eyes.

"You too?" he whispered.

"I, too," she said, "am of the Twice-Born, the Ramas. Even as those whom you know as Berild and Delgaun."

He could not quite take it in. He stared at her in silence, and then asked, "But, then, how many of you are there?"

Fianna shook her head. "I am not sure, but I think only we three are left. And now you know why I follow Berild and serve her. She and Delgaun have the secret of the Sending On of Minds, the true secret. They know where the Crowns of the Ramas are hidden, somewhere here in Sinharat, and I do not know that. They give me life, from one lifetime to another, so that I have lived only at their caprice. And that has been a long, long time."

Without realizing it, Stark had let his hands fall from her and had stepped back. Fianna looked up at him and said, not resentfully but sadly, "I do not blame you. I know what we have been. The ever-young, the ever-living immortals, the stealers of others' lives. It was wrong, wrong, the thing that began here in Sinharat long ago. I have known it was wrong, through all these changing lives. But I will tell you this—most evilly powerful of all addictions is the addiction to life."

Stark stepped forward and again he took her head between his hands. "Whatever you are and have been, Fianna, I think you are my friend."

"Your friend, and the friend of all the Dryland tribesmen from whom I—the real I—sprang. They must not march, and drown Mars and themselves in blood. Will you help me?"

"It is why I am here," he said.

"Then come with me," said Fianna. She stirred the Shunni's body with her foot. "Bring that. It must not be found here."

Stark heaved the body over his shoulder and followed the girl through a twisting maze of corridors, some pitch dark, some feebly lighted by the moons. Fianna moved as surely as though she were in the main square at high noon. There was the silence of death in these cold tunnels, and the dry, faint smell of eternity.

At length Fianna whispered, "Here. Be careful."

She put out a hand to guide him but Stark's eyes were like a cat's in the dark. He made out a space where the rock with which the ancient builders had faced these subterranean ways gave place to the original coral.

Ragged black mouths opened in the coral, entrances to some unguessed catacombs beneath. Stark consigned the body to the nearest pit, but he kept the sword with which the Shunni warrior had planned to kill him.

"You will need it," Fianna said.

Stark listened to the distant sliding echoes from the pit, and shivered. He had so nearly finished there himself. He was glad to follow Fianna away from that place of darkness and silent death.

He stopped her in a place where a bar of moonlight came splashing through a great crack in the tunnel roof. He said, "You want my help in preventing the march and the conquest. But only Kynon's death can prevent that."

"Kynon stands in danger of worse than death, tonight," she said. "We go to save him."

Stark roughly caught her wrist. "Save Kynon? But he planned this bloody thing... he is the man who will lead it!"

Fianna shook her head. "He will not lead it, though he will seem to do so. And he did not plan it, for that was the doing of Delgaun and Berild, who put the plan into Kynon's head."

"There are lies everywhere," said Stark. "I am tangled up in lies. Tell me the truth."

"The truth of Delgaun and Berild is this," said Fianna. "They are tired of wandering secretly through the ages of the world. Even Berild has wearied of living for pleasure only, and longs for power. They, the Twice-Born, should rule the short-lived peoples. So they conceived their plan for empire.

"Berild it was who subtly put into Kynon's mind the idea of using the legended secret of the Sending On of Minds, the lure of immortality, as a bait to lure the fighting-men, to rally Drylanders and Low-Canallers together. Kynon, always ambitious and eager for power, seized upon that. He prepared the hoax, and with the promise of the Crowns, he has gathered the men. It was Delgaun who suggested bringing in the outlanders, and their weapons. More outland vultures will come, drawn by the smell of loot, if the first conquest succeeds. And Delgaun and

Berild will use them to keep the Martian tribes in check, and to prop their evil rule."

Stark thought about Knighton and Walsh of Terra, Themis and Arrod of Mercury and Callisto Colony. He thought of others like them, and what they would do with their talons hooked in the heart of Mars. He thought of Delgaun's yellow eyes.

He said, "You speak of Delgaun and Berild ruling—but would they dare get rid of Kynon, whom all look on as leader?"

Fianna looked at him pityingly. "You don't understand. The will not get rid of Kynon physically. It will still be Kynon whom the tribesmen hail and follow as their leader."

Still Stark could not comprehend. "What do you mean?" Kynon may have been influenced, but he's not one to dance to anyone's bidding."

"I said, they will not get rid of Kynon *physically*," Fianna repeated.

Stark began to understand, and a cold sickness rose in him. "You mean—the Sending On of Minds?"

The sickness in Stark became shuddering repulsion, as from a nightmare. He suddenly felt a violent hatred for this ancient, evil world and of the black things that came up from its past.

"Do you understand now why I need your help?" Fianna was saying. "This final wickedness must not happen. If Delgaun takes the body of Kynon, he'll use it to lead the Drylanders to bloody ruin. You have to help me prevent that."

Stark looked at her, and asked thickly, "Where?"

"Berild's quarters. Kynon is there now, in the trap. Delgaun has gone to bring the Crowns of the Ramas from their hiding-place."

Stark gripped the Shunni sword and said, "Take me there the shortest way."

"Not quite the shortest, but the safest. Come!"

She led him through labyrinthine underground ways, a dark maze that twisted and turned and seemed to go on forever. And he saw things on the way that he had not dreamed existed under the dead pile of Sinharat.

One great cavern was lighted vaguely by a globe of cold green fire that stood upon a pedestal in a corner. It cast a livid glow over masses of piled and jumbled and incomprehensible objects. There were massive silvery wheels and targes, weird reticulations of dusty metal rods, brazen beaks that had once adorned the prows of ships, in the old days when Sinharat was an island rising arrogantly from the rolling ocean.

Relics, possessions, or perhaps only loot—they were of the Ramas and the past that should be dead but not, quite. They set Stark to bristling, and he gripped the sword more tightly, but Fianna did not glance at them.

A flight of dark steps took them up into a passageway that smelled of the upper air. And now a whispering began about them, a muttering and chuckling and piping that he had heard before, and it seemed uncannily to Stark as though the sounds that were called the voices of the Ramas were really voices now. It was as thought the old ones, the Ever-living, watched and gloated over the thing that was about to be done.

"The wind is rising and it will soon be dawn," said Fianna. "We must hurry."

Cold air struck Stark's face as he followed her upward again, this time into a room whose windows let in the light of the flying moons.

"We are there," whispered Fianna. "Now, very quietly, I must know first if Delgaun has returned."

She went softly down a hallway, motioning him to wait. After a moment, without any sound at all, a little crack of light spilled into the corridor and showed Fianna pressed close outside a door she had softly opened.

Stark's pulses thudded as he caught the sound of a silvery voice that he recognized as Berild's. Then the dark silhouette of Fianna moved, making a beckoning gesture.

He came softly to her side and she stepped away so that he might see through the crack in the doorway. He looked, into the lamplit room.

He saw Kynon, in profile, bound by leather thongs to one of the massive stone pillars. There was a great bruise on Kynon's temple, and in his harsh, powerful face there was a look that Stark had never seen on any human face before.

Delgaun stood nearby, but Kynon ignored him and stared fixedly at Berild.

"You may well look, Kynon," she said. "It is the last you will see of Berild, your submissive and patient woman. You great ox of a barbarian! Not in a thousand years have I been so bored with anyone as I have been with you, and your roaring boasts and childish schemes."

"There's no time for this," Delgaun said sharply. "Let us get it done."

Berild nodded, and went to a small coffer of golden metal that rested on a table. She pressed a series of patterned bosses in an intricate sequence, and there was a sharp click of an opening lock. A shiver ran up along Stark's spine as he watched Berild raise the lid of the coffer and reach her hands inside it.

On the slave block of Valkis, Kynon had brought forth two crowns of shining crystal and a rod of flame. But as glass is to diamond, as the pallid moon to the light of the sun, were those things to the reality that now shone forth.

In her two hands Berild had the ancient crowns of the Ramas, the givers of life. Twin circlets of glorious fire, dimming the shallow light of the lamps, putting a nimbus of light around the white-clad woman so that as she walked across the room she was like a goddess walking in a could of stars.

She held them for Kynon to see, mocking him. "You blazoned them on your banner for all the world to see—do not shrink from them now!"

"I say again, we waste time," cut in the sharp voice of Delgaun.

Delgaun came and stood beside bound Kynon, with his back also against the pillar. And Berild raised the two flashing crowns in her hands and bent toward them.

In the ear of Stark, Fianna said, "Now!"

CHAPTER FOURTEEN

STARK WENT INTO the room with the sword up and he went fast, heading toward Delgaun. He had always recognized the infinite dangerousness of this man. And now that he knew that it was backed by countless lifetimes of cunning and experience, he thought that his chances were not good.

Delgaun's yellow eyes flashed amazement, but he reacted with superb speed. He ran swiftly toward the corner of the room, and scrabbled a gun out of its hiding place under a cloak.

And Stark thought, as he plunged, "Of course, he wouldn't have the gun on him when his body was going to be exchanged with Kynon's..."

He had never seen such speed as Delgaun's, turning with the gun. But the Shunni blade went home before the turn was ever completed, and Delgaun pitched and fell, the fall of his body wrenching the sword-hilt out of Stark's hand.

Stark, kneeling to retrieve the sword, head a ringing sound and saw something bright rolling past him. It was one of the crystal crowns, but whatever material they were made of, it was not really crystal, for the crown was unharmed by its fall. Still stooping, grabbing the sword-hilt, he turned swiftly.

Berild had dropped the Crowns, and had drawn a slender knife. In her face was terror. For Kynon was loose, cut loose by Fianna, and the big barbarian was advancing toward her. His face was terrible as he grasped with hungry hands for the woman.

Berild's knife flashed, twice, and then Kynon's great arms closed around her. She screamed chokingly. Kynon's face was as red as the blood that was pouring from his side, his mighty muscles straining, and in a moment, by the time Stark was on his feet again, Berild was broken and dead.

Kynon flung her limp body away, like an outworn, unclean doll. He turned slowly and his hand went to the gashes in his side. He said thickly, "The Rama witch has killed me. My life is pouring out..."

He stood, rocking and swaying, with a numbed expression on his face as though he could not actually believe it. Stark went to his side and supported him.

"Kynon, listen!"

Kynon did not even seem to hear him. His eyes had turned upon the motionless bodies of Berild and Delgaun.

"Witch and wizard," he muttered. "All this time—deceiving me, laughing at me, using me for their own ends. It is good that you killed the man, too."

Stark spoke urgently, "Kynon, their evil will still live and work if the men in the Drylands march! Not Berild and Delgaun, but someone else will spend the blood of the tribes for power."

Kynon seemed dazedly to consider that, and then his eyes blazed fiercely.

"Power that should have been mine… No, by God! Help me, Stark—I have a thing to tell the tribes!"

He was lurching, like an oak about to fall. Powerful as Stark was, he had difficulty supporting Kynon as they went out of the room. Fianna remained, still standing by the pillar and trembling and looking after them.

The dawn lightened the streets of Sinharat, and the morning wind was stronger. Louder came the pipings and flutings from the city. Kynon, his left hand pressed against his side, looked up at the stone faces of the Ramas and then raised his clenched right hand and shook it at them.

They came in the great stairway and started down it. Below them in the sunrise light the vast huddle of tents was awakening. Then a voice yelled, a tribesman pointed wildly to where Stark and Kynon came painfully down the stair, and with a bursting roar of excited voices, the whole camp came to life. The men of Kesh and Shun came crowding in hundreds, then in thousands, their faces fierce and strange in the brightening light as they looked up to where Kynon stood swaying, with Stark steadying him.

Kynon looked down at them without speaking, for a moment. Then he seemed to gather his strength, and his bull voice roared out almost as loudly as it had on the slave block in Valkis.

"I have been deceived and betrayed, and so have you all! Delgaun and Berild conspired to use us of the Drylands, as a sword to hack conquests for them, not us!"

It took moments for them to take it in. Then a low growling sound came up from the thousands below.

A Keshi chieftain leaped up a few steps on the stairway and shook his weapon and shouted, "Death for them!"

And the crowd took up and echoed that fierce shout.

Kynon held up his hand. "They are already dead... and Delgaun was slain by Stark, who tried to save me. But the snake Berild stung me, and I am dying."

He swayed so that Stark had to hold up his massive weight by both arms around him, but then he gathered his strength again.

"I lied when I said I had the secret of the Ramas." Kynon said. "And now I know that that secret would yield only evil. Forget it, and forget the war that you would fight only for the profit of others."

He tried to say more, but did not seem to be able to voice the words. Stark felt the weight of him sagging more heavily, and tried to hold him, but Kynon said thickly, "Let be."

He slid down, still holding his side, to sit upon the steps. He sat there, as the sun rose higher, with the great battlements and towers of Sinharat behind him and with the fighting-men of the Drylands looking silently up at him, and the desert stretching far away. And what thoughts were mirrored in his face, Stark, who stood behind him, could not see.

Kynon said no more. He sat, and his shoulders sagged, and then his whole body sagged down and was still.

For a time, nothing at all happened, Stark stood waiting, and farther back up the stair, Knighton and Walsh and Arrod and Themis stood, peering and stricken, but no one moved.

Then four chieftains of the Shunni came silently up the stair. They did not even glance at Stark. They picked up Kynon's body and went back down the stair with it, and the crowd of warriors divided in front of them.

Stark climbed back up the stairway to where Knight and the others watched, a group of downeast, doubtful men.

"The thing's blown," said Stark. "There won't be any war, and there won't be any loot."

Walsh cursed. He asked, "What happened?"

Stark shrugged. "You heard Kynon."

They were not satisfied at all, but there was nothing they could do about it. They stood pondering, looking with gloomy eyes down at the striking of the skin tents and the loading of the beasts, as the great camp broke up. Knighton said, finally, "I'm getting out. And the rest of you had better go with me, and not back to Valkis or anywhere near it."

The others had already had that thought. Delgaun's lieutenants would be waiting in Valkis, ready for the great stroke against the Border, and they would not be happy with the thing that had happened.

Stark said, "I won't go with you. I'm going to Tarak."

He thought of Simon Ashton waiting in Tarak, and he thought that Ashton would be glad of the word he brought, the word that meant peace and not war.

Walsh, looking at Stark without love, told him, "It's just as well. I think you Jonahed this whole deal, thought I don't know how. There are riding-beasts in the pen behind Kynon's palace."

They turned and went away. Stark looked back down the stairway toward the desert.

The vast encampment was disappearing as if by magic. It was dissolving into streams of men and animals that moved out in long caravans, in many different direction, back into recesses of the Drylands.

One file of men and beasts moved to the sound of booming drums and skirling pipes. Kynon of Shun was going home as a leader should.

Stark walked back through the silent streets of Sinharat, and came again into the room where Delgraun and Berild had died.

Their bodies were not there now. But Fianna sat by the window looking out at the departure of the hosts.

Stark's gaze swiftly searched around the room. Fianna turned, and said, "They're not here, if it's the Crowns of the Ramas you are looking for. I hid them."

"The thought that was in my mind was to destroy them," said Stark.

She nodded. "I had the same thought. I almost did it. But—"

"But the addiction to life is a strong one, indeed," said Stark. "So you said, remember?"

Fianna got up and came to face him, and her face was shadowed by doubt.

"I know this," she said, "I do not want another life, who have had so many. I do not want it now. But when the body finally fails, and death stoops near, it may be different. There will always be time to destroy the Crowns."

"There will always be time," said Stark. "But there will never be the will."

Fianna came closer to him and her eyes were suddenly fierce. "Don't be so smug in your strength! You haven't felt your life guttering out... as I have, more than once! Perhaps when you come to feel that, you would be glad to join me in the Sending On of Minds."

Stark was silent for a moment, and then he shook his head. "I don't think so. Life has not been so soft and sweet for me that I would want to live it over."

"Don't answer me now," Fianna said. "Answer me thirty years from now. And if your answer is 'Yes,' come seek me here in Sinharat. Soon or late, I will always return here."

"I will not return," Stark said flatly.

She looked up at him, and then she whispered, "Perhaps you won't. But don't be too sure."

The throbbing of Kynon's burial-drums was only a faint echo now, and far out on the desert the dust of the caravans receded.

Stark turned. "I am going, as soon as I can prepare. Do you go with me?"

Fianna shook her head. "I stay here, at least for a while. I am the last of my people, and this is my place."

Stark hesitated, then turned and left her.

When night came, he was riding far out on the desert, leading his pack-beasts. The wind was rising, murmuring and piping in the lonesomeness, but he knew it was only illusion that made him seem to hear at this distance the whispering, fluting voices of the city behind him.

Would he someday go back there, questing for another life, seeking out Fianna so that they two might go down through ages as Delgaun and Berild had done?

No. And yet...

Stark turned in the saddle and looked back at the white towers of Sinharat rising against the larger moon.

People of
the Talisman

CHAPTER ONE

THROUGH ALL THE long cold hours of the Norland night the Martian had not moved nor spoken. At dusk of the day before Eric John Stark had brought him into the ruined tower and laid him down, wrapped in blankets, on the snow. He had built a fire of dry lichens, and since then the two men had waited, alone in the vast wasteland that girdles the polar cap of Mars.

Now, just before dawn, Camar the Martian spoke.

"Stark."

"Yes?"

"I am dying."

"Yes."

"I will not reach Kushat."

"No."

Camar nodded. He was silent again.

The wind howled down from the northern ice, and the broken walls rose up against the wind, brooding, gigantic, roofless now but so huge and sprawling that they seemed less like walls than cliffs of ebon stone. Stark would not have gone near them but for Camar. They were wrong, somehow, with a taint of forgotten evil still about them.

The big Earthman glanced at Camar, and his face was sad. "A man likes to die in his own place," he said abruptly. "I am sorry."

"The Lord of Silence is a great personage," Camar answered. "He does not mind the meeting place. No. It was not for that I came back into the Norlands."

He was shaken by an agony that was not of the body. "But I will not reach Kushat."

Stark spoke quietly, using the courtly High Martian almost as fluently as Camar.

"I have known that there was a burden heavier than death upon my brother's soul."

He leaned over, placing one large hand on the Martian's shoulder. "My brother has given his life for mine. Therefore, I will take his burden upon myself, if I can."

He did not want Camar's burden, whatever it might be. But the Martian had fought beside him through a long guerilla campaign far to the south, among the harried tribes of the Dryland borders. He was a good man of his hands, and in the end had taken the bullet that was meant for Stark, knowing quite well what he was doing. They were friends.

That was why Stark had brought Camar into this bleak north country, trying to reach the city of his birth. The Martian was driven by some secret demon. He was afraid to die before he reached Kushat.

And now he had no choice.

"I have sinned, Stark," he said softly. "I have stolen a holy thing."

Stark crouched beside him. "What thing?"

"You're an outlander, you would not know about Ban Cruach and the talisman that he left when he went away forever beyond the Gates of Death."

Camar flung aside the blankets and sat up, his voice gaining a febrile strength.

"I was born and bred in the Thieves' Quarter under the Wall. I was proud of my skill. And the talisman was a challenge. It was a treasured thing, so treasured that hardly a man has touched it since the days of Ban Cruach. And that was in the days when men still had the luster on them, before they forgot that they were gods.

"'Guard well the Gates of Death,' he said, 'that is the city's trust. And keep the talisman always, for the day may come when you will need its strength.' No enemy, you see, could ever harm Kushat as long as it was there.

"But I was a thief, and proud. And I stole the talisman."

His hands went to his girdle, a belt of worn leather with a boss of battered steel. But his fingers were already numb.

"Take it, Stark. Open the boss, there, on the side, where the beast's head is carved."

Stark took the belt from Camar and found the hidden spring. The rounded top of the boss came free. Inside it was something wrapped in a scrap of silk.

"I had to go away from Kushat," Camar whispered. "I could not ever go back. But it was enough, to have taken that."

He watched, shaken between awe and pride and remorse, as Stark unwrapped the bit of silk.

Stark had discounted most of Camar's talk as superstition, but even so he expected something more spectacular then the object he held in his palm.

It was a lens, some four inches across, and made with great skill, but still only a bit of crystal. He turned it about, frowning. It was not a simple lens. There was an intricate interlocking of many facets, incredibly complex. Far too complex, Stark would have thought, for the level of technology that must have existed in Ban Cruach's time. He found that it was hypnotic if one looked at it too long.

"What is its use?" he asked of Camar.

"We are as children. We have forgotten. But it is surely a thing of great power. You will see that, Stark. There are some who believe that if Kushat were threatened it would call Ban Crauch himself back through the Gates of Death to lead us again. I do not know."

"Men seldom come back through the Gates of Death for any purpose," said Stark dryly. "Unless in Kushat those words have another meaning?"

Camar answered, "It is the name of a pass that opens into the black mountains beyond Kushat. The city stands guard before it. No man remembers why, except that it is a great trust."

His gaze feasted on the talisman, in agony and pride.

Stark said, "You wish me to take this to Kushat?"

"Yes. Yes!" Camar looked at Stark joyfully. Then his eyes clouded and he shook his head. "No. The North is not used to strangers. With me you might have been safe, but alone... No,

Stark. You've risked too much already. Go back, out to the Norlands, while you can."

He lay back on the blankets. Stark saw that a bluish pallor had come into the hollows of his cheeks.

"Camar," he said. And again, "Camar?"

"Yes?"

"Go in peace, Camar. I will take the talisman to Kushat."

The Martian sighed, and smiled, and Stark was glad he had made the promise.

"The riders of Mekh are wolves," said Camar suddenly. "They hunt these gorges. Look out for them."

"I will."

Stark's knowledge of the geography of this part of Mars was vague in the extreme, but he knew that the mountain valleys of Mekh lay ahead and to the north, between him and Kushat. Camar had told him about these upland warriors. He was willing to heed the warning.

And now Camar had done with talking. Stark knew that he did not have long to wait. The wind spoke with the voice of a great organ. The moons had set and it was very dark outside the tower, except for the white glimmering of the snow. Stark looked up at the brooding walls and shivered. There was a smell of death already in the air.

To keep from thinking, he bent closer to the fire, studying the lens. An ornament, he thought, probably worn as a badge of rank. Strange ornament for a barbarian king in the dawn of Mars. The firelight made tiny dancing sparks in the endless inner facets. It seemed to gather the light into itself, until it glowed with a kind of throbbing witch-fire, brightening, as though the thing were coming alive in his hands.

A pang of primitive and unreasoning fear shot through him. He fought it down. The part of him that had learned with much pain and effort to be civilized forced him to sit and consider the crystal, when what he really wanted to do was to rid himself of it by hurling it far away into the snow.

A talisman. A promise from a king long dead, the safety of a city. A piece of crystal, encrusted with legend and superstitious faith. That was all it was. The firelight, coupled with Camar's fervor and the approach of death, were making him imagine things.

Only a bit of crystal....

Yet it glowed brighter in his hands, a warm and living thing. It drew his gaze and held it. The wind talked in the hollow stone, and after a while it seemed to Stark that he heard other voices, very faint and distant, tiny thready things that plucked and slid along the edges of his mind. He started up, shaken by an eerie terror, listening, and when he listened all he could hear was the wind and the chafing of the hard snow blowing, and the painful breathing of Camar.

He looked at the crystal, forcing himself to hold it. But he turned away from the fire so that some of the light died slowly out of it and the quivering witch-fires were a little dimmed.

Imagination, he told himself. One might hear anything in a place like this. One might see anything....

Only still the crystal glowed, as though it might be taking life from his own living hands now that the fire was denied it. And the inner facets called his gaze down to dim depths that stretched into somewhere that was not space, into time perhaps, or...

The tiny voices spoke again, scratching, chittering spider-sounds coming from a million miles away where no ear could possibly hear them. But Stark heard them. He heard them this time just long enough to recognize a certain thing about them, and then he yelled and flung the crystal from him in blind atavistic fear, because suddenly he knew that wherever it came from and however it had gotten to Kushat, no human man had made it.

It fell into the banked snow by the doorway, vanishing without a sound. Stark stood shivering violently, and then in a minute or two he began rather uncertainly to curse himself for an idiot. The voices were gone again and he stretched his hearing, trying to catch them and reassure himself that they had been only his oversensitive capacity to find strange gods and evil spirits with every step he took. The primitive aboriginal was still very close under his skin. He knew and recognized it, finding it often a curse and only sometimes a blessing. The naked boy who had run with Tika and Old One among the haunted rocks on the edge of Darkside had been playing tricks again with Eric John Stark.

He stood still, cataloguing the sounds, the many shadings of the wind blowing far, blowing near, the chafing of the snow, Camar's breathing...

But Camar's breathing had stopped.

Stark went to him and knelt down, rather wishing now that he could retract his promise and knowing it was too late. He crossed Camar's hands in the ritual posture and then drew the tattered edge of his cloak across his face. He rose and gave Camar the gesture of farewell, and then turned to where he had thrown the talisman. He was on his knees groping for it in the drifted snow when one of the beasts tethered outside the tower started up from its sleep with a shrill hissing. Motionless he listened, and heard it answered.

Working desperately, Stark probed the icy drift with his fingers, felt the smooth oval of the talisman and plucked it out, placing it in the boss of Camar's belt. He closed it and clasped the belt around his waist, and then, not hurrying now, he found the small flask that lay with his gear beside the fire and took a long pull at it.

Then he waited.

They came silently on padded feet, the rangy mountain brutes moving daintily through the rubble of the sprawling ruin. Their riders too were silent, tall men with fierce eyes and russet hair. They wore leather coats, and each man carried a long straight spear.

There were a score of them around the tower in the windy gloom. Stark did not bother to draw his gun. He had learned very young the difference between courage and idiocy.

He walked out toward them, moving slowly lest one of them be startled into spearing him, yet not slowly enough to denote fear. And he held up his right hand and gave them greeting.

They did not answer him. They sat their restive mounts and stared at him, and Stark knew that Camar had spoken the truth.

These were the riders of Mekh, and they were wolves.

CHAPTER TWO

STARK WAITED, UNTIL they should tire of their own silence.

Finally one demanded, "Of what country are you?"

He answered, "I am called N'Chaka, the Man-Without-a-Tribe."

This was the name his foster-folk had given him, the half human aboriginals who had found him orphaned and alone after an earthquake wiped out the mining community that had been his home; the folk who had raised him, in the blaze and thunder and bitter frosts of Mercury's Twilight Belt. It still seemed to Stark to be his true name.

"A stranger," said the leader, and smiled. He pointed to the dead Camar and asked, "Did you slay him?"

"He was my friend," said Stark. "I was bringing him home to die."

Two riders dismounted to inspect the body. One called up to the leader, "He was from Kushat, if I know the bred, Thord! And he has not been robbed." He proceeded to take care of that detail himself.

"A stranger," repeated the leader, Thord. "Bound for Kushat, with a man of Kushat. Well, I think you will come with us, stranger."

Stark shrugged. And with the long spears pricking him, he did not resist when the tall Thord plundered him of all he owned except his clothes and Camar's belt, which was not worth the stealing. His gun Thord flung contemptuously away.

One of the men brought Stark's beast and Camar's from where they were tethered and the Earthman mounted, as usual over the violent protest of the creature, which did not like the smell of him. They moved out from under the shelter of the wall, into the full fury of the wind.

For the rest of that night and through the next day and the night that followed it they rode eastward, stopping only to rest the beasts and chew on their rations of jerked meat. And to Stark, riding a prisoner, it came with full force that this was the

North country, half a world away from the Mars of spaceships and commerce and visitors from other planets. The future had never touched these wild mountains and barren plains. Not even the present had reached them. The past held pride enough.

Far to the north, below the horizon, the polar pack made a glimmering white blink on the sky, and at night there were the cold flames of the aurora to burn out the stars. The wind blew down from the ice, through the mountain gorges, across the plains, never ceasing. And here and there the cryptic towers rose, broken monoliths of stone, of unknown history and unguessed purpose. The men of Mekh could tell Stark nothing about them, though they seemed to prefer to avoid them.

Thord did not make any mention to Stark about where they were taking him, or why, and Stark did not ask. It would have been an admission of fear. Since there was nothing else he could do at the moment he exercised the patience of the chained beast, and simply waited. But there were times when he found it difficult. Camar's belt sat uncomfortably at his middle. He kept thinking about the talisman and wondering how much of its strangeness was his own imagination and how much was real, and it made for uneasy thinking. All he wanted now was to get as quickly as possible to Kushat and be rid of the thing. And he cursed Thord and his riders, silently but with great viciousness.

In mid-afternoon of the second day they came to a lip of rock where the snow was swept clean, and below it was a sheer drop into a narrow valley. Looking down, Stark saw that on the floor of the valley, up and down as far as he could see, were men and beasts and shelters of hides and brush, and fires burning. By the hundreds, by the several thousand, they camped under the cliffs and their voices rose up on the thin air in a vast deep murmur that was deafening after the silence of the plains.

A war party, gathered now, before the thaw. Stark smiled. He became curious to meet the leader of this army.

They found their way single file along a winding track that dropped down the cliff face. The wind stopped abruptly, cut off by the valley walls. They came in among the shelters of the camp.

Here the snow was churned and soiled and melted to slush by the fires. There were no women in the camp, no sign of the usual cheerful rabble that follows a barbarian army. There were only men, hillmen and warriors all, tough-handed killers with no thought but battle.

They came out of their holes to shout at Thord and his men, and stare at the stranger. Thord was flushed and jovial with his own importance.

"I have no time for you," he shouted back. "I go to speak with the Lord Ciaran."

Stark rode impassively, a dark giant with a face of stone. From time to time he made his beast curvet, and laughed at himself inwardly for doing it.

They came at length to a shelter larger than the others but built exactly the same and no more comfortable. A spear was thrust into the snow beside the entrance, and from it hung a black pennant with a single bar of silver across it like lightning in a night sky. Beside it was a shield with the same device. There were no guards.

Thord dismounted, bidding Stark to do the same. He hammered on the shield with the hilt of his sword, announcing himself.

"Lord Ciaran! It is Thord, with a captive."

A voice, toneless and strangely muffled, spoke from within.

"Enter, Thord."

Thord pushed aside the hide curtain and went in, with Stark at his heels.

The dim daylight did not penetrate the interior. Cressets burned, giving off a flickering brilliance and a smell of strong oil. The floor of packed snow was carpeted with furs, much worn so that the bare hide showed through in places. Otherwise there was no adornment, and no furniture but a chair and table, both dark with age and use, and a pallet of skins in one shadowy corner with what seemed to be a heap of rags thrown upon it.

In the chair sat a man.

He seemed very tall in the shaking light of the cressets. From neck to thigh his lean body was cased in black link mail, and under that a tunic of leather, dyed black. Across his knees he held a sable axe, a great thing made for the shearing of skulls, and his hands lay upon it gently, as though it were a toy he loved.

His head and face were covered by a thing that Stark had seen before only in very old paintings, but he recognized it. It was the ancient war-mask of the Inland Kings of Mars. Wrought of black and gleaming steel, it presented an inhuman visage of slitted eyeholes and a barred slot for breathing. At the top and back of the head it sprang out in a thin roaring sweep of curving metal like a dark wing edge-on in flight.

The intent, expressionless scrutiny of that mask was bent, not upon Thord, but upon Eric John Stark.

The hollow voice spoke again, from behind the mask.

"Well?"

"We were hunting in the gorges to the south," said Thord.

"We saw a fire…" He told the story of how they had found the stranger and the body of the man from Kushat.

"Kushat!" said the Lord Ciaran softly. "Ah! And why, stranger, were you going to Kushat?"

"My name is Stark. Eric John Stark, Earthman, out of Mercury." He was tired of being called stranger. He was tired of the whole business, and the blank mask irritated him. "Why should I not go to Kushat? Is it against some law, that a man may not go there in peace without being hounded all over the Norlands? And why do the men of Mekh make it their business? They have nothing to do with the city."

Thord held his breath, watching with delighted anticipation.

The hands of the man in armor caressed the axe. They were slender hands, smooth and sinewy. Small hands, it seemed, for such a weapon.

"We make what we will our business, Eric John Stark." He spoke with a peculiar gentleness. "I have asked you. Why were you going to Kushat?"

"Because," Stark answered with equal restraint, "my comrade wanted to go home to die."

"It seems a long hard journey, just for dying." The black helm bent forward in an attitude of thought. "Only the condemned or the banished leave their cities, or their clans. Why did your comrade flee Kushat?"

A voice spoke suddenly from out of the heap of rags that lay on the pallet in the shadows of the corner. A man's voice, deep and husky, with the harsh quaver of age or madness in it.

"Three men beside myself have fled Kushat, over the years that matter. One died in the spring floods. One was caught in the moving ice of winter. One lived. A thief named Camar, who stole a certain talisman."

Stark said, "My comrade was called Greshi." The leather belt weighed heavy about him, and the iron boss seemed hot against his belly. He was beginning now to be afraid.

The Lord Ciaran spoke, ignoring Stark. "It was the sacred talisman of Kushat. Without it, the city is like a man without a soul."

As the Veil of Tanit was to Carthage, Stark thought, and reflected on the fate of that city after the Veil was stolen.

"The nobles were afraid of their own people," the man in armor said. "They did not dare to tell that it was gone. But we know."

"And," said Stark, "you will attack Kushat before the thaw, when they least expect you."

"You have a sharp mind, stranger. Yes. But the great wall will be hard to carry, even so. If I came, bearing in *my* hand the talisman of Ban Cruach..."

He did not finish, but turned instead to Thord. "When you plundered the dead man's body, what did you find?"

"Nothing, Lord. A few coins, a knife, hardly worth the taking."

"And you, Eric John Stark. What did you take from the body?"

With perfect truth he answered, "Nothing."

"Thord," said the Lord Ciaran, "search him."

Thord came smiling up to Stark and ripped his jacket open.

With uncanny swiftness, the Earthman moved. The edge of one broad hand took Thord under the ear, and before the man's knees had time to sag Stark had caught his arm. He turned, crouching forward, and pitched Thord headlong through the door flap.

He straightened and turned again. His eyes held a feral glint. "The man has robbed me once," he said. "It is enough."

He heard Thord's men coming. Three of them tried to jam through the entrance at once, and one of them had a spear. Stark took it out of his hands. He used the butt of it, not speaking nor making a sound except the hard cracking of wood on bone. He cleared the doorway and flung the spear contemptuously after the stunned barbarians.

"Now," he said to the Lord Ciaran, "will we talk as men?"

The man in armor laughed, a sound of pure enjoyment. It seemed that the gaze behind the mask studied Stark's savage face and then lifted to greet the sullen Thord who came back into the shelter, his cheeks flushed crimson with rage.

"Go," said the Lord Ciaran. "The stranger and I will talk."

Thord had his sword in his hands and was panting to use it. "But Lord, it is not safe…"

"My dark mistress looks after my safety," said Ciaran, lifting the axe across his knees, "and better than you have done. Go."

Thord went.

The man in armor was silent then, the blind mask turned to Stark, who met that eyeless gaze and was silent also. And the bundle of rags in the shadows straightened slowly and became a tall old man with rusty hair and beard, through which peeped craggy juts of bone and two bright, small points of fire, as though some wicked flame burned within him.

He shuffled over and crouched at the feet of the Lord Ciaran, watching the Earthman. And the man in armor leaned forward.

"I will tell you something, Eric John Stark. I am a bastard, but I come of the blood of kings. My name and rank I must make with my own hands. But I will set them high, and my name will ring in the Norlands.

"I will take Kushat. Who holds Kushat holds the power and the riches that lie beyond the Gates of Death."

Ciaran paused, as though he might be dreaming, and then he said, "Ban Cruach came out of nowhere and made himself half a god. I will do the same."

The old man made a chuckling sound. "I told them, in Kushat. I said it was time to rouse themselves and regain their power. They could have done it easily then, when they still had the talisman. The city was dying, and I told them it was their last chance to live, but they were too content. They only laughed, and chained me. Now they will laugh in a different way. Ha! How they will laugh!"

Stark looked at him with distaste, but he, like Ciaran, was too occupied with his dreams to notice.

And Ciaran said, "Now the city is naked, and I will take it, and talisman or not, I will go beyond the Gates of Death to see what may be there."

He paused again, the dark mask inscrutable and compelling, turned toward Stark.

"Ride with me," he said abruptly. "Yield up the talisman, if indeed you can, and be the shield at my back. I have offered no other man that honor."

Stark asked slowly, "Why do you choose me?"

"We are of one blood, Stark, though we are strangers."

The Earthman's cold eyes narrowed. "What would your red wolves say to that? And what would Otar say? Look at him, already stiff with jealousy and fear lest I answer 'Yes.'"

"I do not think you would be afraid of either of them."

"On the contrary," said Stark, "I am a prudent man." He studied Ciaran. "Very prudent. So much so that I will bargain with no man until I have looked into his eyes. Take off your helm, Ciaran. Then perhaps we will talk."

Otar's breath made a snakelike hissing between his toothless gums, and the hands of the Lord Ciaran tightened on the haft of the axe.

"No," he whispered. "That I can never do."

Otar rose to his feet, and for the first time Stark felt the full strength that lay in this strange old man.

"Would you look upon the face of destruction?" he thundered. "Do you ask for death? Do you think a thing is hidden behind a mask of steel without a reason, that you demand to see it?

He turned. "My Lord," he said. "By tomorrow the last of the clans will have joined us. After that, we must march, as it was planned. But I think it likely that this man is lying. I think it likely that he knows where the talisman is. Give him to Thord for the time that remains."

The blank, blind mask was unmoving, and Stark thought that from behind it came a faint sound that might have been a sigh.

Then...

"Thord!" cried the Lord Ciaran, and lifted up the axe.

CHAPTER THREE

THE FLAMES LEAPED high from the fire in the windless gorge. Men sat around in a great circle. The wild riders out of the mountain valleys of Mekh, sitting with the curbed and quivering eagerness of wolves around a dying quarry. Their eyes were intent, and now and then their teeth showed in a kind of silent laughter.

"He is strong," they whispered, one to the other. "He will live the night out, surely!"

On an outcrop of rock sat the Lord Ciaran, wrapped in a black cloak, holding the great axe in the crook of his arm. Beside him, Otar huddled in the snow.

Close by, the long spears had been driven deep and lashed together to make a scaffolding, and upon this frame was hung a man. A big man, iron-muscled and very lean, the bulk of his shoulders filling the space between the bending shafts. Eric John Stark of Earth, out of Mercury.

He had already been scourged without mercy. He sagged of his own weight between the spears, breathing in harsh sobs, and the trampled snow around him was stained with red.

Thord was wielding the lash. He had stripped off his own coat and his body glistened with sweat in spite of the cold. He cut his victim with great care, making the long lash sing and crack. He was proud of his skill.

Stark did not cry out.

Presently Thord stepped back. He wiped the sweat from his face and looked at the Lord Ciaran. And the black helm nodded.

Thord dropped the whip. He went up to the big dark man and lifted his head by the hair.

"Stark," he said, and shook the head roughly. "Stranger!"

Eyes opened and stared at him, and Thord could not repress a slight shiver. It seemed that the pain and indignity had wrought some evil magic on this man. He had seen exactly the same gaze in a big snow-cat caught in a trap, and he felt suddenly that it was not a man he spoke to, but a predatory beast.

"Stark," he said. "Where is the talisman of Ban Cruach?"

The Earthman did not answer.

Thord laughed. He glanced up at the sky, where the moons rode low and swift.

"The night is only half gone. Do you think you can last it out?"

The cold, cruel, patient eyes watched Thord. There was no reply.

Some quality of pride in that gaze angered the barbarian. It seemed to mock him, who was so sure of his ability to loosen a reluctant tongue. It seemed to say, I have shamed you once before the Lord Ciaran; now I shame you again.

"You think I cannot make you talk," Thord said softly. "You don't know me, stranger. You don't know Thord, who can make the rocks speak out if he will."

With his free hand he struck Stark across the face.

It seemed impossible that anything so still could move so quickly. There was an ugly flash of teeth and Thord's wrist was caught above the thumb-joint. He bellowed, and the iron jaws closed down, worrying the bone.

Suddenly Thord screamed, not for pain but for panic. The rows of watching men swayed forward, and even the Lord Ciaran rose up, startled.

"Hear!" ran the whispering around the fire. "Hear how he growls!"

Thord had let go of Stark's hair and was beating him about the head with his clenched fist. His face was white.

"Werewolf!" he screamed. "Beast-thing! Let me go!"

But the dark man clung to Thord's wrist, snarling, and did not hear. After a bit there came the dull snap of bone.

Stark opened his jaws. Thord ceased to strike him. He backed off slowly, staring at the torn flesh. Stark had sunk down to the length of his arms.

With his left hand, Thord drew his knife.

The Lord Ciaran stepped forward. "Wait, Thord!"

"It is a thing of evil," whispered the barbarian. "Warlock. Werewolf. Beast."

He sprang at Stark.

The man in armor moved, very swiftly, and the great axe went whirling through the air. It caught Thord squarely where the cords of his neck ran into the shoulder, caught and shore on through.

There was a silence in the valley.

The Lord Ciaran walked slowly across the trampled snow and took up his axe again.

"I will be obeyed," he said. "And I will not stand for fear, not of god, man, nor devil." He gestured toward Stark. "Cut him down. And see that he does not die."

He strode away, and Otar began to laugh.

From a vast distance, Stark heard that shrill, wild laughter. His mouth was full of blood and he was mad with a cold fury.

A cunning that was purely animal guided his movements then. His head fell forward and his body hung inert against the thongs. He might almost have been dead.

A knot of men came toward him. He listened to them. They were hesitant and afraid. Then, as he did not move, they plucked up courage and came closer, and one of them prodded him gently with the point of his spear.

"Prick him well," said another. "Let us be sure."

The sharp point bit a little deeper. A few drops of blood welled out and joined the small red streams that ran from the weals of the lash. Stark did not stir.

The spearman grunted. "He is safe enough now."

Stark felt the knife blades working at the thongs. He waited. The rawhide snapped, and he was free.

He did not fall. He would not have fallen then if he had taken a death wound. He gathered his legs under him and sprang.

He picked up the spearman in that first rush and flung him into the fire. Then he began to run toward the place where the scaly mounts were herded, leaving a trail of blood behind him on the snow.

A man loomed up in front of him. He saw the shadow of a spear and swerved and caught the shaft in his two hands. He wrenched it free and struck down with the butt of it and went on. Behind him he heard voices shouting and the beginning of turmoil.

The Lord Ciaran turned and came back, striding fast.

There were men before Stark now, many men, the circle of watchers breaking up because there had been nothing more to watch. He gripped the long spear. It was a good weapon, better than the flint-tipped stick with which the boy N'Chaka had hunted the giant lizard of the rocks.

His body curved into a half crouch. He voiced one cry, the challenging scream of a predatory killer, and went in among the men.

He did slaughter with that spear. They were not expecting attack. Most of them were not armed except for their knives, and they were caught off guard; Stark had sprung to life too quickly. And they were afraid of him. He could smell the fear on them. Fear not of a man like themselves, but of a creature less and more than man.

He killed, and was happy.

They fell away from him. They were sure now that he was a demon. He raged among them with the bright spear and they heard again that sound that should not have come from a human throat, and their superstitious terror rose and sent them scrambling out of his path, trampling on each other in childish panic.

He broke through, and now there was nothing between him and escape but two mounted men who guarded the herd.

Being mounted, they had more courage. They felt that even a warlock could not stand against their charge. They came at him as he ran, the padded feet of their beasts making a muffled drumming in the snow.

Without breaking stride, Stark hurled his spear.

It drove through one man's body and tumbled him off so that he fell under his comrade's mount and fouled its legs. It staggered and reared up, hissing, and Stark fled on.

Once he glanced over his shoulder. Through the milling, shouting crowd of men he glimpsed a dark mailed figure with a winged mask, going through the ruck with a loping stride and bearing a sable axe raised high for the throwing.

Stark was close to the herd now. And they caught his scent.

The Norland brutes had never liked the smell of him, and now the reek of blood upon him was enough in itself to set them wild. They began to hiss and snarl uneasily, rubbing their reptilian flanks together as they wheeled around, staring at him with lambent eyes. He rushed them, before they should decide to break.

He was quick enough to catch one by the flesh comb that served it for a forelock. He held it with savage indifference to its squealing and leaped to its back. Then he let it bolt, and as he rode it he yelled a shrill brute cry that urged the creatures on to panic.

The herd broke, stampeding outward from its center like a bursting shell.

Stark was in the forefront. Clinging low on the scaly neck, he saw the men of Mekh scattered and churned and tramped into the snow by the flying pads. In and out of the shelters, kicking the brush walls down, lifting up their harsh reptilian voices, they went racketing through the camp, leaving behind them wreckage as of a storm. And Stark went with them.

He snatched a cloak from off the shoulders of some petty chieftain as he went by and then, twisting cruelly on the fleshy comb and beating with his fist at the creature's head, he got his mount turned in the way he wanted it to go, down the valley.

He caught one last glimpse of the Lord Ciaran, fighting to hold one of the creatures long enough to mount it, and then a dozen striving bodies surged around him and hid him and he was gone.

Stark's beast did not slacken its pace. It seemed to hope that it could outrun the alien, bloody thing that clung to its back. The last fringes of the camp shot by and vanished in the gloom and the clean snow of the lower valley lay open before it. The creature laid its belly to the ground and went, the white spray spurting from its heels.

Stark hung on. His strength was all gone now, run out of him with the battle-madness. He became aware that he was sick and bleeding and that his body was one cruel pain. In that moment, more than in the hours that had gone before, he hated the black leader of the clans of Mekh.

The flight down the valley became a sort of ugly dream. Stark was aware of rock walls reeling past, and then they seemed to widen away and the wind came out of nowhere like the stroke of a great hammer, and he was on the open moors again. The beast began to falter and slow down. Presently it stopped.

Stark wanted simply to fall off and die, but it seemed a stupid thing to do after he had gone to so much trouble, and anyway if he did it here the Lord Ciaran would find his body and be pleased. So he managed to scoop up snow to rub on his wounds. He came near to fainting but the bleeding stopped and after that the pain was numbed to a dull ache. He wrapped the cloak around him and urged the beast to go on again, speaking to it gently this time, and after it had breathed it obeyed him, settling into the shuffling pace it could keep up for hours.

He was three days on the moors. Part of the time he rode in a stupor and part of the time he was feverishly alert and cunning, watching the skyline and taking pains to confuse his trail, not caring that the wind erased his tracks as soon as he had made them. Frequently he took the shapes of thrusting rocks for riders, and found cover until he was sure they did not move. He made a halter for the beast out of strips torn from the cloak, and he kept the end of it tied to Camar's belt which was still around his waist, so that when he fell or dismounted the beast would not get away from him. That was one of his worst fears. The other was that he would wake up out of a dark unconsciousness to find the Lord Ciaran looking down at him, holding the axe.

The ruined towers marched with him across the bitter land. He did not go near them.

He knew that he wandered a great deal, but he could not help it, and it was probably his salvation. In those tortured badlands, riven by ages of frost and flood, one might follow a man more or less easily on a straight track between two points. But to find a single rider lost in that wilderness was a matter of sheer luck, and this time the luck was riding with Stark. Twice in the distance he saw mounted men and knew they must be Ciaran's. Both times they passed him by a wide margin where he lay hid in snow-choked gullies with the cold white stuff thrown over him and the beast, negating both sight and scent.

And one evening at sunset he came out upon a plain that sloped upward to a black and towering scarp, notched with a single pass.

The light was level and blood-red, glittering on the frosty rock so that it seemed the throat of the pass was aflame with evil fires. To Stark's mind, essentially primitive and stripped now of all its acquired reason, that narrow cleft appeared as the doorway to the dwelling place of demons as horrible as the fabled creatures that roamed the Darkside of his native world.

He looked long at the Gates of Death, and a cold memory crept into his brain. Memory of that nightmare time when the talisman had seemed to bring him the echoes of unhuman voices and the sly touch of unhuman hands.

The weary beast plodded on, and Stark saw as in a dream the great walled city that stood guard before the Gate. He watched it glide toward him through a crimson haze, and fancied that he could see the ages clustered like birds around the towers.

He set his hands on Camar's belt, stiff with blood around his waist, and felt the sweet cruel warmth of hate flood through him. "I will break you," he whispered to the wide moor and the black-mailed rider that was somewhere upon it. "Here in Kushat—or there...." He looked again at the pass and was not afraid, and his fingers clenched hard over the boss. "I will break you, Ciaran."

He rode on, trembling with eagerness, thinking of the power that lay beyond the Gates of Death.

CHAPTER FOUR

HE STOOD IN a large square lined about with huckster's stalls and the booths of wine-sellers. Beyond were buildings, streets, a city. Stark got a blurred impression of a grand and brooding darkness of stone, bulking huge against the mountains, as bleak and proud and quite as ancient as they, with many ruins and deserted quarters.

He was not sure how he had come there. He had a vague memory of the city gate. It had been open and he had passed through it, he thought, behind a party of hunters bringing home their kill. After that he could not remember. But now he was standing on his own feet and someone was pouring sour wine into his mouth. He drank it, greedily. There were people around him, jostling, chattering, demanding answers to questions he had not heard. A girl's voice said sharply, "Let him be! Can't you see he's hurt?"

Stark looked down. His exalted mood, with its dreams of godlike vengeance, had left him. Reality came crowding back upon him, and reality was a slim and ragged girl with black hair and large eyes as yellow as a cat's. She held a leather bottle in her hand. She smiled and said, "I'm Thanis. Will you drink more wine?"

He did, and then managed to say, "Thank you, Thanis." He put his hand on her shoulder to steady himself. It was surprisingly strong. He felt light-headed and strange, but the wine was fusing a spurious sense of well-being into him and he was content to let that last as long as it would.

The crowd was still churning around him, growing larger, and now he heard the tramp of military feet. A small detachment of men in light armor pushed their way through.

A very young officer whose breastplate hurt the eye with brightness demanded to be told at once who Stark was and why he had come here.

"No one crosses the moors in winter," he said, as though that in itself were proof of the evil intent.

"The clans of Mekh are crossing them," Stark answered.

"An army, to take Kushat, a day, two days behind me."

The crowd picked that up. Excited voices tossed it back and forth and clamored for more news. Stark spoke to the officer.

"I will see your captain, and at once."

"You'll see the inside of a prison, more likely!" snapped the young man. "What's this nonsense about the clans of Mekh?"

Stark regarded him. He looked so long and so curiously that the crowd began to snicker and the officer's beardless face flushed pink to the ears.

"I have fought in many wars," said Stark gently. "And long ago I learned that it was wise to listen when someone came to warn me of the attack."

"Better take him to the captain, Lugh," cried Thanis. "It's our skins too, you know, if there's war."

The crowd began to shout. They were all poor folk, wrapped in threadbare cloaks or tattered leather. They had no love for the guards. And whether there was war or not, their winter had been long and dull and they were going to make the most of this excitement.

"Take him, Lugh! Take him! Let him warn Old Sowbelly!"

The young officer winced. And then from someone made anonymous by the crowd there rose a louder cry.

"Let him warn the nobles! Let them think how they'll defend Kushat now that the talisman is gone!"

There was a roar from the crowd. Lugh turned, his face suddenly grim, and motioned to his soldiers. Rather reluctantly, Stark thought, they leveled their spears and moved toward the crowd, which shrank back away from them and became quickly silent. Lugh's voice rang out, harsh and strident.

"The talisman is there for all to see! And you know the penalty for repeating that lie."

Stark's small start of surprise must have communicated itself through his tightened fingers to the girl, for he saw her look at him sharply, with something close to alarm. Then Lugh had swung around and was gesturing angrily at him. "See if he's armed."

One of the soldiers stepped forward, but Stark was quicker. He slipped the thongs and let the cloak fall, baring his upper body.

"The clansmen have already taken everything I owned," he said. "But they gave me something in return."

The crowd stared at the half healed stripes that scarred him, and there was a drawing in of breath, and a muttering.

The soldier picked up the cloak and laid it over Stark's shoulders. And Lugh said sullenly, "Come, then. I'll take you to the captain."

The girl turned to help him with the cloak, leaning her head close to his while she fastened the thongs. Her voice reached him in a quick, fierce whisper.

"Don't mention the talisman. It could mean your life!"

The soldiers were reforming. The girl stood back, casual, finished with her small task. But Stark did not let her go.

"Thank you, Thanis," he said. "And now will you come with me? Otherwise, I must crawl."

She smiled at him and came, bearing Stark's unsteady weight with amazing strength. And Stark wondered. Camar, certainly, had not lied. Otar and Ciaran, certainly, had well known that it was gone. Yet here was this young popinjay bellowing that the talisman was there for all to see and threatening the suddenly-cowed mob with the penalty for denying it.

He remembered that Ciaran had said something about the nobles of Kushat being afraid to let their people know the truth. They would be, Stark thought, and a substitution would be the surest way of covering up the loss. In any case, he decided to heed the girl's warning, and began forcing his weary brain to the task of eliminating from his story not only all mention of Camar but also of Otar and of Ciaran's references to the naked state of Kushat. A wrong word to the wrong person... He was too numb with exhaustion to think out all the possibilities, but he was suddenly and ironically aware that the talisman might prove to be more dangerous to him here in Kushat than it had been in Ciaran's camp.

The captain of the guards was a fleshy man with a smell of wine about him and a face already crumbling apart though his hair was not yet gray. He sat in a squat tower above the square, and he observed Stark with no particular interest.

"You had something to tell," said Lugh. "Tell it."

Stark told them, watching every word with care. The captain listened to all he had to say about the gathering of the clans of Mekh and then sat studying him with a bleary shrewdness.

"Of course you have proof of all this?"

"These stripes. Their leader Ciaran himself ordered them laid on."

The captain sighed and leaned back.

"Any wandering band of hunters could have scourged you," he said. "A nameless vagabond from the gods know where, and a lawless one at that if I'm any judge of men—you probably deserve it."

He reached for the wine and smiled. "Look you, stranger. In the Norlands, no one makes war in the winter. And no one ever heard of Ciaran. If you hoped for a reward from the city, you overshot badly."

"The Lord Ciaran," said Stark, grimly controlling his anger, "will be battering at your gates within two days. You will hear of him then."

"Perhaps. You can wait for him—in a cell. And you can leave Kushat with the first caravan after the thaw. We have enough rabble here without taking in more."

Thanis caught Stark by the cloak and held him back.

"*Sir,*" she said, as though it were an unclean word, "I will vouch for the stranger."

The captain glanced at her. "You?"

"Sir, I am a free citizen of Kushat. According to the law, I may vouch for him."

"If you scum of the Thieves' Quarter would practice the law half as well as you prate it, we would have less trouble," grumbled the captain. "Very well, take the creature, if you want him. I don't suppose you've anything to lose."

Thanis' eyes blazed but she made no answer. Lugh laughed.

"Name and dwelling place," said the captain, and wrote them down. "Remember, he is not to leave the Quarter."

Thanis nodded. "Come," she said to Stark. He did not move, and she looked up at him. He was staring at the captain. His beard had grown in these last days, and his face was still scarred by Thord's blows and made wolfish with pain and fever. And now, out of this evil mask, his eyes were peering with a chill and terrible intensity at the soft-bellied man who sat and mocked him.

Thanis laid her hand on his rough cheek. "Come," she said. "Come and rest."

Gently she turned his head. He blinked and swayed, and she took him around the waist and led him unprotesting to the door.

There she paused, looking back.

"Sir," she said, very meekly, "news of this attack is being shouted through the Quarter now. If it *should* come, and it were known that you had the warning and did not pass it on..." She made an expressive gesture and went out.

Lugh glanced uneasily at the captain. "She's right, sir. If by chance the man did tell the truth..."

The captain swore. "Rot. A rogue's tale. And yet..." He scowled indecisively, then shrugged and reached for parchment. "After all, it's a simple matter. Write it up, pass it on, and let the nobles do the worrying."

His pen began to scratch.

Thanis took Stark by steep and narrow ways, darkling now in the afterglow, where the city climbed and fell again over the uneven rock. Stark was aware of the heavy smells of spices and unfamiliar foods, and the musky undertones of a million generations swarmed together to spawn and die in these crowded tenements of slate and stone.

There was a house, blending into other houses, close under the loom of the great Wall. There was a flight of steps, hollowed deep with use, twisting crazily around outer corners. There was a low room, and a slender man named Balin, who said he was Thanis' brother and who stared with some amazement at Stark, his long thief's fingers playing delicately with the red jewel he wore in his left ear. There was a bed of skins and woven clothes and Stark's body yearned toward it. But he fought off the darkness, sitting on the edge of the bed while Thanis brought him wine and a bowl of food, making quick explanations to Balin while she did so. Stark was too tired for the food, but he drank the wine and cleared the cobwebs out of his mind so that he could think rationally at least for a little while.

"Why," he asked Thanis, "is it dangerous to speak of the talisman?"

He was aware of Balin's brilliant gaze upon him, but he watched the girl's face.

"You heard Lugh when he answered the crowd," she said. "They have put some bit of glass in the shrine and called it the talisman, and those who say they are liars are made to regret it."

In a light and silken voice Balin said, "When the talisman vanished, we very nearly had a revolution in Kushat. The people resented losing it, and blamed the folk of the King City, where the shrine is, for not taking better care of it. Narrabhar and his nobles felt their high seats tottering under them, and the substitution was quickly made."

"But," said Stark, "if the people don't believe…"

"Only we in the Thieves' Quarter really know. It was one of us who took it." There was an odd mingling of pride and condemnation in his tone. "The others—the artisans and shopkeepers, the ones with a little fat under their belts—they would rather believe the lie than bleed for the truth. So it has worked." He added, "Thus far."

Looking Stark very steadily in the eye, Thanis said, "You're an outlander, yet you know about the talisman and you knew that it was gone. How?"

The old instinct of caution held him quiet. He understood now, quite clearly, that the possession of the talisman could be his death-warrant. So he said with perfect if fragmentary truth, "Ciaran of Mekh said it. There is an old man with him, a man of Kushat. His name is Otar..."

"Otar!" said Balin. "Otar? We supposed that he was dead."

Stark shook his head. "He has told Ciaran the talisman was stolen and because of that Kushat is ready for the taking." He recalled Ciaran's words and repeated them. "Like a man without a soul." He paused, frowning. "Does this bit of glass really have such power?"

Balin said, "The people believe that it has, and that is what matters."

Stark nodded. His brief period of grace was over now and the darkness was sweeping in. He stared at Balin, and then at Thanis, in a curiously blank and yet penetrating fashion, like an animal that thinks its own thoughts. He took a deep breath. Then, as though he found the air clean of danger, he lay back and went instantly to sleep.

Hands and voices called him back. Strong hands shaking him, urgent voices speaking his name. He started up, heart hammering and muscles tense, with a confused idea that he had slept only a moment or two, and then he saw that the light of a new sun was pouring in through the window. Thanis and Balin were bending over him.

"Stark," said the girl, and shook him. "There are soldiers coming."

CHAPTER FIVE

HE SHOOK HIS head, groaning with the stiffness of his body as he moved to rise. "Soldiers?" There was a clamor in the street outside, and a rhythmic clinking of metal that meant armed men marching. Full consciousness came back with a rush. His gaze swept the room, marking the window, the door, and archway into an inner chamber, his muscles flexing. Balin took him by the shoulder.

"No. You can't escape. And anyway, there's no need. I think Old Sowbelly made his report, and now you'll be taken to the King City to answer more questions." He faced Stark, speaking sharply. "Now listen. Don't mention Otar or what Ciaran said about the city. They won't like it, and they might well take your head off to keep you from repeating the story to others. You understand? Tell them exactly what you told the captain, nothing more."

Stark nodded. "I understand." Air from the window curled icily around his body and he realized for the first time that he was naked. He had been shaved and washed, his wounds rubbed with salve. Thanis handed him his boots and trousers, carefully cleaned, and a garment he did not recognize, a tunic of golden fur tanned soft as silk.

"Balin stole it from the baths where the nobles go. He said you might as well have the best."

"And a devil of a time I had finding one big enough to fit you." Balin looked out the window. "They're coming up now. No need to hurry. Let them wait."

Stark pulled the clothes on and looked in quiet panic for Camar's belt. There came a pounding on the door and the remembered voice of Lugh demanding entrance. Balin lifted the bar and the room filled with soldiers.

"Good morning," Balin said, bowing with a flourish and wincing visibly at the light dancing on Lugh's breastplate. Lugh ignored the mockery. He was very soldierly and important this morning, a man with a duty to perform. "The Commander of the City will question you, stranger," he said to Stark, and gave a preemptory nod toward the doorway.

Thanis lifted Stark's cloak from a peg on the wall, revealing the belt under it. She brought them both to Stark. "You mustn't keep the Lord Rogain waiting," she said demurely, and smiled. She was wearing a red kirtle and a necklet of beaten metal intricately pierced, and her dark hair was combed out smooth and shining. Stark smiled back and thanked her, and buckled on the belt. Then he threw the cloak over his shoulders and went out with Lugh.

There were people in the street below watching as Stark went down the crazy stairway with the soldiers in single file before and behind him and Lugh walking ahead of all like a young cockpheasant. This time the people only watched and did not say much to the soldiers. The detachment formed up in the street, eight soldiers and an officer to escort one man. Stark thought that they would have been better used to patrol the Wall, but he did not say so. The crowd left them plenty of room. Stark could see the intent faces peering at him and hear the muttered undertone of talk, and he knew that the word he had brought of Ciaran's coming was all over the Quarter now, and probably over half the city.

Lugh did not speak to him again. They marched through the narrow twisting streets of the Quarter, and then left it for the somewhat broader but even more crowded avenues where the shops of the weavers and the armorers, the silversmiths and the potters, the blacksmiths and the stone-masons, all the multifarious crafts and trades necessary for civilized living, lined the ways that led to the King City. People passing by stopped to look curiously at Stark, and he looked at them, thinking of the riders of Mekh and wondering what their prosperous shops and neat houses would look like after another sun or two had passed.

Kushat was built in the immemorial pattern of Martian cities, a sort of irregular, sprawling wheel enclosed by a wall at its outer rim and with the King City at the hub, a walled enclave of its own containing the great towered hall of the king and the houses of the nobles. The dark turrets, some of them ruined and partly fallen, all of them stained and blackened with time, stood up grim and dreary in the cold sunlight, the faded banners whipping in the wind that blew down from the pass. Beyond them, blotting out the northern sky, were the black and ice-seamed cliffs for a backdrop.

Stark shivered, with more than the cold. He hated cities anyway. They were traps, robbing a man of his freedom, penning him in with walls and the authority of other men. They were full of a sort of people that he did not like, the mob-minded ones, the sheep-like ones and the small predators that used them. Yet he had been in cities that were at least exciting, the Low-Canal towns of Valkis and Jekkara far to the south, as old as Kushat but still throbbing with a wicked vitality. Perhaps it was the northern cold that cast such a pall over these streets.

Or was it something more? Stark looked up at the cliffs and the notch of the pass. Was it living so close under the Gates of Death, and fearing whatever it was that lay beyond them?

They passed into the King City through a narrow gate, challenged by the strong guard mounted there. Here the buildings of carved stone stood wide apart, with paved squares between them. Some were no more than skeletons, with blank archways and fallen roofs, but others showed rich curtains in their slitted windows and signs of activity in their courtyards. Lugh marched smartly, his back straight and his chin in the air, making precise military turns at the corners, going toward the towers of the king's hall.

They came out abruptly into the wide square in front of it. And Stark slowed his pace, staring.

The men behind him swore, stepping wide to avoid running into him. Lugh turned to see what the trouble was, prepared to be irritable. Then he saw what Stark was looking at, and decided instead to be condescending to the barbarian.

"That," he said, "is the shrine of the talisman, and the statue of Ban Cruach, who built Kushat."

The statue was the height of three tall men above its pedestal, massively and simply carved, and the weathering of centuries had smoothed away much of the finer detail. Yet it was a powerful portrait, and somehow Stark felt that just so had Ban Cruach looked in his ancient armor, standing with the hilt of his great sword between his hands and his helmeted head uplifted, his eyes fixed upon the Gates of Death. His face was made for battles and for ruling, the bony ridges harsh and strong, the mouth proud and stern but not cruel. A fearless man, one would have said. But Stark thought that he saw in that stone face the shadow of something akin to fear-awe, perhaps, or doubt, or something more nameless, as though he stared at the portal of some dark and secret world where only he had ventured.

"Ban Cruach," Stark said softly, as though he had not heard the name before. "And a shrine. You spoke of a talisman?"

Lugh motioned to the soldiers to march nearer to the statue. The pedestal on which it stood was not a solid block of masonry, but a squat building having a small barred window in each side and no door that Stark could see. Entrance to the chamber must be through some hidden passageway below.

"The talisman," Lugh said, "was the gift of Ban Crauch to the city. As long as it is here, Kushat will never fall to an enemy."

"Why?" asked Stark.

"Because of the power of the talisman."

"And what is that?" asked Stark, the rude barbarian, simple and wondering.

Lugh answered with unquestioning certainty, "It will unlock the power that lies beyond the Gates of Death."

"Oh," said Stark. He leaned close to the little barred window. "That must be a great power indeed."

"Great enough," said Lugh, "that no enemy has ever dared to attack us, and no enemy ever will as long as the talisman is there." His voice was defiant, a little too emphatic. Stark wondered. Did Lugh really believe that this was the talisman, or was he only trying to believe it, trying very hard?

"I thought that yesterday in the market place I heard someone say..."

"A wild rumor started by the rabble in the Thieves' Quarter. You can see for youself. It is there."

Certainly something was there, set on a block of polished stone. An oval piece of crystal, very like the talisman in shape and size, so much like it that they could not be told apart except that this was a bit of crystal and nothing more, inert, hollow, reflecting the light with shallow brightness. Remembering the eerie glow, the living flickering shifting radiance of the talisman, Stark smiled inwardly. And paused to wonder how under heaven Camar had managed to steal the thing.

"I see," said Stark aloud. "It is. And those are coming who will test its strength—and yours." He glanced at Lugh. "How is it used to unlock this power you speak of?"

"When the time comes to use it," Lugh said curtly, "it will be used. Come, the Lord Rogain is waiting."

In other words, Stark thought, you don't know how it is used any more than I do.

As he moved to fall in again with the soldiers, Lugh added with positive viciousness,

"And I do not believe your barbarian army any more than the captain does."

He strode off, the soldiers matching step behind him. They marched across the square and into the courtyard of a massive building on its eastern side, where the stone figures of men in ancient mail stood sentry, some without their heads, or arms, some shattered into fragments by the cracking frosts of a thousand winters. Here the soldiers were left behind, and Lugh escorted him through high draughty corridors hung with dim tapestries and through a series of guard rooms where men-at-arms halted them and made Lugh give his name, rank, company, and errand. At length a guard swung open a massive bronze-plated door and Stark found himself in a surprisingly small room, heavily curtained against the cold, smelling of smoke from a couple of braziers, and filled with an assortment of irritated men.

Stark recognized the captain of the guard. The others, old, young, and intermediate, wore various harness indicating rank, and all of them looked as though they hated Eric John Stark, whether for presenting them with unpleasant problems or for routing them out of their warm beds at such an early hour he did not know. Probably both.

Behind a broad table that served as a desk sat a man who wore the jeweled cuirass of a noble. He had a nice, kind face. Gray hair, mild scholarly eyes, soft cheeks. A fine man, Stark thought, but ludicrous in the trappings of a soldier.

Lugh saluted. "Here is the man, sir," he said. Rogain nodded and thanked him, and dismissed him with a flick of the hand. Stark stood still, waiting, and Rogain studied him, taking his time, his gaze probing and thoughtful.

"How are you called?" he asked.

Stark told him.

"You are not of the Norlands."

"No. Nor of Mars. My parents came from the third planet. I was born on the world nearest the sun." He paused, meeting Rogain's eye without either arrogance or deference. "I say this because I wish you to understand that I am a wanderer by birth and by nature."

Rogain nodded, with just the hint of a smile. "In other words, I need not enquire what business you had on the northern moors in winter. Or any other time, for that matter."

The captain of the guard muttered something audible about the business of rogues and outlaws. Stark said to Rogain,

"Ask what you will. I was in the south, where I had come to fight with the Drylanders in a war against the Border States. But things went wrong, and that war was never fought. There was nothing for me to do there, and I had never seen this part of Mars. So I came north."

"You are a mercenary, then?" asked Rogain, and one of the others, a heavy-jawed man with insolent, stupid eyes, made a gesture of relief.

"There is your answer, Rogain. He brings a great tale of war in the hope of selling his services."

"What do you say to that, Stark?" asked Rogain mildly.

Stark shrugged. "I say that the proof of my story is easily gained. Only wait a day or two." He looked from one to the other of the assembled faces, finding them hopelessly wanting. They were civilized men, all of them, good, bad, and indifferent—so civilized that the origins of their culture had been forgotten half an age before the first clay brick was laid in Sumer. Too civilized, Stark thought, and far too long accustomed to the peace Ban Cruach had bequeathed them, a peace that had drawn their fangs and cut their claws, leaving even the best of them unfit for what was coming.

"You will defend Kushat or not, as you choose," he said. "But in either case, my services are not for sale."

"Oh?" said Rogain. "Why?"

Very softly Stark said, "I have a personal quarrel with Ciaran of Mekh."

The man who had spoken before gave a derisive laugh. Rogain turned to look at him with pointed interest. "Can you no longer recognize a man when he stands before you?" he asked, and shook his head. The man's wattles turned a dull red, and the others looked startled. Rogain turned again to Stark.

"Sit down," he said, pointing to a chair beside the desk. "Now. I would like to hear the story from your own lips."

Stark told it, exactly as he had told the captain. When he was finished Rogain asked him questions. Where was the camp? How many men? What were the exact words of the Lord Ciaran, and who was he? Why had he ordered Stark to be scourged? Stark found answers for them all that were truthful and yet made no mention of Otar and the talisman. Rogain sat then for some time, lost in thought, while the others waited impatiently, not quite daring to offer their opinions. Stark watched Rogain's hand moving abstractedly among the seals and scrolls upon his desk—a scholar's hands, without a callus on them. Finally he sighed and said, "I will arm the city. And if the attack comes, Kushat will owe you a debt for the warning, Stark." An astonishingly unpleasant look came into his eyes. "If it does not come—we will talk further about the matter then."

Stark smiled, rather cruelly. "You still hope that I am lying."

"This part of the world has laws of its own, which you neither know nor understand, and therefore it is possible for you to be mistaken. Firstly..."

"No one makes war in the winter," Stark said. "That is exactly why Ciaran is doing it."

"Quite possibly," said Rogain. "But there is another thing. We have a power here that guards our city. It has sufficed in all the time past." His voice was very quiet, deceptively unemotional. "Why now should the barbarians suddenly lose their fear of the talisman?"

There was now a stillness in the room, a sense of held breath and stretching ears, of eyes that glanced swiftly at Stark's face and then away again, afraid to be caught looking lest they betray the intensity behind them. A duller man than Stark would have been able to smell the trap that had opened so innocently under this feet. Stark gave no notice that he was aware of anything, but any thought he might have had of telling Rogain the truth and surrendering the talisman to its rightful owners died then and there. He was on the edge of a trap, but these men were in one. They had lied to their own people to save their skins, and they did not dare admit it. If he told them that Ciaran knew the talisman was gone they would kill him to keep the word from spreading. If he gave them the true talisman, they would weep with relief and joy, and kill him even quicker. The last thing they could afford was to have word get about the city that the true talisman had returned.

So Stark said, "The Lord Ciaran is no common barbarian, and he is a hungry man, far too hungry for fear. If your talisman is as powerful as you say, I would guess he means to take it for himself." The stillness hurt his ears. He sat with his heart pounding and the sweat flushing cold on his skin, and he added casually, "Sooner or later there is always someone to challenge a tradition."

It was as though the room relaxed and drew breath. Rogain nodded curtly and said,

"We shall see. For the moment, that is all."

Stark rose and went out. Lugh was waiting to march him out of the building and across the square under the looming statue of Ban Cruach, past the shine, and back to the grimy Quarter under the wall.

CHAPTER SIX

AT THE FOOT of the stair Lugh stopped and gave Stark one last bitter look.

"Sleep well," he said, "while better men than you walk freezing on the Wall."

He marched his men away and Stark looked after them, hearing the petulance in the clang of Lugh's iron-shod boots on the stones. He could find it in his heart to pity this young man, who was going to be forced so soon to dirty his beautiful armor with blood. Then he turned and climbed the stair, and was appalled at the effort it took. Twice he had to stop and hold on to keep from falling.

Part of his faintness was from hunger. He knew that as he entered the room and saw Thanis bent over a brazier stirring something savory in a blackened pot. Balin sprawled gracefully on the bench bed that ran along one crooked wall. He sprang up to catch Stark's arm and steady him to a seat, and Stark muttered something about food, unable to remember how long it was since he had eaten. Thanis waited on him gladly, and they did not speak until he was finished, drinking the last of his wine and feeling human again, feeling strong enough to think, and thinking, scowling into his cup.

And Balin asked, "What happened?"

"They will arm the city," Stark said.

"Will they hold it?"

Thanis said, "Of course they'll hold it. We still have the Wall."

"Walls," said Balin, "are no stronger than the men who defend them." He asked again. "Will they hold it?"

Stark shook his head. "They'll try. Some of them will even die gloriously. But they're sheep, and the wolves will tear them. This is my belief.

He rose abruptly and went to stand by the window, looking out at the ancient uneven roofs, above them to the distant towers of the King City, and then beyond to the black line of the cliffs. The cold air stirred his hair, and he shivered and said,

"Balin, could they hold it if they had the talisman?"

There was a quiet, in which he could hear the wind chafing and whining at the walls outside. He pulled the curtain tight and turned, and Balin was looking at him with smoky cat eyes, his body poised like a bent bow.

"This is your city, Balin. You know. I can only guess. Could they hold it?"

Slowly and softly Balin answered, while Thanis sat stiff and still as ivory, and as pale, watching the two men.

"They *are* sheep, Stark. And they're worse than that. They're liars. And they have forgotten the knowledge that was entrusted to them. They do not remember any more how the talisman was used, or what it called forth from beyond the Gates of Death. If they had ten talismans, they could not hold the city."

And he added, "Why do you ask that question?"

"Because," said Stark grimly, "I have decided to trust you with my life." He slipped the belt from around his waist. "I've done what I promised. I have finished a journey for a friend—a man named Camar, who had a burden on his soul." He saw Thanis start at the sound of that name, but Balin did not stir and his eyes never wavered from Stark's. The silence thrummed between them. Stark's nerves twitched and tightened, and his fingers curved around the hollow boss of the buckle.

"The talisman belongs to Kushat. But on that journey I bought a small share in it, Balin, with my blood. Both Otar and Ciaran were sure I could give it to them, and they did their best to make me. Now I say that if the city falls to Ciaran he must not get the talisman. And someone—you or I, *someone*, must live to use it against him." He paused. "If there truly is a power beyond the Gates of Death..."

"For an outlander," Balin said, "you have a strong love for Kushat."

Stark shook his head. "Kushat may stand or fall as it will without breaking my heart. But I have a score to settle with Ciaran, and I will hale the devil out of hell to do it, if I have to."

"Well," said Balin, and smiled, and was suddenly relaxed and easy. "In that case our ways lie close enough together that we can walk them side by side." Casually he laid back the covering on the couch beside him, and the thin sharp blade of a throwing knife glittered in the chill light. He picked it up and placed it in his girdle. "Oh," he said, "and Stark, don't be too concerned about trusting me with your life." His fingers plucked something from the folds of his tunic and held it up—a bit of crystal, gleaming with subtle witch-fire, seeming to draw to itself all the light in the room.

Thanis cried out, "Balin...!" and then was still, her eyes wide as moons.

"I knew Camar too," said Balin. "He once showed me the secret of that buckle. So I have had your life in my hands since last night."

Thanis whispered, "And you did not tell me..."

"Of course not," said Balin. "I might have had to kill him, and I recognize the light in your eye, little sister. These things are unpleasant enough without additional fussing." He leaned forward, placing the talisman on a low table, and then looked up at Stark.

"As you say, Kushat is my city."

Stark said slowly, "I will be damned." He stared at Balin, as though he were looking at a new and different man. Then he laughed and flung himself down on the couch, being careful to avoid the talisman. "Very well, comrade. How do we plan?"

"If the Wall holds and the city stands, then the plan is simple enough and Narrabhar's high seat will be quickly emptied. But if the city falls..." Balin sipped his wine reflectively. "We here in the Quarter are more like rats than sheep, and so perhaps poverty is useful, since it has kept our teeth sharp. I think that we are the ones who must survive, Stark." He looked at the talisman and added in a strangely awed and almost frightened voice, "We are the ones who will have to carry that beyond the Gates of Death."

"So long as I go with you," Stark said.

"We need you," Balin said simply. "We are thieves by trade, killers only by accident. I myself have never drawn blood in anger. You will have to make us into fighting men."

"If you have the will," Stark said, "the method is not hard to teach." He yawned.

"The will we have."

"Good." Stark lay back on the soft furs. "There will be very little time. What we do must be done quickly. Talk to your people, Balin, the best men. Assume that the Wall will be breached. Arrange a rallying place, and if it is possible, plan a way out of the city. We'll need supplies, food and warm clothing, all we can carry without being burdened. And no more women and children than you can help. They're more likely to die in the mountains than they are here, and we must be able to move fast."

Balin had risen. He looked down at Stark and said, "Friend, I've been at this since I found the talisman."

"So much the better," Start said, and swore. "I hate this planning in the dark. I can see clearly enough between Kushat and the Gates of Death, and after that I am in darkness. Is it possible, Balin—truly possible, that no one ever goes into that pass, even a little way, to tell us what it's like? Even Otar didn't say he had."

Balin shrugged. "From time to time men have tried it, in spite of the tabu. Sometimes their bodies return to us in the spring floods. Mostly they never come back at all. The law and the legend of Ban Cruach both say that Kushat was built to guard the pass, and that only with the talisman can a man go through it and live."

"Does the legend say," asked Stark, "why Kushat guards the pass?"

"Didn't Camar tell you that?"

"He said no one remembered why, except that it was a great trust."

"And that is true. But one may guess that the power hidden beyond the pass is too great to be loosed by chance or whim, and so must be protected. In the beginning, of course, Ban Cruach gained that power for himself somehow, and used it to build his own fame in the Norlands..."

"Which Ciaran hopes to do again." Stark nodded. "Otar has turned his brain with desire."

"Otar," said Balin, and shook his head. "He was always daft. He used to make speeches in the market places, the wine shops, anywhere that people would listen to him, saying that Kushat was dying and it was time we took the power beyond the Gates and made ourselves great again. He became so troublesome that Rogain chained him up a time or two, and after that he vanished."

"He found someone to listen," said Stark. "Is there more to the legend?"

"It is believed that the building of Kushat was part of the bargain that Ban Cruach made to get the—whatever it was he got...."

"Bargain?" Bargain with whom?"

"Or with *what*. No one knows. It does not seem that anyone but Ban Cruach knew even then, though it is all so long ago that nothing is sure. Perhaps there never was a bargain. But this you can depend on. Regardless of what gods or devils may be waiting there, there is enough danger in the Gates of Death without them. Crevasses, ice and mist and grinding rockfalls, starvation and cold.

"Well," said Stark, "those things won't stop the Lord Ciaran, so they can't stop us. As for what else may or may not be there, I suppose we'll find out when the time comes. Until then we may as well forget it."

"At any rate," said Balin, "we have the talisman. So if there is truth in the legend... Stark?"

Silence.

Thanis said, "He's asleep."

Balin swore a long and involved Norland oath, and then smiled wryly. "I'm not at all sure it's entirely human, but I'm glad to have it on my side, anyway."

"Would you really have killed him?"

"Let's put it this way. I'd have tried." He measured the thickness of Stark's shoulders and shook his head. "I'm extremely relieved that I didn't have to."

Thanis turned again to the talisman, not going close to it but standing with her hands clasped tightly behind her back and her head bent, her eyes sober and shadowed. Suddenly she said, "I'm afraid, Balin."

He touched her shoulder gently. "So am I. But the thing has come home and the gods have put it into our hands, and we must do what we can."

He took the crystal reverently in his fingers and returned it to the hollow boss, closing it carefully.

Thanis had not moved, except to let her hands drop to her sides. Now she lifted them and brushed the black heavy strands of hair from her forehead, and it was an old woman's gesture, infinitely weary.

"It's all to be broken, isn't it?" she said.

The one small word encompassed everything, the city, the Quarter, the street, this building, this room, these few belongings, this way of life. Balin experienced something of Stark's personal hatred of the Mekhish bastard who would do this breaking, and he wanted very much to comfort Thanis, but it was no use lying and so he did not. He said,

"For a time, I'm afraid. For a time, anyway."

He hung the belt over the wall peg under Stark's cloak, threw his own cloak around him and went out. The cold air struck him with the familiar winter smells of frost and smoke. The dark roofs glinted in the sunlight, lying against one another like the discarded counters of a game of hazard, and above him the great Wall rose as it had risen since his eyes first opened on the world, massive and comforting and secure. Balin went down the hollow steps, his hands touching the worn stone at his side. He moved slowly. He moved like a man with a knife in his heart.

CHAPTER SEVEN

IT WAS EVENING again when Stark awoke and lay stretching, still sore in all his muscles and ravenously hungry, but feeling pretty much himself. He became aware of sounds that had not been there before, the pacing of men on the Wall above the house, the calling of the watch. Thanis heard him stir and came from where she had been standing at the doorway, looking out into the dusk.

"There is still no sign of attack," she said.

"It will come." Stark sat up. There was something different about the room. In a moment he realized that all the small things were gone, the little useless things that made a room something more than merely a box in which to shelter like a captive animal. Presumably they had been hidden somewhere. The utilitarian things, clothing and such, were arranged in two small piles in a corner, where they might be quickly chosen from, and a supply of food was beside them, wrapped in cloth. The room was already vacant. No one lived in it any more. People were only camping here, waiting to move on. He glanced up at Thanis. Her eyes hurt him, so big and full of unshed tears.

He said, "I'm sorry."

"Don't be," she answered with unexpected fierceness, and suddenly her eyes blazed. "Just tell me what I can do to fight."

"You've made a good beginning." He smiled at her, pleased. "Is there anything to eat without breaking into the iron rations?"

"Oh, yes. I've had a good day in the markets." She brought him cold meat and bread with wine. She watched him eat for a minute or two and then began herself to eat, very hungrily. And again Stark smiled.

"I see the knot has come untied."

She seemed surprised. "How did you guess?"

"I've known a time or two myself when the food choked me. Here, have some wine. It's warming to the gut and cheering to the nerves." He poured her cup full and she smiled and drank it, and they were companionable in that bereaved room, with the thick shadows gliding in to cover the empty places and a pleasant warmth from the brazier.

"Where is Balin?"

"Talking. Planning. He'll be home soon."

"I should thank you. Both of you, for taking me in, but especially you, for helping me there in the market place."

She looked at him briefly, steadily, and smiled a little, and said, "Thank me if you will. There'll be little enough of kindness soon." She glanced away from him around the room, and outside on the Wall the boots rang on cold stone and the voices challenged harshly.

Stark reached over and pulled her to him and kissed her, feeling the warm sweet-smelling firmness of her body, felling the immensely thrilling fact of life in her, beating in her throat under his fingers, stirring in the lift and fall of her breathing, her own individual and separate being. And she clung to him, almost desperately, and did not speak, and all at once it was as though he held a child, small and frightened and seeking comfort.

Something in his manner must have changed, because she pushed away from him, laughing a little and shaking her head. "I need more wine, I think." She lifted the cup and then paused, listening, and gave Stark an urchin's grin.

"Anyway, here is my brother."

Balin was in a taut, keyed-up mood. He sat down at first with them to eat, but then rose and moved restlessly about the room, his eyes too bright, his voice edged and brittle, talking about all he had been doing.

"I've had to be very careful, Stark. Only four other men know about the taliman, and them I trust as I do my own right hand. One word—just one word in the wrong ear, and the three of us here would never live to see what happens to Kushat."

"You have a rallying place?"

"Yes. The Festival Stones. They lie outside the city..." He sat down beside Stark and dipped his finger in the wine, drawing with it a map on the table-top. "Here, to the northeast, some two miles. There is a ceremony there every year at the spring solstice, mostly for the children now, though in older times it was a more serious thing."

Stark nodded. The sun rose and set for all the planets, and on each one of them the worship of the Shining God was old as the first men, as old as life.

"Everyone knows where it is," Balin was saying, "and from there the way is clear to the pass. That is all arranged. Each man will find his own way out of the city. There are a hundred ways and every thief knows them. In its under-levels, Kushat is a honeycomb."

Again Stark nodded. This was so with every Martian city he knew.

The challenge of the watch sounded on the Wall. Suddenly the room was stifling. "I would like to go out," Stark said, and rose. "Is it possible?"

"Oh, yes. As long as we stay in the Quarter." He jumped up, caught by a new idea and eager to go again. "We will go around and let the men see you, so they'll know you when the time comes."

"And," said Stark mildly, putting on his cloak, "you might show me one or two of these ways out of the city that every thief knows. Just in case we become separated in the heat of battle...."

Balin said cheerfully, "I told you, I'm not a soldier. Come on." He touched Thanis on the shoulder. "Try and get some sleep, little one. You'll need it."

She gave them an uncertain smile, and they left her and went out into the cold night. Both moons were up, painting the tumbled roofs of the city in a wild pattern of black and greenish silver, doubled-shadowed and constantly ashift. The towers of the King City rose up as though they would catch the nearer moon out of the sky, and it shone maliciously through them where their walls were broken away, revealing them for the sad ruins they were. Below in the streets there was mostly darkness, except for the watchfires in the squares, with here and there a torch lighting a tavern sign, or a dim gleam behind a shuttered window.

Stark noticed that Balin went ahead of him rapidly down the stairs and did not pause to look. He shook his head sympathetically and followed him. High above on the Wall the iron-shod boots tramped rhythmically.

"The city seems very quiet," Stark said, walking beside Balin along the crooked street.

"They still do not quite believe," said Balin. "Even here in the Quarter. No one has ever seen an attack, and no one has ever thought of such a thing in the winter. Winter is a safe time, when the tribesmen are too busy scratching a living to be bothered with making war. In the summer they try to plunder the caravans we send to trade with cities farther south, and they attack our hunting parties, but that is all. Most people in Kushat are of Thanis' opinion, anyway—regardless of the talisman, the great Walls still protects us." He looked up at it. "And when I see it I cannot help but feel in my heart, no matter what my mind tells me, that the Wall is proof against any enemy."

"Nevertheless," said Stark, "show me these hidden ways."

Balin showed him. There was a place in the Wall itself where a slab of stone swung open into a dark tunnel. There was another place where a paving block, hidden in a narrow mews, tilted open to show a rusted ladder of iron pegs going down into what Balin said was the system of ancient drains that carried the spring floods under Kushat.

"Very good," said Stark. "But we may be driven back out of the Quarter. Supposing that I am running for my life somewhere between here and the King City. Where would I go?"

"In that case," said Balin, "your best way would be by the Quarter of the Tomb-Robbers. That is only our name for it, of course—the artisans call it the Quarter of the Blessed. It is a burying ground." He led Stark up onto a roof-top and pointed out the way as well as he could, and then described in detail how to find the entrance to the hidden rat-runs that pierced the many levels below the surface, through the layers of detritus built up over the centuries to the deep rock that underlay it all. "Stay with the main tunnel. It will bring you out under the Wall and well away." He paused and added, "It leads under the King City. That was the road that Camar took when he left Kushat. He might have come back that way unseen.... Of course the men who use these ways go chiefly to meet the outland traders and dispose of items that cannot well be sold in Kushat. Trade moves briskly in summer, at the time of the caravans." Again he paused. "Poor Camar. The sin of pride. But perhaps after all he has done the city a great service."

"We'll know soon," said Stark, feeling the weight of the belt around his waist. "Doubtless sooner that we wish." And he stored all the information Balin had given him very carefully in his mind, knowing that by it he might live or die.

They went after that to a succession of poor tavern rooms, thick with smoke and the smell of people and old used leather garments. They sat for a little while in each one, drinking a cup of the sour wine that came by caravan from places with a kinder climate, and in each one lean dark-faced men took note of Stark but did not speak. When they walked home the nearer moon was closer upon the Wall and the black figures of the sentries moved hugely against it.

Thanis lay at one end of the bench bed, sleeping. They lay down quietly and did not disturb her.

The night wore on.

Very late, when the farther moon was sloping to the west, Thanis woke and knew that she was not going to sleep again. The room was very quiet except for the deep breathing of the men. The sentries on the wall had ceased their pacing. Thanis lay in the dark quiet until she could not stand it any longer and then she rose and went to the window and opened the heavy curtains. Wind and moonlight swept around her, leaning on the sill and looking out at the slumbering city.

Stark stirred uneasily, turning one way and then another. His motions grew violent. Thanis turned, and then crossed the room and touched him.

Instantly he was awake.

"You were dreaming," she said softly.

Stark shook his head. His eyes were still clouded, though not with sleep. "Blood," he said, "heavy in the wind."

Thanis whispered, "I smell nothing but the dawn."

Stark got up. "Wake Balin. I'm going up on the Wall."

He caught his cloak from the peg and flung open the door, standing on the narrow steps outside. The moonlight caught in his eyes, pale as frostfire. Thanis turned from him, suddenly trembling.

"Balin," she said. "Balin..."

He was already awake. Together they followed Stark up the rough-cut stair that led to the top of the Wall.

Stark looked southward, where the plain ran down from the mountains and spread away below Kushat. Nothing moved out there. Nothing marred the empty whiteness.

Stark said, "They will attack at dawn."

CHAPTER EIGHT

THEY WAITED.

Some distance away in either direction a guard was huddled down over a small brazier, each one making a sort of tent out of his cloak to hoard the heat. They glanced incuriously at the three civilians, apparently content merely to survive these last hours of the night, when a man's will and courage ran out of him like water from a cracked vessel. The wind came whistling down through the Gates of Death, and below in the empty streets the watchfires shuddered and flared.

They waited, and still there was nothing.

Balin said at last, "How can you know they're coming?"

Stark shivered, a shallow rippling of the flesh that had nothing to do with cold, and every muscle of his body came alive. The farther moon plunged downward. The moonlight dimmed and changed, and the plain was very empty, very still.

"They will wait for darkness," Stark said. "They will have an hour or so, between moonset and the rising of the sun."

He turned his head, drawn inevitably to look toward the cliffs above Kushat. Here, close under them, they seemed to tower outward in a curving mass, like the last wave of eternity rolling down, crested white with the ash of shattered worlds.

He looked into the black and narrow mouth of the Gates of Death, and the primitive ape-thing within him cringed and moaned, oppressed by a sense of fate. By this means and that he had been led across half a world to stand here with the talisman of a long-dead king in his hands. If things went as he supposed they would, he would soon be following the footsteps of that long-dead king into whatever strangeness might lie beyond that doorway—a strangeness, perhaps, that spoke with little spidery voices....

He shook with the memory of those voices and fought down a strong desire to take off the belt and drop it outside the Wall. He reminded himself of how he had ridden toward Kushat, looking up at the pass and lusting after the power that he might find there, power to destroy Ciaran of Mekh, and he laughed, not with any very great humor, at his own inconsistency.

He said to Balin, "Camar told me that Ban Cruach was supposed to have gone back through the Gates of Death at the end. Is that true?"

Balin shrugged. "That is the legend. At least, he is not buried in Kushat." It occurred to him to be surprised. "Why do you ask that?"

"I don't know," Stark said, and turned back to his contemplation of the plain. Deimos touched the horizon. A last gleam of reddish light tinged the snow and then was gone.

Thanis pressed closer to Balin for warmth, looking uneasily at Stark. There was a sort of timeless patience about him. Balin was aware of it, too, and envied him. He would have liked to go back down where there were warmth and comfort to help the waiting, but he was ashamed to. He was cold and doubtful, but he stayed.

Time passed, endless minutes of it. The sentries drowsed over their braziers. The plain was in utter darkness under the faint, far northern stars.

Stark said, "Can you hear them?"

"No."

"They come."

His hearing, far keener than Balin's, picked up the little sounds, the vast inchoate rustling of an army on the move in stealth and darkness. Light-armed men, hunters, used to stalking wild beasts in the snow. They could move softly. But still they made a breathing and a stirring, a whispering that was not of the wind.

"I hear nothing," Balin said. And Thanis shook her head, her face showing pale from the folds of Balin's cloak.

Again they waited. The westering stars moved toward the horizons, and at length in the east a dim pallor crept across the sky. The plain was still shrouded in night, but now Stark could make out the high towers of the King City, ghostly and indistinct. And he wondered who would be king in Kushat by the time this un-risen sun had set.

"You were wrong," said Balin, peering. "There is nothing on the plain."

"Go kick that sentry awake," Stark told him, and strode off to rouse the other one. The man snarled at him and Stark straight-ened him up with a rough hand, pushing the brazier over into the street below. "There is something out there that you should see," he said.

Swiftly now, in the thin air of Mars, the dawn came with a rush and a leap, flooding the world with harsh light. It flashed in cruel brilliance from sword-blades, from spearheads, from helmets and burnished mail, from the war harness of beasts. It glistened on bare russet heads and on coats of leather, and it set the ban-ners of the clans to burning, crimson and gold and green, bright against the snow.

For as long as a man might hold a breath there was no sound, not a whisper, in all the land. Then the sentry turned and ran, his iron-shod boots pounding on the stone. A great gong was set up on the parapet. He seized the hammer and began to beat the alarm, and the sound was picked up all around the cir-cumference of the Wall where other gongs added their brazen booming.

Out among the tribesmen a hunting horn sent forth one deep cry to split the morning. The wild skirling of the mountain pipes came after it, and the broken thunder of drums, and a wordless scream of exultation that rang back from the Wall of Kushat like the very voice of battle.

The men of Mekh began to move.

They came slowly and raggedly at first, the front ranks going at a walking pace that quickened and quickened as the press of warriors behind them pushed forward, until all at once they were running and the whole army began to break and flow, and the barbarians swept toward the city as water sweeps over a broken dam.

They came in knots and clumps of tall men, running like deer, leaping, shouting, swinging their great brands. Riders spurred their mounts until they raced with bleeding flanks and their bellies to the ground. There was no order, no array of neat and studied ranks advancing according to a plan. Behind the runners and the riders came more and more men and beasts until they became indistinguishable as such and were simply a motion, a tossing and rushing and trampling that shook the ground.

Ahead of them all came a solitary figure in black mail, bearing a sable axe and riding a tall beast trapped all in black.

Stark became aware that he was leaning far over the parapet and that Balin was trying to pull him back. "Did you have some idea of single combat?" Balin asked, and Stark stared at him, and Balin drew back, away from him. "One favor, friend. Don't become my enemy, please—my nerves would never stand it. But your turn against Ciaran must come later."

He pointed along the parapet where soldiers were running toward them, shouting at them to get off the Wall. Stark shrugged and followed Balin back down the steps and then up another set to the roof of the bulding. Thanis followed them, and they clambered out over the cold slates to watch. And again Stark was withdrawn into his stony patience, but only when Ciaran was hidden from him did he take his eyes off the black helm.

Kushat had come violently to life. The gongs still bellowed intermittently. Soldiers had begun to pour up onto the Wall. There seemed to be very many soldiers until their numbers were balanced off against the numbers of the barbarians and the length of the Wall. Mobs of citizens swarmed in the streets, hung out of windows, filled the roofs. A troop of nobles went by, brave in their bright mail, to take up their posts in the square by the great gate.

"What do you think now?" asked Balin softly, and Stark shook his head.

"This first attack won't carry. Then it depends on whether Ciaran is leader enough to hold his men at the Wall." He paused. "I think he is."

They did not speak again for a long while.

Up in their high emplacements the big ballistas creaked and thrummed, hurling boulders to tear great gouges in the flesh and bone of the attackers. From both sides the muted song of the horn bows became a wailing hum, and the short bone arrows flew in whickering showers. Slingers rattled their stones as thick as hail. War was a primitive thing there in the Norlands, as it was now over all of Mars except where the Earthman's weapons had been brought in, not for lack of ingenuity but for lack of metal and chemicals and power. Even a drained and dying world could still find hide and stone and bone and enough iron to forge a blade, and these simple, ancient ways were efficient enough. Men fell and were carried or kicked off the ledges by their fellows, and below them the barbarian dead began to lie in windrows. The blood-howl of the clans rang unceasingly on the frosty air, and Stark heard the rap of scaling ladders against stone. And he began to think that he was wrong and this first charge was going to carry after all. The soldiers of Kushat fought bravely, but it was their first and only battle and they were indeed like folded sheep against the tall killers of the mountains.

Still the Wall held. And by mid-morning the barbarian wave had beaten its strength out on the black stones. The men of Mekh grew silent and moved sullenly back across the plain, carrying their wounded with them, leaving their dead behind.

Thanis said, "You see, Stark? The Wall—the Wall protects us." Her face was drawn and over-bright with hope. "You see? They're going away."

Stark said, "They have left their dead. Among the tribes I know, the men of Kesh and Shun, this is a pledge that they will return. I would guess that these have the same custom. And look there." He pointed out across the plain. "That black banner with the lightning stoke. That is Ciaran's standard, and see how the chiefs are gathering to it."

Looking at the thinned ranks of the soldiers on the Wall, Balin said, "If this is victory, one is all we can afford."

But the city screamed with joy. People rushed into the streets to embrace the soldiers. The nobles rode the circuit of the Wall, looking well pleased. And on the highest tower of the king's hall a crimson banner shook out on the wind.

Stark said to Thanis, "Bring us food, if you will. There'll be little time later on."

She said fiercely, "I don't believe you, Stark. They're beaten." But she went and brought them food. The sun rose higher, and they waited.

A little after noon the barbarian army began to move again. It spilt itself into three spearheads, with a fourth body of men in reserve. Two spearheads launched themselves at two widely separated segments of the Wall, while the third simply waited. And Stark nodded.

"This is what Ciaran should have done at first. But barbarians are independent and have to be crushed once before they'll listen. Now we'll see. And the nobles had better get their reserves on the Wall."

The reserves came, running wildly. The forces of the defenders divided themselves raggedly and rushed to the two threatened points to repel the tribesmen already swarming up their ladders onto the parapet. Now the rest of the Wall was only thinly guarded.

The third barbarian spearhead hurled itself at the great gate.

Now the city was silent again except for the noises of battle. And Thanis said abruptly, "What is that—that sound like thunder?"

"Rams," Stark answered. "They are battering the gate."

He became very restless, watching as the officers tried to meet this new danger with their increasingly inadequate forces. The party attacking the gate was well organized. The sweating red-haired giants who swung the rams were protected by shield-men who locked their long hide shields together overhead to form a roof, warding off missiles from above. Other shield-men knelt to provide cover from which bowmen and slingers could sweep the Wall. Out on the plain, by the black standard, Ciaran waited with some of the chiefs and the impatient body of reserves, who were beginning to howl and cry like hounds chained up in sight of the hunt.

Stark said to Balin, "It would be better if you went now. Take the talisman, gather your men…"

Balin struck his fists down hard against the slates. "Not one man will leave Kushat without fighting for it." He glared angrily at Stark, who shrugged.

"Their chance is coming." He nodded to where press gangs were starting to beat the Quarter for men. "Let's go and meet them, then." He stood up and turned to Thanis. "You asked me last night to tell you how you could fight." He took off the belt and fastened it around her body underneath her cloak. "Take this, and what food and blankets you can carry, but above all this. Go and wait for us at the Festival Stones."

She seemed about to defy him, and he told her gently, "You have the talisman. It's up to you to see that its not taken."

She stared at him wide-eyed, and Balin said impatiently, "Will you stand all day?" He kissed her on the cheek and then pushed her bodily ahead of him off the roof and down the stairs. As they passed the door of the room he added, as though to make sure she understood, "And *wait*. Someone will come."

He ran on past her, down the steps. Stark smiled and said, "Be careful." He followed Balin. At the foot of the steps he glanced back and she was gone inside the room, taking with her Camar's belt and the talisman. He felt light and free, as though he had been relieved of a heavy stone.

They joined a thickening flow of men who needed no urging from the press gangs to go and fight for their city. Balin ran beside Stark, and his face was so set and white around the lips that Stark said, "When you run the first one through and he screams, and you reflect upon your mutual humanness, remember that he came here of his own free and greedy will to kill you."

Balin snarled at him. "Thanks, but I don't expect to have that trouble."

"Nevertheless," said Stark, "you will."

The weapons of the dead and wounded soldiers were heaped together in piles to supply the citizenry. Stark and Balin armed themselves and went up onto the Wall.

CHAPTER NINE

IT WAS A waste of time, and Stark knew it. He thought that probably a fair number of the men swarming up with them knew it too, and certainly for the thieves at least it would have been much easier simply to slip away out of Kushat and avoid the inevitable. But he was beginning to have considerable respect for the people of Kushat. To his simple way of thinking, a man who would not fight to defend what was his did not deserve to have it and would not have it for long. Some people, he knew, professed to find nobility in the doctrine of surrender. Maybe they did. To him it was only a matter of making a virtue out of cowardice.

At any rate, they fought, these men. Thief and weaver, butcher and blacksmith, stonemason and tavern-keeper, they fought. They were not very good at it, and the officers who ordered them this way and that along the Wall were not much better. The intermittent thunder of the rams still boomed from the gateway. The barbarian spearheads attacking the Wall began to play a game of shift, striking and then withdrawing to strike again in another place. "Playing with us," Stark thought, and noticed that the supply of arrows seemed to be exhausted, as more and more of the defenders threw away their bows. He looked out at the black standard, where it waited on the plain.

And then the wait was over.

The mounted standard-bearer lifted the banner and rode with it to the forefront of the reserve force. The black-mailed form of Ciaran rode in its shadow. The pipers set up a thin wild crying, and the mass of men was suddenly in motion, coming down on Kushat like a thunderbolt.

Stark said to Balin, "Don't wait too long, friend. Remember there is a second battle to be fought."

"I know," said Balin. "I know." His face was agonized, watching the death of his city. He had not yet found occasion to flesh his blade.

The occasion came swiftly.

A ladder banged against the stones only a few feet away. Men came leaping up the rungs, fierce-eyed clansmen out to avenge their fallen brothers and wipe out the defeat they had suffered that morning. Stark was at the ladderhead to greet them, with a spear. He spitted two men through with it and lost it as the second one fell with the point jammed in his breastbone. A third man came over the parapet. Stark received him into his arms.

Balin stood frozen, his borrowed sword half raised. He saw Stark hurl the warrior bodily off the Wall and heard the cry as he fell, and he saw Stark's face as he grasped the ladder and shoved it outward. There were more screams. Then there were more ladders and more red-haired men, and Stark had found a sword and was using it. Balin smelled the blood, and suddenly he was shaken with the immediacy of it, the physical closeness of an enemy come to slaughter him and destroy everything he loved. A fever burned through him. He moved forward and began to chop at the heads that appeared over the Wall. But it was as Stark had said, and at first he found that it was easier if he did not look too closely into their faces. Because of this one of them got under his uncertain guard and almost gutted him. After that he had no more difficulty.

Things had become so hot and confused now that the officers had lost control and men fought wherever they wished and could. And there was fighting in plenty for all, but it did not last long. The barbarians gained the Wall in three places, lost it in two and then regained it in one, and from these two footholds they spread inward along the ledges, rolling up the defenders, driving them back, driving them down. The fighting spread to the streets, and now all at once the ways leading back into the city were clogged with screaming women and children. Stark lost sight of Balin. He hoped that he was still alive and sensible enough to get away, but however it might be he was on his own and there was nothing Stark could do about it. So he forgot it and began to think of other things.

The great gate still held against the booming rams. Stark forced his way through to the square. The booths of the hucksters were overthrown, the wine-jars broken and the red wine spilled. Tethered beasts squealed and stamped, tired of their chafing harness and driven wild by the shouting and the smell of blood. The dead were heaped high where they had fallen from above. The last of the defense was here, soldiers and citizens forming a hollow square more or less by instinct, trying to guard their threatened flanks and their front, which was the gate, all at the same time, The deeps thunder of the rams shook the very stones under them. The iron-sheathed timbers of the gate gave back an answering scream, and toward the end all other sounds grew hushed. The nobles had come down off the Wall. They mounted and sat waiting.

There were fewer of them now. Their bright armor was dented and stained, and their faces had a pallor on them. Still they held themselves erect and arranged their garments and saw that the blazons on their shields were clean of blood. Stark saw Rogain. His scholar's hands were soft, but they did not tremble.

There was one last hammer-stroke of the rams. With a bitter shriek the weakened bolts tore out and the great gate was broken through.

The nobles of Kushat made their first, and final, charge.

As soldiers they went up against the riders of Mekh, and as soldiers they held them until they were cut down. The few who survived were borne back into the square like pebbles on the forefront of an avalanche. And first through the gates came the winged battle-mask of the Lord Ciaran.

There were many beasts tied among the ruined stalls with no riders to claim them. Stark mounted the nearest one and cut it free. Where the press was thickest, there was the man in black armor, riding like a god, and the sable axe drank life wherever it hewed. Stark's eyes shone with a strange cold light. The talisman was gone, the fate of Kushat was nothing to him. He was a free man. He struck his heels hard into the scaly flanks and the beast plunged forward.

It was strong, and frightened beyond fear. It bit and trampled, and Stark cut a path through the barbarians with the long sword, and presently above the din he shouted, "Ciaran!"

The black mask turned toward him. "Stark."

He spurred the beast again. "I claim my sword-right, bastard!"

The remembered voice spoke from behind the barred slot. "Claim it, then!" The black axe swept a circle, warning friend and foe alike that this was a single combat. And all at once they two were alone in a little space at the heart of the battle.

Their mounts shocked together. The axe came down in a whistling curve, and the red swordblade flashed to meet it. There was a ringing clash of metal, and the blade was shattered and the axe fallen to the ground.

There was a strange sound from the tribesmen. Stark ignored it. He spurred his mount ruthlessly, pressing in.

Ciaran reached for his sword, but his hand was numbed by the force of the blow and lacked its usual split-second cunning. The hilt of Stark's weapon, still clutched in his own numb grip and swung viciously by the full weight of his arm, fetched Ciaran a stunning blow on the helm so that the metal rang like a flawed bell. He reeled back in the saddle, only for a moment, but for long enough. Stark grasped the war-mask and ripped it off, and got his hands around the naked throat.

He did not break that neck, as he had planned to do. And the clansmen all around the circle stopped and stared and did not move.

Stark knew now why the Lord Ciaran had never shown his face.

That throat he held was white and strong, and his hands around it were buried in a mane of black hair that fell down over the shirt of mail. A red mouth passionate with fury, wonderful curving bone under sculptured flesh, eyes fierce and proud and tameless as the eyes of a young eagle. A splendid face, but never on any of the nine worlds of the sun could it have been the face of a man.

In that moment of amazement, she was quicker than he.

There was nothing to warn him, no least flicker of expression. Her two fists came up together between his outstretched arms and caught him under the jaw with a force that nearly snapped his neck. He fell backward out of the saddle and lay sprawled on the bloody stones, and for a moment the sun went out.

The woman wheeled her mount. Bending low, she caught up the axe from where it had fallen and faced her chieftains and her warriors, who were as dazed as Stark.

"I have led you well," she said. "I have taken you Kushat. Will any man dispute me?"

They knew the axe, if they did not know her. They looked from side to side uneasily, completely at a loss. Stark, lying on the ground, saw her through a wavering haze. She seemed to tower against the sky in her black mail, with her dark hair blowing. And he felt a strange pang deep within him, a kind of chill fore-knowledge, and the smell of blood rose thick and strong from the stones.

The nobles of Kushat chose that moment to charge. This strange unmasking of the Mekhish lord had given them time to rally their remnants together, and now they thought that the gods had wrought a miracle at last to help them. They found hope, where they had lost everything but courage.

"A woman!" they cried. "A strumpet. A drab of the camps. A *woman!*"

They howled it like an epithet, and tore into the barbarians.

She who had been the Lord Ciaran drove the spurs in deep, so that the beast leaped forward screaming. She went, and did not look once to see if any had followed, in among the men of Kushat. The great axe rose and fell.

She killed three and left two others bleeding on the stones. And still she did not look back.

The clansmen found their tongues.

"Ciaran! Ciaran! Ciaran!"

The crashing shout drowned out the sound of battle. As one man they turned and followed her. These tall wild children that she led could see only two choices, to slay her out of hand or to worship her, and they had chosen to worship. From here on they would follow her anywhere she led, with a kind of devotion different from and more powerful than any they could have given to a man—so long as she did nothing to tarnish the image they had of her, as a goddess.

Stark almost laughed. Instead of killing Ciaran, he had succeeded in giving her power and freedom she had never had before. Now nothing short of death could stop her.

Very well, he thought, in some dark corner of his mind. Very well, if that is the way the thread is woven.

Feet trampled him, kicked him, stumbled over him. Men were fighting above him, and the padded hoofs of beasts came stamping toward him. His head cleared with a panic rush. He got his knees under him and started to rise, and the movement attracted the attention of a warrior who must have thought he was dead, judging from the expression of surprise. He yelled and started the lunge that was meant to run Stark through, and then suddenly he dropped down flat as an old sack, with the back of his neck shorn through, and somebody was telling Stark bitterly, "Pick up his sword, damn it, pick up his sword, I can't hold them off alone."

It was Lugh, filthy, battered, bleeding, and a hundred years older than he had been the last time Stark saw him. Stark bent quickly and caught up the sword. He stood beside Lugh and they fought together, moving with the flow of the fight, which was becoming a rout so swiftly square. Here in the narrow, crooked streets, the press of refugees was simply too great. Clots of men formed like corks, bottling up the ways, and the barbarians cut them down happily at leisure. Stark grunted. "There's no profit in this. Can we get clear?"

"What matter?" said Lugh. "We might as well die here as anywhere."

Stark said, "There is a second line of battle, if you'd rather fight than die."

Lugh looked at him out of haggard eyes, a man's eyes where only a few hours ago they had been the eyes of a petulant boy. "Where, Stark? Where? The city is lost."

"But another thing has been found." The barbarians held all the streets under the Wall now. There was no way back to the places Balin had shown him. He took Lugh sharply by the shoulder. "If you can point me the way to the Quarter of the Blessed, I'll show you."

Lugh looked at him for a moment more. They were hemmed in by the press of people, jammed against the cold stone of the buildings. Lugh shook his head. "I can point the way, but we must still go over or through this mob."

Stark nodded. The walls were solid, and in any case one street would be no better than another. The roofs were a blind alley, and the houses traps. "We'll go through, then. Stick close."

He began to forge his way by main strength through the press, being perfectly ruthless about it, and he thought that very quickly now Ciaran of Mekh would be looking for him. She—it still came very strangely to think of Ciaran as "she"—would have killed him when he challenged her because no leader could violate the customs of single combat, but he knew that she would vastly prefer to have him alive. There was still that matter of the talisman. Only the shock of the unmasking and the subsequent necessities of the battle had saved him in the square. He moved faster and harder the more he thought about it. Men cursed and struck at him, but he was bigger and stronger than most of them, and a little more coherently desperate, and with Lugh to back him up he found himself before too long at the other side of the jam, where the press began to thin out into streams of people blindly running.

Stark ran too, but not blindly, with Lugh coming at a sort of loose-jointed weary gallop beside him. They passed through the gate of the Thieves' Quarter, where they had passed before on their way to the King City. The streets of the artisans had in them only the first stirrings of chaos. Mostly the shops were shuttered, the houses quiet. The folk had left them to watch the fighting, and now the buildings stood in the winter sunlight as peacefully as on a holiday afternoon.

Lugh sobbed, an abrupt, harsh sound. "They betrayed us," he said. "They lied."

"About the talisman? Yes."

"They *lied*!" A pause. Their feet rang on the paving stones. "But that wasn't the worst. They were fools, Stark. Idiots!"

"Fools are plentiful everywhere. A man has to learn to think for himself."

"They're dead," said Lugh vindictively. "They were paid for their folly."

"Fools generally are. Did they die well?"

"Most of them. Even Old Sowbelly. But what good is courage at the last minute, when you've already thrown everything away?"

"Every man has to answer that question for himself," Stark said, looking back. People were pouring through the gate now, and over the low wall. Over their heads he saw mounted men, forging their way in a tight group through the refugees. There were eight or nine of them and they looked as though they were hunting for something. "You were satisfied well enough with your leaders yesterday, so it might be said that you deserved them. Now let's drop the subject and think about staying alive." He shoved Lugh bodily aside into a transverse street. "Which way to the Quarter of the Blessed?"

Lugh opened his mouth, shut it again hard, and then made a wry gesture. "I can't argue with that," he said. "This way." He started to walk.

"Faster," said Stark. "Ciaran's riders are on the hunt."

They ran, looking frequently over their shoulders.

"She won't forgive you," Lugh said, and swore. "What a shame to us, to be defeated by a woman!"

Stark said, "Kushat has been taken by a warrior, and never forget it."

The street had curved and twisted, shutting off the view of the main avenue, but Stark's quick ears caught the sound of riders coming, the feet of the beasts making a soft heavy thudding as they ran. He caught Lugh and pulled him into an alley that led between the buildings, no more than three feet wide. They fled along it and into a mews behind the crumbling rear premises of the street, and Stark realized that most of these buildings had been abandoned long ago. The windows gaped and walls had spilled their carefully-cut blocks into the mews, where they were drifted over with dust and the wind-blown sloughings of a city. The sounds of war and death seemed suddenly very far away.

"How much farther?" Stark asked.

"I don't know... not much farther, I think."

They floundered, slipping and scrambling over the debris, their flanks heaving. And then the mews ended in a blank wall some eight feet high, and Lugh said,

"There. On the other side."

CHAPTER TEN

STARK HAULED HIMSELF up onto the wall and sat there, breathing hard and looking at the Quarter of the Blessed.

It was not a happy prospect. Kushat was a very old city, and a great deal of dying had been done in it. The area of this quarter was greater than any of those housing the living, and it had grown vertically as well as horizontally. Above ground the squat stone tombs had fallen and been leveled and rebuilt on their own debris until most of them now stood on humped mounds higher than the wall. Beside each one stood a tall stela, carved with innumerable names, most of them long obliterated, and these stelae sagged and leaned in every direction, bowed down with their weight of time, a dark sad forest with the cold wind blowing through it and the winter sun making long erratic patterns of shadow. Below ground, Balin had said, the rock was riddled with the even older shaft graves. Except for the wind, the silence was absolute.

High overhead, the somber cliffs brooded, notched with the gateway of the pass.

Stark sniffed the cold and quiet air, and the aborigine in him recoiled, shivering. He hunched around on the wall, looking back toward the increasing sounds of war and rapine. Columns of smoke were rising now, here and there, and the screaming of women had become incessant. The barbarian tide was rolling rapidly inward toward the King City. On the high tower of the king's hall, the crimson banner had come down.

Lugh had clambered up on the wall beside him. He watched Stark curiously. "What is it?"

"I'm thinking that I'd rather go back where the fighting is hot, than in there where it's far too peaceful."

"Then why go?"

"Because Balin told me of a way used by the tomb-robbers."

Lugh nodded, looking at Stark and smiling a crooked smile. "But you're afraid."

Stark shrugged, a nervous twitch of his shoulders.

Lugh said, "I was hating you, Stark, because you're too damned much of a man and you make me feel like a child. But you're only a child yourself under all that muscle." He jumped down off the wall. "Come on, I'll keep you safe against the dust and the dry bones."

Stark stared at him. Then he laughed and followed him, but still reluctantly. They went between the tombs and the leaning stelae, mindful of Ciaran's riders and darting like animals between the covering mounds. Then Lugh stopped and stood facing Stark and said,

"When you told me, 'Another thing has been found' what did you mean?"

"The talisman."

The wind rocked Lugh back and forth where he stood, and his eyes were wild and bright, looking into Stark's.

"How do you know that, outlander?"

"Because I brought it here myself, having taken it from the hands of Camar, who was my friend and who did not live to return it."

"I see." Lugh nodded. "I see. Then that morning at Ban Cruach's shrine…"

"I knew you were lying. Yes."

"No matter. Where is it, Stark? I want to see…"

"It's in safe hands, and long out of the city." He hoped that he was right. "Men are rallying to it, at the Festival Stones."

"That's where we're going?"

"Yes."

"Good enough," Lugh said. "Good enough. Where is the door to this rat-run?"

Stark pointed toward the arched ceremonial gate that pierced the wall at the end of the street they had left. "I must count from that. Keep an eye out for Ciaran's men."

There was no sign of them. It was possible they had turned back. It was also possible that they had come ahead of Stark and Lugh into the Quarter of the Blessed and were now hidden from sight among the tumuli. He picked up his guide mark as quickly as he could and counted the stelae as Balin had told him, going past one that was cracked in half, and one that was fallen, and one that had carved on its top a woman's face. "Here," he said, and stopped below a tomb with a great slab of rock in its side, no different from any other in appearance. He began to climb up the tall mound, flinching from the icy touch of the stone and rubble that seemed somehow colder than other stones, and Lugh came scrambling up like a dog on all fours behind him.

"Stark," he said abruptly, "what happens if you have counted wrong?"

"We go back and start over again."

"I think not."

Stark turned his head, startled. Lugh was looking off to his left. There was movement there among the tumuli. Stark saw the gleam of a bare red head in the sunlight, and then at a distance another as two riders came into view in the twisting lanes between the mounds. From those two he could extrapolate the whole company of riders. They had come ahead to the burying ground, while Stark and Lugh were struggling on foot along the mews. Now they were fanned out in a long line and working their way back toward the gate, hoping to flush out their quarry.

One of the men saw them and yelled, and Stark flung himself upward toward the stone slab.

If he *had* counted wrong…

He set his hands on the stone in the way Balin had told him, and he pushed in the way Balin had told him, and for a moment nothing at all happened and the red-haired riders were racing toward them. Then the slab tilted, with a sudden harsh groan. There was a puff of dead-cold, dead-stale air in his face, and the side of the tomb was open. He shoved Lugh into the dark aperture, glancing back as he did so at the riders. They were not quite going to make it, and both of them had their arms lifted for the throw. Behind them other riders were coming into sight, gathering to their shouts. Stark dived for the opening as the spears flew. One grazed his leg, cutting a gash across the back of the calf. The other came through the opening beside him, passed between him and Lugh and clattered harmlessly against the far wall of the tomb. "Close it up," Lugh was saying. "Close it up, we'll have the bastards in with us." They flung themselves against the stone and it went back with a clang on its pivots, shutting out light and sounds.

They sat for a moment, getting their breath and their bearings. Very quickly there came a pounding on the stone and the faint shouting of angry voices.

"Can they open it?" Lugh asked.

"Not likely. The stone is cleverly made."

The pounding increased, and now there were new sounds, of men clambering over the vaulted roof and probing with their spear-points for a likely crack. "They won't get far with that," Stark said, "but it won't take them long to commandeer some men with picks and sledgehammers. We'd best be going."

"What about light?"

Stark groped and fumbled in the darkness, remembered Balin's instructions. "Even tomb-robbers need light to ply their trade. Here—if I can find it..."

He found it, neatly set out in a corner—a lantern, a supply of slow-burning candles, and a flint-and-steel lighter with an impregnated wick that gave out a tiny flame the second time Stark snapped it. He stuck one candle into the lantern and thrust the rest into his tunic along with the lighter. Let Ciaran's men find their own. The banging and hammering on the outside was reaching a peak of angry frustration. Stark examined the gash on his leg. It was not deep but it was bleeding enough to be annoying. He stood while Lugh bound it up with a strip of dirty rag torn from some part of his garments, studying the tomb chamber in the dim glow of the lantern. It was quite large, and quite empty. The stone ledges had been used for nothing besides the storage of loot.

"All right," he said, when Lugh had finished. "That stone over there, with the ring in it. It lifts aside."

Underneath it was a pitch black and narrow shaft, with niches cut for the hands and feet. Lugh peered down it. Stark glanced at his face and grunted.

"What happened to your courage, fearless one?"

"It's not the dust and the dry bones that bother me," Lugh said. "It's thinking what will happen if I miss my footing."

"I'll go first with the lantern." Stark lowered himself over the edge, feeling for the niches, and started down, the lantern slung by a thong from his wrist. He looked up at Lugh. "*Don't* miss your footing," he said.

Lugh followed him, slowly and painfully, saying nothing.

It was a long way down. The upper part of the shaft had been constructed over many centuries, extending up through the layers of rubble as they formed. At the moment Stark had no interest in archaeology, but it was impossible not to observe the strata as he crept down through them. Then the shaft widened and the walls were of solid rock, and he knew that he was in the original, the gods knew how ancient, shaft. They had cut it deep, those long-gone builders, and Stark cursed them for every foot of it, the sweat starting on his forehead and his muscles aching, his attention shifting anxiously between his own next foothold and the soles of Lugh's boots scrabbling uncertainly so close above his head.

He stood at last in the fine vaulted chamber at the bottom and waited for Lugh to stop shaking. The lantern glow showed the outlines of bas-reliefs as sharp and clear as the day they were finished. Otherwise the chamber was empty except for a few ambiguous fragments and a pinch of dust swept into a corner as though by some untidy housewife. The air was musty and stifling, though the candle burned well enough. Stark fought down a choking claustrophobia, holding himself firmly in hand. There was a doorway leading out of the chamber, crudely cut and brutally ruining one of the reliefs. Stark went through it, into a narrow rough-walled tunnel.

He had no idea how old this tunnel might be. Even more he had no idea why men would have gone to the immense and back-breaking labor of constructing it, unless every tomb it connected with was as rich as Tut-ankh-Amen's, and even then it seemed as though it would have been easier just to work for a living. It did pass through a succession of chambers, all stripped bare except for an occasional heap of bones or potsherds. Side tunnels led off presumably to other tombs. Stark supposed that this tunneling had gone on since the first shaft grave was sunk in Kushat, and that had been time enough for a lot of expansion.

"Did you know about this?" he asked Lugh.

"There are tales about all sorts of holes and byways underneath the city. We never took much stock in them." He added, "That's only one of the mistakes we made, and not the worst, either."

Their voices sounded dim and muffled in that place, and made little furtive echoings in the side passages. They did not speak again.

After a while Stark realized that it had been some time since they passed the last tomb-chamber. He guessed that they had now left the Quarter of the Blessed and were under the King City.

The tunnel became a doorway into a vastly wider space. Stark held the lantern high, peering into the dim-lit obscurity. And now he understood the reason why the tunnel had been built.

"The catacombs," said Lugh, whispering. "The tombs of the kings of Kushat."

The words scattered softly away in the hollow darkness. Lugh held out his hand to Stark. "Light a candle."

Stark lighted him one at the stub in the lantern, and then replaced that with a fresh one. Lugh ranged ahead, looking here, looking there, his face shocked in the candle-glow.

"But they were so carefully sealed," he said. "There are three levels, and each gallery was sealed so that no one could ever break into it...."

"From above," said Stark. "Where it would be noticed. That's what they did with the talisman. Camar must have come at it from below."

"Oh," said Lugh, shaken with indignation. "Oh, but see what they've done!"

The kings of Kushat had been buried royally, each one carefully embalmed and sitting upright on a funerary throne, presumably wearing all the trappings of kingship and surrounded by the weapons and the wine cups, the offertory bowls and the precious ornaments suitable to his estate. The beautifully polished stone of the ceilings and walls had been carved in reliefs showing events in the lives of the rulers, who had sat stiffly all down the length of that very long, wide hall, each in his own space. The remains of hooks set into the roof showed where rich hangings had once served to separate these throne-rooms, and Stark could imagine carpets on the cold floor, and a great deal of color. There were many holes for sconces, and he thought that it must have been a fine sight here with the torches blazing and the long procession of priests and nobles and mourning women following slowly as a king was borne on his long shield to the place where he would hold court forever. At the back of each room was a rock-cut chamber, equally splendid in its own way, for the queen and other members of the royal family.

Of all that immeasurable splendor, the tunneling thieves of Kushat had taken every crumb. Even the metal sconces had been dug out of the walls. Nothing was left, except the thrones, which were stone and immovable, and the kings themselves, who were not worth the carrying. Stripped of their robes and their armor and their jeweled insignia of office, the naked corpses shivered on their icy thrones, and the irreverent thieves had placed some of those that were still sturdy enough in antic poses. Others were broken in bits and scattered on the floor or heaped like kindling in the throne seats.

"All this time it's been like this," Lugh was muttering. "All this time. And we never knew."

"I expect that by now Narrabhar is in much the same case," said Stark, and added, "Let's get the hell out of here."

He blew out Lugh's candle and hurried on, treading once or twice on the brittle fragments of royalty.

From the catacombs the way led straight enough, with only two side tunnels leading off to some other sources of plunder, perhaps the other catacombs Lugh had mentioned. Stark moved as fast as he dared, in a tearing rush to get out into the world again. At the same time he was calculating how long it would take Ciaran's men to break into the tomb and follow them, and how long it would take Ciaran to think of sending patrols out around the city. In any case, the sooner he and Lugh got clear of this rathole the better.

He came to the end of it almost before he realized it. He had been watching for daylight and there was none, or so very little of it that he did not notice it at once. It was a change in the air, a fresh clean smell that warned him. He blew out the candle, and then he was able to see ahead of him a ragged patch of darkness much less absolute than that surrounding them. He touched Lugh's arm, enjoining caution, and moved much more slowly and carefully to the end of the tunnel.

It opened into the bottom of a deep cleft in the rock, where the shadows were already black. Overhead he saw the sky with pale sunlight still left in it. There was no sight or sound of anything human nearby. Stark emerged from the tunnel, breathing deeply and covered suddenly with a cold sweat, as though he had just escaped some deadly peril.

"There is a path," said Lugh, pointing to a narrow thread that slanted up the side of the cleft.

They climbed it, coming out at length in a sheltered place among the rocks where the plain sloped upward from Kushat. Here for thousands of years thief and merchant had met to bargain over the furniture of kings and rich men and the golden hair-pins of their wives. Now Stark and Lugh looked out between the rocks and saw the black smoke rising from the city, and heard the voices, thin and distant down the wind. Lugh's chin quivered like a child's.

"The Festival Stones lie there," he said, and led off at an abrupt trot.

Stark turned to follow him. And high above him on his right hand, so close now that he could hear the huge whistling of the wind in its stony throat, was the Gates of Death.

CHAPTER ELEVEN

THE FESTIVAL STONES, a broken ring of cyclopean blocks, stood alone on a great space below the pass, a space so flat and smooth that Stark knew it must have been levelled artificially. And he knew that whatever the original purpose of the stones might have been, it had nothing to do with sun-worship. He recognized them, with a lifting of the hair at the back of his neck, as soon as he could see them clearly. They were the foundation courses of a tower like the one in which Camar had died. The rest of the structure, apparently shaken down in some ancient cataclysm, lay tumbled over the rock, the cut stones so worn now by time and frost and the gnawing wind that they had lost their precise shapes and might have been only a casual scattering of boulders.

The circle was full of people, and more were coming, straggling in little bands across the plain from Kushat. They were, on the whole, quiet, but it was a bitter, angry quiet. From time to time an eddy of the wind brought a taint of smoke from the city.

Lugh looked around, estimating the numbers and the ratio of women and children to men. "Not much of an army," he muttered.

"It will have to do," Stark said. He moved through the huddled groups, searching for Thanis, and he was beginning to get panicky when he saw her. She was helping some other women patch up the wounded, her face pulled into a deep frown of weariness and concentration. He called her name. She started and then ran to him and threw her arms around him. She did not say anything, but he felt the tightness of her grip and the way she trembled, and he held her until she drew a long unsteady breath and stood away from him, half smiling. She began to unbuckle the belt from around her waist, as though she could not get rid of it fast enough.

"Here, you can have this back," she said. "It's too big for me."

Stark took it and put it on, feeling a great number of eyes watching him. "Where's Balin?"

"Out with some others, rounding up refugees. Some got away that were not from our Quarter, and he thought they might be useful."

"Every man helps." He smiled briefly. "Yes, even he." Thanis was looking at Lugh in a way that should have felled him on the spot. Lugh bore it patiently, without resentment, and presently Thanis shrugged and dropped her gaze.

"I suppose you're right," she said. "We're all here together, now."

Stark said, "Yes." He put his hands on the boss of Camar's belt and turned and looked at the people who were gathered there inside the great circle of stone. He looked up at the pass high above them, with the long rays of the sun touching the icy rocks to flame so that it burned as it had when he first saw it, with the sullen fires of hell, and it seemed to him that the wind that blew down from it carried a hint of strangeness that plucked at his nerves. He remembered with a sudden and shocking vividness how the talisman had glowed between his hands, and how from somewhere far away the tiny unhuman voices had spoken.

He clenched his hands firmly around the boss and walked to the center of the ring, where a kind of altar had been made by piling together some of the fallen stones. He stood on this and called to the people, and while they came closer to hear him he watched the smoke rise up from Kushat and thought of Ciaran and the lash and the dark axe, and hardly at all of night-black hair and white skin and a beautiful woman's face.

He said aloud to the people, "Most of you know that the talisman of Ban Cruach was stolen by a thief named Camar."

They did, and said so, and many of them cursed his name. And some others said, in an ugly mood, "Who are you, outlander, to be talking about the talisman?"

Two of the men that Stark had seen in the taverns on the night before the attack climbed up on the altar beside him. "Balin vouches for him," they said. "And he has something to say that you would do well to listen to." They sat down on the top of the altar, their knives bare in their hands.

Stark went on. "I was a friend of Camar. He died on his way here, to return that which he had taken. Because I owed him a debt, I finished the journey for him."

He opened the boss, and took from it the bit of crystal wrapped in silk.

"Most of you knew, or guessed, that the so-called talisman in the shrine was only a piece of glass put there by the nobles to hide the loss." He waited until the angry growl had quieted, and then he held up his hands, with the crystal cupped between them. And he said, "Look now at this."

He laid back the covering of silk. The level sunlight struck against the crystal, and it seemed to draw the light, to feed on it, to suck it down and down into its many facets until each one glowed with a separate radiance. Stark caught his breath sharply and held himself rigid, watching the crystal brighten into a small sun between his hands. It was warm now. It dazzled his eyes.

And the voices spoke. In his ear. Over his shoulder. Close, immediate, just beyond... just beyond...

"Stark!"

It was Balin's voice. The sound of it broke through the other voices and shocked him back into the sane world. He caught a brief reeling glimpse of the people staring, their eyes stretched and their mouths gone slack with awe, and he realized that they were looking at him as much as they were at the talisman. He closed his hands over it, shutting off the radiance but not the warmth, and huddled the silk wrapping over it and hid it again in the boss, and all the time Balin was pushing through the crowd toward him. In the background where Balin had left them, was a party of refugees, and Stark recognized Rogain among them.

Balin stood at the foot of the altar, looking up. "Stark, there are riders coming from Kushat."

"Well," said Stark. "Then we had best be moving." He bent down, still dazed and acting more by instinct than by conscious thought, and gave Balin a hand up beside him. "You know Balin," he said to the people. "Hear him speak."

Balin said, "Stark and I will take the talisman through the Gates of Death, and see what power we can find there to drive the tribesmen out of Kushat. Let everyone who wishes follow us."

He sprang down from the altar, with Stark behind him. They started for the opening in the ring of stones. A tremendous cry went up, a confusion of cries, and the whole untidy crowd began to coalesce and form itself into a solid band. Someone shouted, "Ban Cruach!", like a war cry, and others took it up. Lugh appeared at Stark's elbow, yelling, "The talisman! Follow the talisman!" The people began to pour out of the circle. Stark gave Lugh the lantern and candles he had brought from the tunnel.

"Lead on ahead," he said. "The first place you come to that can be fortified and held by the number of men we have—get about it. Even the children can haul stones."

"I would like to go with him," said someone at his shoulder. It was Rogain. The day had worn hard on him. He was wounded and beaten, and his scholar's hands were stained with blood. But he stood proudly and gave Stark look for look without apology or comment. Stark nodded, and he went to join Lugh, walking stiffly, with his head up.

"There's a good man," Stark said. "A pity he wasn't a better general." He began to shout to the people. "Let the women and the young ones go first. The men stay behind—we may have to fight. Balin, keep them moving there. Hurry on now. Hurry on!"

In the reddening light of late afternoon the men and women and children streamed upward toward the pass, where the fires burned brighter as the sun sank. Stark and Balin were the last to leave the circle. They looked back toward Kushat and Stark could see the riders, a company of fifty or more picking its way over the frost-wracked and gullied surface of the plain. In the forefront was a figure in dark mail.

"Can that be Ciaran leading them?" asked Balin, astonished.

"Why not?" asked Stark.

"But she has barely taken the city. Any other chieftain…"

"…would be baying after loot and women. She has no use for either. All that concerns her is her ambition."

They followed on up the naked slope, and Stark thought that it was a measure of Ciaran's power that she could find fifty men willing to leave the plundering of Kushat. Probably they were clan chiefs whose men were bound to give them their share in any case. Or perhaps the lure of the talisman was great enough to draw them.

Balin said hesitantly, "Stark… when you stood there with the talisman in your hands, just before I called your name…"

"Yes?"

"Your face was strange. It was like the face of a madman—or a god."

"Something spoke to me," Stark said.

Balin looked at him, startled, and Stark shook his head. "Something. Voices. But I seemed to know that they were there, beyond the pass."

"Ah," said Balin, and his eyes were bright. "Then we may hope to find help there as Ban Cruach did."

"The gods know," Stark said. "For an instant, just before you spoke, I thought I understood…"

He broke off, shivering involuntarily, "Time enough for that when we're through the pass." He glanced back at the riders. "They're gaining."

"And look there," said Balin. "Beyond the Festival Stones."

Tribesmen had appeared on the plain as though out of nowhere. Stark nodded. "I was expecting them. They came after us through the tunnel." They had seen the people going up into the pass, and they began to run. They were closer, but the mounted men were faster. Stark judged that both groups would reach the pass at about the same time, and that the time would be much sooner than he wanted it.

"What shall we do?" Balin asked.

"Be ready for a rear-guard action, but keep ahead of them if we can." They ran up the slope, urging the men to go faster, driving them on. The lower parts of the plain were lost now where the dusk flowed over them. In the high places there was still light, and it shone into the pass so that the people seemed to move in a bath of blood. Stark thought how small they looked under those vast sheer cliffs, and how quickly they vanished into the narrow jaws of the Gates of Death. He left Balin and pushed on, past the line of march, in a fever to see the place before the daylight left it altogether.

It was an evil place, a crack in the mountain wall with towering sides that leaned together overhead, a thousand feet or more, and the wind came viciously through it. Stark hated it. He hated it as an aborigine, sensing the unknown and unnatural and cringing from it. And he hated it as a rational man, because it was a death-trap.

Balin had said that this was a place of grinding rockfalls, and that at least was no myth. The floor of the pass was heaped with detritus, and Stark, who knew his mountains well, having grown up where all the world was mountain, could look up at the looming sides and see where the rock was rotten and treacherous, ready to crash down at the slightest disturbance. He caught up to Lugh and Rogain and cautioned them to be careful. They sent his word back along the line and went on.

Stark stayed where he was, standing aside on a pile of boulders and looking up at the cliffs.

The people hurried by him, burdened women, older children carrying younger ones who were too tired now to walk, the men with some of the wild zeal sweated out of them by the climb. Finally Balin came and saw him and stopped.

"They're close behind us, Stark. Hadn't we better prepare to fight?"

"I think," said Stark, looking upward, "there's a better way. Get me a spear." Balin took one from one of the men. Stark laid it by. He stripped off Camar's belt and give it to Balin, along with every other thing that he could spare, and then rigged a thong to hold the spear across his back. While he did this he told Balin what he had in mind.

Balin squinted up at the cliffs and shuddered. "I won't even offer to help you."

"Don't," said Stark feelingly. "Just keep them moving on. I want everyone clear, around the bend there." He pointed ahead to where the pass turned around a jutting shoulder. "Do we have any slingers?"

"A few, I think. They came with Rogain and some others."

"Station them there, behind the shoulder. Keep them well out of sight."

Balin nodded, muttering something about the gods lending Stark strength. He ran on.

Stark went across the floor of the pass and began to climb up the cliff.

The aborigines had taught him how to climb, and he had spent the years of his boyhood clinging to rocks with his fingers and toes and the pores of his naked skin, slithering up and down on his belly like the lizards he hunted. It was a skill that he had never lost, any more than he had ever forgotten now to breathe, because for so long the two functions had been interdependent. He found now that the going was easier than he thought. The rock was rougher than it had looked from below, and its inward slope was greater. He had picked his place carefully, where the rock was sound and the holds did not crumble under this hands and feet. He swarmed up fairly quickly, toward a narrow ledge that angled across the cliff face. The daylight was fading much faster than he could climb, receding upward ahead of him as the sun went lower, but he thought that he would have all he needed. The thing that he was shortest on was time.

He climbed almost recklessly, leaning into the rock, merging with it, moving his four limbs as he had learned to do in imitation of the great rock-lizard, so that he looked like one himself, going claw-over-paw up the cliff and lacking only the balancing tail. He reached the ledge and hauled himself onto it, lying still to get his breath. In the pass below him he heard the clink of arms and harness, and he looked down. The shadows were thickening there, but enough light still reflected from the sky and the high cliffs to show him the riders. The narrowness of the pass had strung them out in a long line and the treacherous footing had slowed them down. The unmounted tribesmen presumably were somewhere behind them. At the head of the line was Ciaran in her black mail. Her voice rose up to him, a thin thread of sound much broken by the wind. He could not understand the words, but it was obvious that she was impatient and urging the others to move faster. Stark smiled. She must feel that the talisman was already in her hands.

He rose and went along the ledge. Ciaran drew level with him, passed him by. Behind her came the Mekhish chiefs, grumbling and cursing at the evil nature of the place and at the growing dark. Some of them had torches and paused to light them, fighting the wind. Stark was not in any hurry now. He came to where the ledge was blocked by stones fallen from above, and he stopped and undid the thong that held the spear across his back. The wind tore at him, beating him back against the cliff. He set his head against it. He thrust the long stout blade of the spear in among the rocks, and set his feet, and pried.

Beyond the point where he stood the cliff face had rotted inward, where frost and the summer melt had eaten away the softer veins. The detritus had fallen, and piled, and slipped, and piled again, and now there were countless tons of rock poised and ready to slide. All that was needed was a touch.

Stark heaved up on the butt of the spear. The dislodged boulders went bounding down with a heavy ominous clashing, like a series of hammer-strokes.

Stark turned and ran.

CHAPTER TWELVE

THERE WAS AN outcry of startled voices, and after that a complete cessation of sound from below. Stark could picture them sitting stiffly in their saddles, stretching eye and ear in the darkness, listening. The hammer-strokes died away in a booming rattle as the boulders hit the floor of the pass and wore out their momentum. For a brief space it seemed that there was silence, except for the wind. Then there began to be other sounds, of stones rolling and clacking together, and knocking, and shifting. The sounds overlapped each other, growing louder, and underneath them was a deep groaning grinding bass. Stark thought that he had heard voices shouting again, very loud this time. The ledge began to quake under him. He threw himself flat, hugging the inner surface. The grinding noise exploded into a great roar. Behind him a section of the cliff face disappeared downward into darkness and a mighty cloud of dust.

Stark clung to the ledge, his arms over his head, his face pressed grinning against the rock. He howled triumphant obscenities that neither he nor anyone else could hear. And it was better than he had hoped. His deafened ears picked up, as though they were echoes, the crashings of three lesser rockfalls touched off by the first one. Very quickly after the last one there came a sort of stunned quiet, stitched through with a trickling of pebbles and a faint screaming.

Stark got to his hands and knees and looked down. The dust hung in the air like smoke, but it was heavy and the wind was tearing it. Below it was a mass of rock completely blocking the pass. And it had fallen like a portcullis between Ciaran and her men, except for a handful that Balin's slingers should take care of.

Stark laughed and began leisurely to climb down the cliff.

He did part of the climb in complete darkness, a task that left him no margin of attention for what was going on below. He could hear cries of pain and anger, and what he thought was Balin's voice raised in some rather violent demands, or orders. There were other sounds, all confused, and all of them at the moment of no interest to him. The nearer moon swung overhead and after that it was easier, though not nearly as easy as it had been going up. By the time the light of a high-held torch reached to him, and hands caught him to ease him down, he was glad of the help.

Balin's face appeared in the torchlight, wild with excitement "We have her. We have her! And the pass is closed."

"For a while," Stark said. "For a while."

He flexed his legs, bending to rub the aching stiffness out of them. It dawned on him that he was tired enough to drop right where he stood. "Has anybody got wine? I could do with a drink." Somebody handed him a leather bottle and he drank thirstily. Balin was still talking, telling how Ciaran and the seven or eight men who had kept up with her had tried to break back at the first sound of falling rock, and how three of the chieftains had been caught under the slide. Before the rest could gather their stunned wits together Balin's slingers had dropped them out of their saddles. Ciaran had tried to charge them with her axe and they had dropped her, too, and Balin had thought that she was dead. Then a great many of the people of Kushat had rushed back from around the bend. They had killed the chieftains on the ground, those who had not been slain outright by the stones, and they had wanted to kill Ciaran too when they found that she was still breathing.

"I had to mount guard over her myself," Balin said. "Then I thought they were going to kill *me*. I had the devil of a time convincing them."

"We may need her," said Stark. "Her men will start pulling away those rocks with the first light. I think there are three more falls, though not such big ones, between here and the mouth of the pass, and it will all take them time, but sooner or later they'll clear the way. When they do we must have the means to destroy them—or else we must buy our way free."

A considerable crowd had gathered. They had been cheering Stark, but now there was some growling and muttering, and

Stark said, "Don't be so impatient. You can always kill her later on, if we find we don't need her."

Thanis pushed her way to him. "Stark, why don't we trade her to them in exchange for Kushat? They'd give up the city to get her back."

Apparently there were many who agree with her. Stark shook his head. "Of course they would. And you'd have Kushat for just as long as Ciaran would need to rally her men and retake it. And then you would wish that you had killed her."

Thanis considered that, walking beside him and Balin as they started through the crowd. "We could say that we would give her back, and then as soon as they left the city we could kill her…"

Stark looked at her. "That's treachery. And it's also bad business. The tribesmen would stamp your city flat and use the stones for butcher's blocks." He found himself suddenly shouting at them all. "Can't you understand? You couldn't hold the city with every man and every weapon you had, and you can't hold it now, with nothing. You lost Kushat, and you'll never get it back unless the talisman gives you the power." They were silent, startled by his anger and impatience. "If it does not, we may buy our own lives with Ciaran, but don't hope for more."

He tramped on ahead and they let him go. Even Thanis stood away from him. He passed the bodies of the chieftains and went around the shoulder where the pass turned. On the other side was a bay or pocket in the cliff, cut out by the waters that had poured through here over the millennia. It offered a partial shelter from the wind, and here the women and children were huddled in a makeshift camp, sharing out cold rations and trying to cover themselves against the night. There was nothing with which to make fires, and only two or three torches burned. Stark saw the dim glow of the candle lamp and made for it. Lugh and Rogain were there, and between them, sitting erect with her back against the cliff wall, was Ciaran.

She had been stripped of her armor, down to the dark close-fitting leather she wore beneath it, and someone had wrapped a tattered cloak around her. Her hands and feet were bound. Her forehead was cut, marred with a purpling bruise. There were streaks of dried blood all down her cheek and her white neck. And still she sat like a king. Stark looked down at her. Her eyes met his without wavering, without pleading or softness or a hint of tears. She did not speak.

He passed on by her. Lugh gave him a robe. He wrapped it around him and lay down on the cold stone and was instantly asleep. When he woke again, stiff and chilled in the predawn dark, Ciaran seemed not to have moved at all, and he wondered whether she had slept, and what her dreams were like. He did not ask her.

"Keep her close behind us," he said to Lugh and Rogain. "I want her guarded well."

They ate their meager breakfast and started on through the Gates of Death. Stark thought that he had never seen a more shivering, miserable army on its way to a blind destiny. He walked at the head of it, with Balin beside him. Lugh and Rogain came with Ciaran just behind. After that the people were strung out as they pleased, since for the present there was no more danger from the rear.

For Stark there began an ordeal.

The sun came up, but now they were going deeper into the pass, and the walls stretched higher, and the light was dim and strange at the bottom of that cleft. The wind boomed and howled. It spoke with many tongues in the unhuman voices that had spoken to him as he held the talisman. Balin had given Camar's belt to him, saying he deserved the honor. Stark thought it was more that Balin had an uneasy passion to be rid of the thing. Now again it was a burden to him, and he hated it. In this place he was more conscious than ever of the strange powers that lived in that bit of crystal, and the fact that the answer to them lay somewhere up ahead, he could not tell how close, and that he was being forced inevitably into seeing what they were, whether he wanted to or not.

He did not want to.

He tried to reason with himself. He tried to force his attention to stay fixed on realities, the ever-present and highly important realities of the pass, which was no less dangerous here than it had been where he had brought down the slide. In spite of himself, his nostrils twitched to the smell of evil, ancient and dusty and old but still living, a subtle unclean taint on the wind that only a beast, or one as close to it as he, can sense and know. Every nerve was a point of pain, raw with apprehension. The thin veneer of civilization began to slough away from him no matter how hard he grasped at it, so that the farther he went the more his very body changed, drawing in upon itself and flattening forward, bristling and starting and pausing to test the wind, more like a four-footed thing than a man walking upright.

The worst of it was that he knew Ciaran watched him, and understood. All that morning she walked with bound hands between her guards, and never once spoke. But he felt that her eyes never left him.

When they stopped to rest and eat a little more of their scanty food he went to where she sat, on a heap of boulders off to one side, away from the others. She had not been given anything to eat or drink, and she had not asked for anything. Stark broke off half of his dry cold hunk of bread and handed it to her. She took it and began to eat, rigidly controlling what must have been her very great hunger. Stark sat down on the rocks facing her and nodded to Lugh and Rogain, who were glad enough to leave their charge. He held out a bottle with some dregs of wine left in it, and they shared that too.

He said, "You're thinking how you may kill me."

"Yes." The wind tumbled her hair across her face and she shook it aside impatiently. "You've been a curse to me, Stark."

"I'm not a forgiving man." He nodded at the people of Kushat. "Neither are they."

"They had no choice," she said. "You did. I made you an offer once." She looked at him with honest curiosity. "You have no more loyalty to these people than I have. Why did you refuse?"

"Two reasons. I had made a promise..."

"To a dead man."

"To a friend."

"That is only one reason. Go on."

"You and I," said Stark, "are much alike. I think you said that yourself. Much too much alike, for one to lead and the other to follow. Besides, I had no desire to take Kushat." He handed her the wine again. "I suppose you might say I lack ambition, but you have too much. You were lord of Mekh. You should have been content."

"Content!" she said. "Are you content? Have you ever been content?"

He considered that. "Not often. And not for long. But the spurs are not so deep in me."

"The wind and the fire," Ciaran said. "One wastes its strength in wandering, the other devours. Well, we shall see who was wiser when the battle is over. But don't talk to me of contentment."

Her face had a white blaze to it, a strength and an iron pride. He studied her, sitting tall and straight on the cold rock, with her long legs and her splendid shoulders, and the fine hands that seemed forlorn without the axe to fondle.

"I would like to know," he said, "what made you as you are?"

She said impatiently, "A man is free to be what he will without questions, but a woman is supposed to be a woman and nothing more. One gets tired of explaining." She leaned back against the boulders, and there was a certain triumph in her eyes. "I did not ask for my sex. I will not be bound by it. I did not ask to be a bastard, and I will not be bound by that, either. So much I have accomplished, if I die today."

She was silent for a time, and he thought that she was through talking. Then she said softly, "If I live, there will be more to do. Kushat was only a stepping-stone."

Her eyes looked somewhere else, far off, and what they saw was bitter.

"A stepping-stone?" asked Stark. "To where?"

"To Narrissan." Her voice was very low. "That is a walled city, Stark, much like Kushat, but farther south, and far more rich and powerful. My grandfather was king in Narrissan. By the time I could walk, I was a servant in his house. I don't think he ever knew it. He came upon me and my mother once in the passageway, and he looked at me as one might look into a mirror. 'So that's the brat,' he said. My mother spoke, complaining, I believe, though I hardly heard her, and he cut her off sharply, saying, 'Be thankful it's a girl-child. Otherwise I would be afraid to let it grow. It's too much in my image.'"

She smiled. "After that he forgot about me. But when I was old enough I left my scrubbing of floors to practice arms with the young boys. I was beaten for it every day, but every day I went. My father was a good man of his hands, and as he said, I was made in his image. I learned. When I had learned enough I started out to make my own fortune. With these two hands, Stark," she said, holding them up. "With what I am myself, and what I can do, not what I can trick and wheedle and whore out of others by the ancient usages of the bed-chamber."

Stark nodded. "And that is why you wanted the talisman so badly—because it might help you to take your father's city."

"To take Narrissan. My father is dead these three years and I was his only issue. I hope the gods allow him to be amused..." She shook her head, looking at Stark. "If you had fought with me instead of against me...Well, that is past. But who knows what lies ahead?"

She gave him a keen glance. "You have a hint, I think. And it frightens you."

"We'll soon know," Stark said, and rose, going back to the head of the straggling column. He did not bother to tell Ciaran that if ever they did face each other again it would still be as man to man and equal to equal, with no regard for her sex. He knew that she knew that. And he knew that it would be more than a little foolish to say so, since in any case the choice was not his.

The line of march formed up and moved on again.

The pass dropped lower and the uncanny twilight deepened to a kind of sickly night. There was nothing but rock and ice. Yet the sense of danger increased, so that Stark moved against it as a man might move against water. And not he alone was oppressed. Balin, Lugh, Rogain, Thanis, all of the people now moved grudgingly and in silence. Even Ciaran's face began to show apprehension under the stoic mask.

Then suddenly the rock walls dropped away. The pallid darkness lifted to a clear daylight. They were through the Gates of Death.

Beyond them was a stony slope widening out and down into a great valley locked between the mountains. They filed out of the pass and stood there on the slope. The cessation of the wind that had hammered and howled at them in the narrow cleft made it seem that the valley was terribly quiet.

They stood a long time. Thanis came up between Stark and Balin, her cloak wrapped tight around her, her dark eyes wide and stricken.

"What does that mean?" she asked finally.

Stark answered, "I don't know."

CHAPTER THIRTEEN

THERE WERE THREE towers. Two were roofless, long abandoned. All around these two were ruins, sheathed in ice, and they were the strangest ruins that Stark had ever seen, on a world that was rich in ruins and in strangeness.

The eye could follow even yet the spiderweb pattern of streets, pick out what might have been the market places and the temple squares. All along these streets the hollow skeletons of buildings stood like the shells of fantastic sea-things with their soft flesh all eaten away. The ice made the color blurred and luminous, added a lustre to soaring curves and empty arches where they caught the sun.

"Did they build the place all of swords and spear-points?" said Balin, staring.

"Something like it," Stark said. In that land where stone was the obvious material for building, nothing was made of stone but the great towers. The light and graceful bones of the city were all of metal, colored in some fashion so that the black valley shone with an icy mockery of spring greens and yellows and soft blues, with here and there a spurt of crimson or coral pink. The taller structures had crumpled down. The smaller ones leaned. Nothing had lived there for a very long time.

The third tower was still whole and sound.

Stark looked at it, feeling the cringing, snarling, hateful fear rise in him, and knew that his was how Camar's tower and all the others beyond the pass had looked in the days of their strength. It was alien. It was arrogant. It was massive and very high, the stonework tapering in close at the top, and on its highest point was a glimmer of something unfamiliar, like a captive star. Only the star did not shed light. It sent out instead a cloudy shimmering, visible more as a distortion in the air than as a definite emanation. The mountain peaks behind it seemed to float.

Underneath that cloudy shimmer, filling almost a third of the valley, was a portion of the city that was not in ruins, although the ruined areas joined it. Obviously all had once been part of the same complex, and obviously the dead parts of the city had once been covered by the same kind of force-field, from the abandoned towers. The line of demarcation was quite clear. The ice and the broken buildings ended at the edge of the field. Beyond there were streets as bare as summer. Arches soared up straight and free. The many-colored walls stood squarely. Nowhere was there any sign of frost, or decay.

Or of life. In all those long avenues, nothing moved. And in all that valley there was no living sound except what the people of Kushat had brought with them.

Stark heard Ciaran laugh, and turned to face her. She was looking past him at the bright-colored desolation.

"It seems," she said, "that myths die as well as men."

Stark moved his head as an animal does when it listens to something far off. "There is life there yet."

He put his hands on the belt and felt the talisman as a point of fire under them.

"There must be life," said Balin. "Look at the tower. I don't know what its purpose is, but it still functions. There must be someone—something there to tend it."

The others caught that up. They were eager, desperate to believe. Balin went on, gesturing at the tower.

"That is power, certainly. Perhaps the very kind of power Ban Cruach brought away with him, though not in that form. What do you think it is, Stark? A defense?"

Stark said slowly, "I think it's a defense against the ice and cold. See how warm the city looks."

"And how quiet," Lugh muttered. "Why should we lie to ourselves? The place is dead. As dead as Ban Cruach."

Only Stark heard him. The people had begun to crowd and clamor. They shouted for the talisman, and some of them moved on down the slope, too impatient to wait for their leaders. This was their last hope. On it rested everything they had left behind, city, home, the remnants of their families. With the power they might find here they could regain them all. Without it, even though they might buy their lives with Ciaran and go free, they would be only stateless wanderers on the face of Mars, utterly destitute.

"It would be wiser for them to wait here," Stark said. Balin only shook his head, and Stark did not press the point. Perhaps they knew best what they wanted.

He opened the box and took out the talisman, wrapped in silk. He handed it to Balin.

"It belongs to Kushat," he said. "Not to me."

Balin looked at him with wry and bitter mirth. "True. And I thank you for the honor. But I am not Ban Cruach. If I drop the thing, you may have to pick it up."

He held it stiffly and did not remove the wrappings.

They walked on together, and the people followed them closely. Stark was very conscious of external things, the soft breathing and trampling of the group and the way their voices fell silent, the slippery frost-buckled pavement that replaced the rock under his feet, the lengthening shadow of the western wall of mountains. He was extremely conscious of Ciaran walking behind him, and of Thanis at his side. But there was something else, something he could not put a name to, that he sensed more powerfully than any of these things. He still walked against fear as a man walks against water, just as he had in the pass, in spite of the fact that now he was in the open sunlight and clear air.

The colors and fantastic shapes of the ice-sheathed ruins rose around him, marked off by transverse streets that glittered like ribbons of glass.

"These folk were never part of our past," said Balin. His voice was small and low, so as not to wake any echoes. He held the talisman tight in his closed hands. "We never built like this, even when the world was young and rich."

No, thought Stark. No race on Mars ever built like this. I have seen the old, old cities. Jekkara and Valkis of the Sea-Kings, Barrakesh, and sand-drowned ruins by the Wells of Tamboina. I have even seen Sinharat the Ever-Living. But the people who built them were human. Even the Ramas were human, and so the wickedness that clung around Sinharat was human too, and understandable. But no human ever conceived and shaped these curving walls and enormously elongated arches. No human hands ever opened these strange narrow doors. No human mind could endure for long surrounded by this geometry.

I suppose perhaps they might, he added to himself—but I know that they did not. I have heard the voices.

He said aloud, "They once held all the country beyond the Gates of Death. Even the place where Kushat stands. The Festival Stones were once a tower like that one. You can see the ruins of others all through the Norlands."

"But there are no traces left of any cities like this one."

"No. The metal would have been carried off and beaten into useful things, every scrap of it, ages gone."

Balin grunted. The pace of the whole column had imperceptibly slowed and the people were bunched together closely now, very quiet, mothers hanging tight to their children, husbands close to their wives. The avenue they had been following led straight in under the edge of the shimmering cloud. The line of demarcation was close ahead now. No more than a hundred feet.

Balin gave Stark a queer desperate look. He lifted the talisman as though he might be going to hand it to him, or throw it away. Then he set his jaw tight and said something that Stark could not hear, and he took the silk wrappings away so that the crystal lay bare in his hands.

The people sighed. Thanis gave Balin a look of fierce pride. "Lead us," she said. He held out the talisman in his cupped palms and walked ahead. Stark ceased to watch Balin. Instead he looked up and on either side, going close behind him, his body tensed like a spring, trying to see through walls and hear through silence and feel through the intangible.

Balin paused under the edge of the cloud and nothing happened, except that after a step or two he halted and said with almost childish surprise, "It's warm."

Stark nodded. He was still looking warily around, seeing nothing. The city lay in a kind of summer dream, full of sweet color and soft shadow and the drowsy stillness of sleep. Overhead the sky had vanished in a quivering mirage.

And it was warm. Too warm, after the bitter cold. It gave a feeling of ease and pleasant languor. The people began to loosen their cloaks. Then, as they went on, they laid aside their burdens, piling them neatly together with the unwanted garments, mindful that they would have to be picked up again when they returned.

The avenue was wide. On either side the buildings marched, or on occasion fell back to form an odd-shaped square. Here where they were undamaged and free of ice the strangeness of their shaping was more vividly apparent. They gave an illusion of tallness though actually they were not, being limited by the height of the tower. Some of the structures seemed to have no useful purpose at all. They shot up in twisted spires, or branched in weird spiky arms like giant cacti done in pink and gold, or looped in helical formations, sometimes erect, sometimes lying on their sides. Ornaments, Stark thought, or monuments, perhaps with some religious significance. And then it struck him that they were more like the markers in some monstrous game. It was an unpleasant thought. He did not know why he had it. Then he realized that the odd forms were repeated, distributed throughout the checkerboard streets of the city according to an unknown but definite plan.

Passing close by one of the cactus-shapes, he saw that the metal spikes were long and very sharp, and that there were traces on them of some dark stain.

Thanis' urgent voice said, "Balin? Balin…"

The talisman had been warming and glowing between his hands. Now it shone softly in the growing dusk, under that unnatural sky. And Balin had stopped. His face was ashen. He was like a man in shock. He made a moaning sound and then by sheer convulsive reflex he flung the talisman away from him, exactly as Stark had long ago in the tower. The crystal rolled a little way and lay gleaming.

The people stood still, appalled. Thanis put her hand on Balin's shoulder and looked frightenedly at Stark. Ciaran watched them from between her guards, attentive as a hawk.

Stark said to Balin, "You heard the voices?"

"Yes." Balin caught his breath and straightened up, but his face was still bloodless. "Clearly, in here." He touched his head. "I heard them louder and louder and all of a sudden I understood. I *understood* them, Stark." He looked around at the enclosing buildings, afraid with no ordinary fear. "This is an evil place." He shouted at the people. "Go back! Get out. Get out!"

He started to run. Stark caught him. The people hung on the edge of panic. He said to them, "Wait. Stay together." They milled uncertainly. Those in the back were too far away to see or know what was happening. They only knew that something was wrong. A woman's voice cried out, shrill with fear. In desperation Stark spoke to Lugh and Rogain. "Keep them together! If we start running we're lost." They left Ciaran and went rapidly down the line, shouting in brisk, authoritative voices although both of them were white around the lips. Stark looked at Ciaran. "Here is your chance. Take it, if you will."

She shook her head and smiled, holding up her bound hands. Her eyes looked past him at the city.

Stark shook Balin and said fiercely, "Will you stand now?"

"I'll stand," he whispered. "But we must go, Stark. We must get out."

"All right. But wait."

Stark went to where the talisman lay. He knew now what it was, and that took some of the terror out of it. Even so his hands shook as he picked it up. If it had not been for all the lives that might depend on it, he would have let it stay where it was till doomsday.

The thing glowed and glimmered in his hands. He looked at it, and the voices burst inside his skull.

Not true voices. Probably these creatures had physical voices, but the crystal was not designed to carry them. It transmitted the thought-words that had to come before the spoken ones. At first they were a weird jumble, amplification of the tiny chitterings he had heard from so far away. Their un-humanness then had shocked him into breaking contact. Now it was overwhelming. Because he knew that his own selfish survival depended on it as well as everybody else's, he fought it out this time. He hung on until the voices slipped suddenly over the edge of comprehension.

He understood them. Partly. No human would ever understand all of what these minds were thinking and talking about. But he understood enough. The crystal was unselective. It brought him all the flying fragments of speech within its range. Stark's mind became a sort of camera obscura looking on nightmare, where narrow doorways opened into bright-lit chambers, briefly flashing, each one a shred of lost sanity, each one shining with the phosphorescence of decay. And each one gleeful. That was the worst of it. The laughter. They were happy, these creatures. Terribly happy.

Most of them. Not all. Some of them were disturbed. Some of them had become aware.

Alarm broke the contact for him this time, at least enough that he could push the voices back. He clawed desperately for a grasp at the real world again, not easy since the real world that surrounded him was their world and so not immediately recognizable. There was a pale blur close to him that seemed familiar. It resolved itself gradually into Thanis' face.

"It's too late to go," he said. "they know we're here."

He turned to speak to Balin and the others. At the back of the line a woman screamed abruptly. Men's voices followed, crying out harshly. Lugh appeared, not quite running. "Stark," he said, and pointed. "Stark..."

Stark moved aside, where he could see down the long wide avenue past the line of march.

Back beyond the pink-and-gold structure with the blood-stained spikes, five figures had appeared in the street. Three of them held longish tubes with globed ends that might be weapons. They were very tall, these figures, towering over the people of Kushat, towering even over Stark, but they were excessively slender and they moved with swaying motion like reeds before the wind. They were dressed in an assortment of bright-colored garments and queer tall caps that exaggerated their elongated narrow skulls. Their skin was a pale golden color, stretched tight over a structure of facial bones that seemed to be all brow and jaw with little in between but two great round eyes like dark moons.

They did not speak. They only stood and held the weapons and stared at the people of Kushat.

Thanis caught her breath in a little cry. Stark looked around.

Six thin tall creatures fluttering in rainbow silks moved out to stand across the way. Four of them held tubes.

One of them spoke. His voice was a kind of high-pitched fluting, quite musical, like the call of some strange bird. The talisman brought the meaning of the sounds clearly to Stark.

"Our weapons are invincible. We can destroy you all. Ban Cruach protects us! His promise and his talisman!"

There was a moment's pause, a moment that seemed a hundred years long to Stark as he stared in astonishment.

Then he shouted, "Ban Cruach!"

He walked toward them, holding out the talisman.

CHAPTER FOURTEEN

THE NAME CRASHED in metallic echoes from the surrounding walls. The creatures started back, swaying this way and that, and their huge eyes fixed on the talisman. Now that he was closer, Stark could see the vestigial noses and the small mouths, reptilian in their neatness of tight lips and little even teeth.

"Ban Cruach," he said again.

They swayed and fluted among themselves. The talisman glowed between Stark's hands. Their thought-voices clamored in his head.

"He has the Word of Power!"

"The talisman! He holds the talisman…"

"What are these creatures? What do they want here?"

"They have his form. Perhaps they're his people."

The same thought was suddenly arrived at and projected by several of them together, and it was full of fear.

"They've come to take him away from us!"

"No!" said Stark. He made gestures of negation, having no idea whether they would understand. They stopped fluting and stared at him. He came closer, close enough to be aware of their bodies as living things, breathing, stirring, smelling oddly of a dry dusty perfume like the odor of fallen leaves. They horrified him, not because of their physical difference but because he had eavesdropped on their unguarded conversations and knew at least a fraction of the things these bodies were capable of doing. The creature who had first mentioned Ban Cruach was ornamented with streamers of blue and green attached to his arms and legs and around his body with no possible function other than ornamentation. His conical cap was pink. Stark set his teeth on his rising gorge and approached him. He indicated that he should touch the talisman.

He did, with four long golden fingers and a thumb like a gamecock's spur, tipped with an artificial talon of razor-sharp steel.

"Do you understand me now?" Stark asked aloud.

The dark moon eyes regarded him, alert and frighteningly clever but without comprehension.

"What is it trying to do?" said one of the aliens. This one wore a green cap, a long strip of coral down the front, and a set of amethyst-blue streamers that went down the back then on down both legs, where they were fastened to the ankles by jeweled bands. Start realized all of a sudden that this was a female. There was remarkably little difference. She swayed her thin gold body with a strange angular grace, her arms moving like a dancer's, expressing fear.

"Kill him," said a third one, dressed in russet and brown. "Drive your spur in, Hrillin. Take away their power…"

Stark stepped back abruptly, with the talisman, and half drew his sword. The one called Hrillin looked at him with a sudden blaze of understanding.

"Now I see! When we speak, you hear us, through the talisman." His long arms were motioning his fellows to silence, warning them. "If this is so, raise your hand three times."

Stark obeyed.

"Ah," said Hrillin. He stared at Stark, and stared, and then he laughed. "And is *this* the true nature of the talisman?"

Complete amazement, echoed by the others. More than amazement. Consternation. And the female in coral and amethyst-blue fluted on a shrill note of panic.

"But if that is true…"

"We shall see," said Hrillin, smoothly shutting her off. "It is certain he understands what we say."

"His talisman speaks for us," said another, this one enveloped in a great swirl of flame-colored silk that hid him completely from neck to heels. "Perhaps our talisman will speak for him."

Well, and of course, though Stark. One tuned to their wave-output, one to ours, because the two systems are not compatible. I should have realized that. Otherwise I would have picked up all the human chatter around me as well.

Hrillin was watching him. He raised his hand again, three times.

Hrillin beckoned. "Come then."

Stark beckoned in his turn, to Balin and the others.

"No," said Hrillin. "Only you. Let the others rest."

Stark shook his head. He smiled mockingly and made certain motions, remembering one or two of the things he had learned from the talisman during the time that he listened to the voices of the city.

Hrillin and some of the others laughed. It was a sound as musical as falling water, but Stark did not find it at all pleasant. They turned and moved up the broad street with their swaying, capering steps. Hrillin called to his fellows down the street to let the others come.

"Remember," he said to Stark. "We can destroy you all, in one second, if we wish."

Stark raised his hand, saying yes. But to Balin he said, "Maybe." He explained what Hrillin had said. "It's possible. Pass the word down to stay together. No panic, and no provocations. But there's something wrong here. They're frightened."

The thin gold woman tossed her arms like the branches of a wind-torn tree, pantomiming destruction.

They moved in a long line down the avenue. Stark repeated what had been said, so that Balin and the others would know.

"Ban Cruach protects *them*?" said Balin. "*They* have a talisman?" He seemed unable to believe this. So did Thanis, and those others like Lugh who were close enough to hear. Only Ciaran said,

"Ban Cruach appears to have been a generous man. Let us hope that he keeps his promises—all of them."

Stark warned them to silence when the aliens should hold their talisman.

It was growing dark. In the shadowy cross-streets and the squares along the way, more and more of the thin tall figures gathered, circling, following, watching. All at once, all over the city, lights sprang on.

Thanis gasped, and then whispered, "How can anything that hateful be so beautiful?"

The streets were filled now with a soft radiance of color. The tall thin shapes in their fluttering silks moved through pools of gold and green, blue and violet, orange and blood-red. All the windows of the buildings showed a clear silver-white against the colors. Rank after rank they passed by, giving a million narrow glimpses into public halls with many slender pillars, and the odd-shaped rooms of houses, all deserted.

Stark listened to the fluting calls of the creatures who followed.

"There are not many of them," he said quietly. "I think not as many as we. They seem to have no real leader. Hrillin happened to be the first to see us, so that apparently entitles him to lead for this..." He hesitated. "'Game' is the only word." The wild disorder of their talk was appalling. "Their whole existence here seems to be one great anarchic game. They murder for fun. Not simple murders. They do all kinds of things for fun, and physical torture is one of the least of them. They've had thousands of years to invent perversions."

"I heard them," Balin said. "Only briefly, but enough."

Lugh said, "But if they have no leader, and they are so few, how do they force the victims..."

"They don't have to," Stark said. "The victims get more fun out of it than anybody. It seems to be their moment of supreme fulfillment."

Thanis said furiously, "Ban Cruach would never have promised his help to these monsters."

"That was a long time ago," Stark said. "I doubt that they were monsters then." He looked around at the city, with the massive bulk of the tower rising over it. "They live in prison. They die in prison. They've been dying for a long time. It's small wonder they've gone mad with it."

"I do not pity them," Balin said with a shiver of repulsion.

"Nor I," said Stark. "Any more than they would pity me while they were watching me die."

They came into an enormous circle. In the center of the circle was a pavilion, the roof curved and peaked, upheld on many columns, the whole thing done in shades of purple. Hrillin beckoned Stark and the others on, and from all sides now the aliens began to gather closer. Broad stripes of gold like sunrays laid into the pavement led to the heart of the pavilion, where there was a low dais holding a glitter of crystal.

Embedded in the crystal was the body of a man, a human man, and quite old, dressed in antique armor. Stark recognized him. He had seen that face before, carved in stone and turned forever toward the Gates of Death. He was looking at Ban Cruach.

A wave of awe swept over the people of Kushat. They pushed and crowded, delicately, as though they were in a temple, but determinedly, surrounding the crystal coffin, and all through what followed there was a constant motion as those in front gave way to others moving up from behind to see.

From some secret niche beside the coffin Hrillin took the mate to Ban Cruach's talisman and held it up, and stared while it warmed and glowed between his hands.

"Now," said Stark, "do you understand me, Hrillin?"

The alien flinched, as though he found the impact of human speech as distasteful as Stark had found theirs.

"I understand."

"This is as Ban Cruach and your forefathers wished. Your people made these things we call talismans so that our two races might talk together."

Hrillin glanced aside at Ban Cruach, lying still in his crystal bed.

"He promised to protect us," Hrillin said. "He promised to guard the Gates of Death so that his world could never trespass onto ours."

The aliens echoed that, swaying and tossing their arms. The fluting voices rang from the pavilion roof. "He *promised!* By the power of the talisman…"

"And he kept that promise," Stark said, "as long as his people held Kushat."

Hrillin started. He stared at Stark.

"Kushat? Kushat has fallen?"

A wild crying broke out among the aliens. They pressed closer around Hrillin, around the humans. Some of them apparently in an ecstasy of excitement, pricked themselves and each other with their steel nails, drawing blood.

"Yesterday," Stark said.

"Yesterday," repeated Hrillin. "Yesterday Kushat fell." Suddenly he swayed forward and screamed. "You had no right! You had no right to let it fall!"

The fluting voices shrieked in rage, in hysteria and fear. The tall thin bodies swayed wildly, whirled and tossed. Stark thought the creatures were going to attack, and perhaps they might have, but the men of Kushat drew their weapons and the aliens moved back, circling round and round. More began to gash themselves. The game was not going quite as they had though, Stark felt. And yet they were becoming more and more excited by it, perhaps simply because it was unpredictable and new.

He said to Hrillin, "The men of Kushat died defending their city. They could hardly do more." He could not keep all of what he was thinking out of what he was saying; the words formed themselves in his mind and Hrillin read them before he could suppress them. Some inscrutable emotion flickered in Hrillin's eyes.

"We do not like each other," he said. "Let it rest at that."

"Very well. But now we come to you because Ban Cruach made us a promise too."

"A promise? A promise?" Hrillin was scornful. "His promise was to us. We gave him a strong weapon to fight his wars and in exchange he gave us peace." He placed his hand with the cruel thumb-spur affectionately on the coffin. "When he was an old man he left his people and came to us. We were a great city, then. All this valley was warm and populous. He walked our streets and talked to our philosophers and wise men. It is said that he wrote our history, in the human tongue, though no one knows if that is true." He paused, looking at the humans. "We are the oldest race on Mars. We knew you before you walked erect. We built our cities when you lived in holes in the rock and barely understood fire."

The aliens swayed, lifting their long arms.

"But," said Hrillin, "you bred faster. And we grew old. We built our towers in the cold lands, and for a long time we were not troubled. But even the planet grew old, and men were everywhere, and one by one we abandoned our cities because there was no one left to live in them. This valley was our last stronghold."

"It is a stronghold no longer," Stark said. "Men are on their way. And this was Ban Cruach's promise to us, the other side of your bargain. If ever need arose, we were to bring the talisman through the Gates of Death, and the great power Ban Cruach once had would be given to us again."

He held up the talisman in a gesture of finality.

"Give us that power. We will drive away these men who are enemies to us both, and Kushat will continue to guard the Gates as she always has. Otherwise..."

He let his hands fall.

"Otherwise you must fight this battle by yourselves."

"Fight," said the fluting voices. There was a whirl of laughter, strange and cruel.

"Give them the power, Hrillin, why not?"

"Yes, give them the power!"

"Let them be strong like Ban Cruach and fight the world away from us."

"Shall I?" said Hrillin, swaying, dancing where he stood, gesturing with malicious arms. "Shall I?" He bent to Stark. "Will you go?"

"Give us the weapons, Hrillin, and we'll go."

"Very well," said Hrillin, and turned to his people. "Give them the weapons! Bring all we have. Give them! These are the sons of Ban Cruach our protector. Give them the weapons!"

They began to chant. "Give them the weapons!" Those who carried the bulky tubes pressed them into human hands. Others ran away and returned quickly with more. In a few minutes the men of Kushat had forty of the globed weapons.

"Are you joyous now?" asked Hrillin, and thrust the last of the tubes into Stark's hand. "See, thus and thus do you do with it, but be careful. It will kill much more than you think."

He drew back. All the aliens drew back. Balin held a tube in his own hands. He looked at it, his face alight with triumph, and then he turned to the crystal coffin where Ban Cruach lay. "He did it, Stark. He kept his promise." There was a glitter of tears in his eyes. "I thank you," he said to the aliens. "We of Kushat all thank you." He turned suddenly and faced Ciaran. "Now you can watch your red wolves die."

He shouted to the people, "You have the power now—the power of Ban Cruach! Let us go and take Kushat!"

The people roared. They started to move out of the pavilion and into the street, with Balin running on to lead them. They shouted, "Kushat! Kushat!" until the echoes struck through the city like the ringing of flawed bells. They poured back along the avenue. And now Stark was at the rear of the march with Ciaran, and Lugh and Rogain, who were armed with the alien weapons. Thanis had raced ahead to be with Balin, seeing already the way her room would look with everything back as it had been before.

The people were in a hurry and they moved fast, through the pools of colored light. Stark watched from side to side, and he saw that Ciaran was doing so too.

He could not see anything. There seemed to be no reason for alarm. Yet he was alarmed. And in his hand the talisman of Ban Cruach brought him not one single word.

He had a horrid picture of the aliens bending and swaying with their fingers pressed to their lips, their eyes bright with the excitement of playing a game where no one was allowed to speak.

Still they went on, and nothing happened.

The people began to pick up their burdens again from where they had left them. They put on their cloaks and shared their bundles and hurried along toward the terminus of the warm zone. They were in high spirits, their mouths full of the sweet taste of victory. Ciaran walked with her head high and her face a mask of stone. Lugh and Rogain fondled the strange weapons. Stark, impatient and nervous, kept looking back and seeing nothing, and straining toward the clean cold air ahead.

Perhaps half the people had left the city when the talisman brought Stark one unguarded cry, quickly silenced.

The cry was "Now, *now!*" and it held such a note of hungry eagerness that Stark did not wait for more. He shouted to the people to leave their belongings and run. He pushed Ciaran ahead of him, yelling at Lugh and Rogain to be ready with their weapons. They all began to run. And then all at once the lights went out.

Stark blundered into someone and stopped. It was as though he had been struck blind. He looked up at the sky. The stars were hidden by a shimmering cloud and the whole city was black as the pit. People were stumbling about, yelling, on the edge of panic.

Then the screaming began.

Stark felt something close by him, smelled a scent like the odor of dry leaves, and he knew suddenly that they were all around, keeping very quiet, their narrow feet soundless on the pavement, moving among the people. They must have come by secret ways of their own, through the empty houses and the unused halls. Now, above his head in the darkness, there was a little sound of suppressed laughter, horribly like a giggling child. A long thin finger brushed his face.

He yelled and lashed out violently with the globed weapon that he could not fire because of his own people. But the sharp thumb-spur had already pricked his neck, and whatever drug was on it acted very swiftly. He did not know whether the blow landed. Vaguely, very vaguely, as long arms wrapped around him and dragged him into unconsciousness, he heard sounds of panic as the people of Kushat rushed blindly toward the outer night.

CHAPTER FIFTEEN

THE LIGHTS WERE on again.

He lay in a pool of light. The pool was deep orange, a suffocating color, very rasping to the nerves. Things moved in it, tall things that pranced and fluttered, trailing bright streamers.

"He's awake," they said.

The talisman lay on his breast, between his crossed hands.

"See?" they said. "His eyes are open..."

He sat up convulsively, his brain still unsteady from the drug. He was naked and unarmed. Only the talisman was left. He looked up at them and hated them, futilely, and feared them with a cold sick fear. His body had tiny cuts all over it that stung and pulled when he moved.

Hrillin came and bent above him, holding the other talisman. "You lost Kushat," he said, and Stark knew that Hrillin was referring not to him alone but to all the humans. "You lost Kushat and so the world rolls in on us." He raked himself with his free hand and blood ran down his narrow chest. His eyes burned. He twitched and swayed with a lunatic joy. "Do you feel the greatness of this time? Here we end. All the long, long ages, piled and gathered, and we bear them into the dark."

The figures behind him danced stiffly, fluting wild cries without words.

Stark said, "But you gave us the weapons..."

"The weapons!" Hrillin whirled and took from one of his fellows a tube, perhaps the same one Stark had been carrying. He pointed the globed end at Stark and pressed the firing stud. He pressed it and pressed it, laughing.

"I said these would kill more than you thought! Not enemies. Hopes, and dreams, and faith, but not enemies." He ceased to press the stud and held the weapon upright like a club. "Ban Cruach promised you power. We have no power. The city warms us and lights us and gives us food and drink because it was built to do so, but beyond that we have nothing. All else is dead, worn

—229—

out, corroded, crumbled, useless. Now the city ends, and that is the end of everything. The end of the promise..."

He brought his two hands together, striking the useless weapon hard against the talisman, and the talisman shattered and fell.

"The end!" cried Hrillin. "This is our night of carnival. We dance toward oblivion, laughing, shouting the name of Ban Cruach."

He struck the talisman out of Stark's hands and broke it, and the contact was gone. Forever.

They swooped on him in the orange light, in a swaying semi-circle, and began to prick him with their spurs. And as Hrillin had said, they were laughing.

Stark ran.

He fled along the colored streets. They had brought him to a part of the city that was strange to him, away from the avenue. The great stone tower rose high above the roofs in one direction, and in the other, toward the perimeter of the city, he thought the lights chopped off short, as though the aliens had left a barrier of darkness against the people of Kushat.

By now the people would have learned that the precious weapons were useless. How many of them would dare to come back into the city, through total darkness and armed only with their swords, he did not know. He did not think there would be enough to be useful to him, and there was also a question of time.

The lighted streets were alive with excitement, with joy and murder.

Stark was not the only human they had taken in their stealthy raid. He could hear cries from other streets. Once he saw a man go stumbling across an open space ahead, with his tall pursuers deliberately matching stride and driving him. And at a place where two streets met there was a pink-and-gold cactus with a woman impaled on its spikes.

He was a swift runner, but he knew that they could outdistance him. He proved it fairly quickly, trying to break back down a long wide avenue that he was sure must lead to the outside. There was not a sign of a pursuer when he entered it, but at the second cross-street there they all were, laughing and springing toward him with blue light glinting from their spurs. He turned, and they let him run, but one—he thought it was the female with the amethyst streamers down her back—caught up and gashed his buttocks lightly, just to prove she could, before dancing away out of his reach.

So he ran, but he knew that there would come an end to running. And he looked all around, searching, his empty fingers flexing hungrily.

They drove him. At first he did not realize that, because sometimes they would disappear and he would think perhaps they had gone off on some other insane pursuit. Then as he would turn a corner or start across some square they would be there, and he would have to go another way. His control began to slip. He wanted to rush them and tear at them with his teeth and bare hands, but he knew that they could kill him any time they wanted to, and that they would merely enjoy his savaging as long as it pleased them. So he went on.

He began to find bodies. Some of them were human. Some of them were not, and in one broad pillared hall done all in bronze and gray he saw two of the creatures with bright cords stretched between neck and ankles, strangling themselves in a state of ecstasy while others watched, swaying like trees in a hot wind.

In the middle of a deserted square he found Rogain. He recognized him by his hands, the fine scholar's hands stained with blood. A sword lay across the body.

Stark straightened and looked around. There was no one to see, but he knew they were watching. He knew he had been driven here deliberately. The sword was clean, both hilt and blade, and Rogain had never used it. It had been put there for him to find.

"All right," he said to them, and added an obscene name. "I'll do what you want."

He picked up the sword. It felt very good in his hand. He thought perhaps they had made a mistake.

He took his bearings from the tower and started again toward the outside. They did not stop him. But from this square there was only one way that he could go.

He went, through the colored lights. A band of aliens came upon him suddenly from out of a tall pavilion. They were carrying between themselves two of their females who were either dead or close to it. All of them were bleeding from self-inflicted wounds. Stark wondered if they were drugged. Perhaps, or perhaps the euphoria of self-immolation was enough to make them as strange as they were. They laughed and pointed, and some of them came toward him. Stark had a weapon now, and his wisdom was all gone out of him. He bounded toward them like a big dark cat, and suddenly he was as lunatic as they, prancing and whirling with vicious grace as he drove the steel in. He could not avoid their spurs entirely. His shoulders bled, but he hardly noticed. He rushed on and the others swayed aside from the blade, apparently content to wait a little longer. After a bit he looked back and they had ambled on, dragging their wounded with them.

Then for a space it was quiet. The street led on between high walls. The light changed, blue, gold, violet, soft pink. And then there was another little square all enclosed in a fencing of fine wrought work in a pattern of strange leaves that must have been a memory of another place and a far gone time. At the far side of it, the street was covered by a series of elongated arches that receded in perspective, and the light was red. Coming toward him through the arches, in the bloody light, was a tall white-bodied long-striding woman, with black hair covering her shoulders and a sword in her hand.

Ciaran.

He stopped and waited. She saw him. She came into the square and stopped also, and said his name.

"I think I understand now," she said, "why they gave me this." She held up the sword.

Stark said, "Yes. And mine, too."

"But how did they know..."

"You were a captive. And they heard what Balin said to you about your red wolves. They would know you had something to do with the taking of Kushat."

He glanced from her in the red light, to the wrought work that fenced the square. Through the openings he could see them gathering to watch, their great eyes luminous. Then he looked beyond her through the arches.

"They are behind you now," he said.

She nodded. "And behind you. They're waiting for us to fight."

They faced each other, two naked humans in a strange far place, with swords in their hands.

Stark said, "Will you fight me, Ciaran?"

She shook her dark head. "No. Not to please them."

"Will you fight with me, then? Will you be the shield at my back?"

She smiled. "No. But I will fight beside you, and we can guard each other's backs." She looked at the tall peering creatures and added, "I have never wanted more to kill." Her white skin was marked like his with the pricking of their spurs.

"Good," he said. "Then there are two of us." He lifted his blade, feeling a new surge of hope and hot vengefulness. "Let us fence while we think how we can best use ourselves."

They made the ceremonial gesture. Their blades range together. They moved lightly, their flexing bodies pale in the red glare.

Stark saw how her eyes lighted and glowed. "Remember this is play," he said, and she laughed.

"I'll remember, Stark."

They circled, and the heads in the bright conical caps bobbed to watch them. There was much fluting talk and the smell of dry leaves was strong.

Ciaran said, "I think the outside lies that way. We could try cutting our way through."

They circled, and Stark's eyes rested between strokes on the stone tower.

"It's a long way to the outside," he said, "and doubtful if we could make it. Remember, they expect to die. They could smother us by sheer numbers." He parried a stroke and the blades clashed. "But if we took them by surprise, the tower is much closer. We might have a chance of reaching it."

"The tower? And what would be gained by that?"

"That is the heart of the city. If it dies, all this dies too." She parried him expertly. He was almost sorry that they would not truly fight. It would have been interesting. "I doubt," he said, "that they could stand the cold for long."

"Well," said Ciaran, "we are not likely to live the night through in any case, so let us throw for the highest stakes."

Stark nodded. "Quick, now."

They turned from their fencing and sprang at the creatures that had filled the entrance to the street down which Stark had come.

And they almost perished there.

The creatures were close-packed, and they were tall, and their arms were long. Even in dying they could reach and claw. They fluted and screamed and fluttered and Stark had a nightmare feeling that he and Ciaran were being pecked to death by a flock of ungainly birds. He swung his blade in a frenzy of disgust, literally cutting his way through, and glad of Ciaran's strong shoulder beside his. He saw the street clear before them and they ran with all their might, and behind them the creatures began to stream from around the square and after them. Stark listened to the unmistakable tone of their voices and said between gasps, "They're delighted. The game is going better than they hoped."

Now that he was trying to reach it, the tower that had seemed so close looked as far away as the moons. He tried to approach it obliquely, as much as he could without losing distance, so that perhaps they would not understand his purpose until it was too late, and apparently at first they did not. They played as they had before, letting the quarry go and then heading them, only now there were more than had hunted Stark, quite a lot more. He and Ciaran obediently allowed themselves to be driven until they were level with the tower. Then Stark said, "We go now."

They turned sharply, and the tower was directly ahead of them, set in a great wide circle beyond the end of the avenue.

They ran. And the creatures came striding on their long thin legs out of a side street, to bar the way.

Behind them, Stark heard others coming to close off their retreat. Ciaran heard too. She said, "I think the game has ended."

Stark grunted. "Break through them now—we won't have a second chance."

If only their damned arms weren't so long. The spurs jabbed and clawed for his eyes. He swung the swordblade high, around his head. This worked cruelly well, and Ciaran was using the same trick, alternately stooping low for the hamstring. They trampled over thin gold writhing bodies and through the line, but others were already pecking and pawing at their backs, and still others ran ahead to close them in again. They set their backs together and moved out across the open, keeping a vicious blur of steel between them and the probing spurs. They had stopped trying to kill. Their only interest now was in staying alive long enough to reach the tower.

"Look for a door," Stark said.

"I see one. This way..."

They fought their way to the wall and around it, and it was easier now because the creatures could only come at them from three sides. And there were fewer of the creatures able to fight. But now they knew what the humans were up to, and for several minutes there had been loud calls as though for help.

They reached the door, a high and narrow door of metal set deep in the stone. "See if you can open it," Stark said, and faced outward to hold the creatures off. Then he realized a surprising thing. They were drawing back. More and more of them drifted into the great circle, all that were left, he imagined, and suddenly a strange quiet was coming over them. They stood swaying gently, their bright streamers dabbled all with blood, and those who had come dragging after them the trophies of the chase now laid them down. Behind him Ciaran panted and cursed at the door, and then she said, "It's open..."

It was a moment before Stark turned. A tall creature in stained flutterings of blue and green was walking among the crowd, his arms held high, calling out in a sort of chant. Apart from that there was no more sound nor movement in the circle. Stark listened. The whole bright city had gone silent.

He turned abruptly and went through the door into the tower.

"I'll stand guard," Ciaran said.

He shook his head. "No need. This is the end of the game."

In the dark outer rim of the city, Balin and twenty-three men picked their way with drawn blades along the nighted avenue, starting at their own footsteps, their bellies cold with fear, cursing the pride that would not quite let them go without at least an attempt at rescue, or failing that, revenge. Far ahead of them the colored lights glowed.

There had been sounds. Now it seemed that there were no more.

Balin whispered, "Stop..."

They stopped. The world ached with silence. Even in his fear, Balin thought he could sense a waiting, a gathering, a rushing toward some tremendous and final moment. Ahead of him the lights flickered and went down. There was a deep hollow groan, more felt than heard. High overhead there was one vivid flash and then the stars sprang out clearly in the sky.

Very quickly, it began to grow cold.

It was morning. They stood on the slope at the mouth of the pass, Stark and Ciaran dressed in borrowed clothing and wrapped in borrowed cloaks. Of eleven men and women the aliens had taken, only they two survived. Behind them, the city lay quiet under the sun, rimed white with frost.

"We would have done better," Balin said, "all of us—to forget Ban Cruach and his talisman, and hew our own wood as it came to hand."

"Myths are unchancy things to lean on," Stark said, and turned to Ciaran. Her hands were not bound this morning, and that was

at Stark's insistence. "Now you know that there is no power beyond the Gates of Death, and now that you have fed your red
wolves with plunder, will you take your pack and leave Kushat in
peace?"

She looked at him, with the cold wind blowing her hair. "I
might do that—on one condition. Now that I cannot count on the
talisman, I must look elsewhere for help. Ride beside me, Stark,
to Narrissan, and we will guard each other's backs as we did last
night. Or have you made some other promise?"

"No promise," Stark said. He remembered her eyes, glowing
as the swords swung. A deep excitement stirred in him. "This
time I'll ride with you."

Thanis came forward, and he caught her quickly up and kissed
her to silence the angry words before she could speak them. "I
owe you my life, little one, you and your brother. I do this for you,
and for your Kushat. Build a new city, and build it in the world, so
that your people will never end like they did." He nodded toward
the other city, dead and shining in the sun.

He set her down and took Balin's hand. "Let us go ahead. By
the time you come, the tribesmen will be clear of Kushat." He
held Balin's strong grip a moment longer. Then he turned and
walked with Ciaran, back through the Gates of Death.

ABOUT THE AUTHOR

Though Leigh Douglass Brackett (1915–1978) was one of the most prominent science fiction authors of her time, she was equally adept in both crime fiction and westerns. While many of her early stories, beginning with "Martian Quest" in 1940, were science fantasy adventures, her first novel, "No Good From a Corpse" (1944), was a hard-boiled detective mystery that so impressed director Howard Hawks that he had his staff call in "this guy Brackett" to help William Faulkner write the script for *The Big Sleep*. The film, starring Humphrey Bogart and Lauren Bacall, is considered a shining example of film noir, and launched Brackett's scriptwriting career, which would go on to include such notable pictures as *Rio Bravo*, *The Long Goodbye*, and the first draft of *The Empire Strikes Back*, which was written shortly before her death and later revised significantly. During this time, however, she maintained her status as a pulp science fiction icon, writing numerous stories and occasionally collaborating with protégé Ray Bradbury or husband Edmond Hamilton. It was during this busy period that she created her most famous character, criminal and wild man Eric John Stark, an anti-hero who allowed her to explore colonialism's affect on native cultures, a theme that pervades much of her work. Despite her death from cancer in 1978, Brackett's works live on today as some of the most important in the genre.